Dinghies

&

Deceit

The Intelligencers  Book Four

BY

JANE GLATT

Dinghies & Deceit

The Intelligencers ⚓ Book Four

By
Jane Glatt

TYCHE BOOKS LTD.

Published by Tyche Books Ltd.
Calgary, Alberta, Canada
www.TycheBooks.com

Cover Design by Indigo Chick Designs
Interior Layout by Ryah Deines
Editorial by Karley Hauser

First Tyche Books Ltd Edition 2021
Print ISBN: 978-1-989407-31-8
Ebook ISBN: 978-1-989407-32-5

Author photograph: Eugene Choi
Echo1 Photography

This book was funded in part by a grant from the Alberta Media Fund.

To everyone, everywhere who is doing their best to get through this #@*& pandemic. And a shout out to Leslie and Yvonne, my fellow live-alone, Friday-night-wine companions who sat outside on my patio through 4 seasons (so far). Here's hoping we can visit indoors next winter.

Books by Jane Glatt

The Mage Guild Trilogy
Unguilded
Unmagic
The Unmage

The Conjurers Duology
The Bookbinder's Daughter
The Shaman's Son

The Intelligencers
Pirates & Privateers
Traits & Traitors
Sailors & Spies
Dinghies & Deceit

CHAPTER 1

PIA JOLTED AWAKE. She held her breath and listened for the sound that had disturbed her sleep. A snort echoed across the partially empty warehouse, and someone swore a few feet from where Pia and Frida had laid out their bedrolls. The sound of her little sister's steady breathing calmed her, and Pia settled back onto her bedroll.

Snoring and belching woke her up multiple times a night, a hazard of sleeping in close quarters with almost half a dozen other people coupled with her constant worry about Frida's safety.

Pia hadn't wanted to go to Lavais Port with Kaja, so when the Intelligencer student suggested this warehouse as a safe place, she'd agreed.

Solvig Madsen, the older woman who owned the warehouse, hadn't even asked any questions. She had simply put them to work with the rest: an assortment of woodcutters, volunteers, and refugees from burned out villages along the coast. And all of them, along with the three fishermen who lived here, were tasked with finding and storing food to fill this warehouse.

Pia tried to ignore the sounds of sleeping people and instead Concentrated on the safe feeling she got from the growing stores of food. No more begging Ottosen's staff for scraps for Frida and her; no more stealing food from servants who would report her to the Clan Freeholder and put her sister's life at risk. And no

1

more nights holding a hungry Frida when they lay just a single locked door away from a kitchen full of good things to eat.

Just hard work to make sure they paid their own way and earned their food and shelter.

And the anonymity of being two more displaced souls among many. The very best disguise she could have ever wished for. Almost as important were the invaluable lessons on finding and preserving local food that she was learning.

In the half a dozen days they'd been here, Pia had learned how to recognize a handful of edible tree nuts and seeds as well as some wild vegetables. She'd volunteered to help Solvig lay out the salt fish tomorrow, a task none of the men seemed to want. But she didn't mind. The more she learned, the more control she could have over her life.

She never wanted to have to rely on anyone else ever again. And with the ability to find and preserve her own food, she was closer to that than she'd thought possible.

On the trip south, Kaja had treated Pia as though she was just like her, a fully committed Intelligencer student. But that had been Ottosen's plan for her, a way to use her to forward his own agenda. And he had forced her compliance with incredible cruelty by imprisoning Frida. By restraining a child, physically punishing her, and even starving her in order to make Pia do his bidding.

Pia had diligently learned everything the Intelligencer school was willing to teach her. And the whole time, every single day for three years, she had been looking for a way to save Frida—and kill Ottosen.

Now, thanks to Lauma Strauskas and the Intelligencers, Frida was safe. But Ottosen was still alive.

She rolled over and nestled into her sister's back, and Frida seemed to sigh and relax into her, even in sleep recognizing the safety of her big sister.

Frida needed her. That was the only reason why she wasn't already planning Ottosen's death. But once she and Frida were self-sufficient, once they were safe and on their own, Pia would head north to Nordmere. And Henrik Ottosen would find out that he had created the weapon that would destroy him.

DAG STARED OUT across the water at Tarklee—and the people

waiting on shore for her and Saulia Holt.

"The barge is ready," Calder said, joining them.

"Thank you," Dag said. "I'll let your mother know you won't be coming ashore."

"Tell her I'm disappointed," Calder replied. "And I promise I will see her next time, but the less time we spend in port, the earlier we can return to Messanos."

"I'll be back as soon as I can," Dag replied before following Saulia to the stern, where a grinning Jaak was shouting over the gunwale at someone below.

"I'm taking your hammock if you don't make it back on board," Jaak called out. Dag leaned over just as a sailor standing in the fully laden barge gestured rudely up at them. When he saw her, he quickly dropped his arm, and Jaak laughed and turned to her.

"Don't mind us," Jaak said. "Pall and me have a long-standing argument about who has the best berth. Ready to go ashore?"

"We are," Dag replied. "Saulia, you first."

Jaak helped Saulia over the gunwale, and Dag stared out at the harbour. Nothing seemed out of place, at least not to her eyes. But without ships, there was little work, and without work, there was no pay.

"Now you," Jaak said.

"See you soon," Dag said and hauled herself over the gunwale and down the rope ladder to the deck of the barge. She found a spot close to Saulia, but she was too keyed up to sit, so instead she stood and stared at the city as the barge was rowed towards shore.

As soon as the barge was close enough, she jumped onto the dock and took a deep breath.

She was home.

"I might as well get this over with," Saulia said as she passed Dag on her way along the dock to where Lauma and Nadez waited.

"Saulia Holt, I am very glad to see you," Lauma said, stepping forward. "We have much to discuss."

"My parents are dead," Saulia said. "And I've been told I must trust you."

"Our clans have never been enemies," Lauma replied. "I am sorry about your parents. What about the rest of your household?"

"Any that travelled with us are dead," Saulia said. "I am all that's left of my clan. But do not think for a moment that I am weak." She nodded and stepped past Lauma, who looked at Dag with raised eyebrows.

"She's angry," Dag replied. "And has no one she can trust."

"Yes," Lauma said. She turned and they both watched Saulia, who had stopped a few steps from the shore. Suddenly the young woman cried out and launched herself at the figure standing a few feet in front of her. "That's why I asked Mykol, her father's former assistant, to work for her." She smiled a sad smile. "I will miss his knowledge, and I desperately hope I don't live to regret it, but I thought she would need at least one friend."

"I'll be keeping an eye on them," Nadez said. "Once I've dealt with the food shipment. It's good to have you back."

"It's good to be back," Dag said. "But I'm only here for as long as it takes to unload the ship."

"Is my son not coming to see his mother?"

"Sorry, but he has tasks on board, and we don't want to risk any delays," Dag said. "We need to return to the Sapphire Sea as soon as possible. It's late in the season to buy food, and we're hoping to make two more trips before the supplies are gone." Inger was trying to secure goods in Messanos for them, but there was no guarantee she would be successful. The Arressan council may have approved her twin's appointment, but that did not mean the locals would sell to her. Rahm's influence was the only reason they were able to buy what they were delivering now. They hoped his influence extended to Inger and her purchases, but they didn't know if it would.

"All right," Lauma said. "I asked Mykol to bring Saulia to my office once they had a chance to speak in private. Nadez will join us once the goods are offloaded and stored."

"Will you be distributing the food?" Dag asked as they walked away from the docks and into the streets of the city.

"Yes," Lauma replied. "Nadez wants this shipment split and sent north and south. If winter hits before you make it back with another full hold, some areas, especially far north, might be unreachable."

"And the city is calm?"

"There are no food riots," Lauma said. She turned down a

familiar laneway to the small door that led into the Hall. "We're using the warehouses to feed and house anyone who needs it." Lauma tugged the door open, and Dag followed her into the narrow corridor.

"Who's paying for that?" It was a good idea, but it would be very expensive.

"The Alliance is," Lauma said. "As it should. It turns out that previous Grand Freeholders have been amassing huge sums of coin from taxes and fees and not using it to do anything for the people." Lauma turned to her and shook her head. "I figure that feeding people is cheaper than paying for more guards to keep the peace."

"Not to mention more compassionate," Dag replied. She followed Lauma through a door and into the outer office of the Grand Freeholder. "I'm surprised previous Grand Freeholders left any surpluses from taxes."

"Oh, I'm certain they took what they could for themselves without raising any alarms," Lauma said as she sat down behind her desk. "But not using the funds to help our people should not be allowed."

Saulia entered the office, looking slightly less belligerent than she had when they'd landed.

"Where's Mykol?" Lauma asked.

"My uncle is in the city: Mykol has gone to let him know I've returned and that my parents have not," Saulia said, sitting down. "Thank you. Mykol said it was your idea that he be my assistant instead of staying with you. It was very thoughtful."

"Yes, well, we all need you to be effective, and Mykol is a wonder. Come into my office."

"Did Mykol let you know about your quarters?" Lauma asked.

"Yes," Saulia replied. "He said both the apartment in the Hall and the house are ready. The entire staff did not come with us, so there will be some familiar faces."

"That's good. I hate to rush you, but the Nordmere contingent is pushing to seize your clan holdings in light of your father's suspected treason."

"Already?" Dag asked. "Do they have any evidence?"

"I haven't seen any," Lauma replied. "But that doesn't mean they don't have it. But none of that matters now that you are here. You have proof that your parents are dead?"

"Yes," Dag said. "Eyewitnesses, including me."

Lauma visibly relaxed. "Even Ottosen can't fault the word of an agent of the Fair Seas Treaty Alliance."

"You think he would contest my right to inherit?" Saulia asked.

"I think he and Heikki very much want to control all of Nordmere," Lauma said. "By whatever means they can. I fear that you will need to be careful even after you are declared Clan Freeholder."

"Can we have someone guard her?" Dag asked. "What about Gustav? He's proven to be very resourceful."

"No," Saulia said. "I don't trust him."

"He's not available anyway," Lauma said. "Oh, there's Mykol. Come, join us."

Mykol stood next to Saulia. "Clan Freeholder Seppa is on his way," Mykol said. "Along with half a dozen of his guards."

"That solves that problem," Dag said. "As long as Saulia agrees."

"Yes," Saulia said. "My uncle will keep me safe."

"When he arrives, we can formally declare you Clan Freeholder," Lauma said. "We have verification of the deaths of your parents and, once your uncle vouches for you, proof that you are the heir." Lauma turned to Saulia. "Unless you wish more time to grieve."

"I don't need more time," Saulia said. "And as soon as I am named Clan Freeholder, I will declare my uncle as my heir."

"That's a very wise move," Lauma said and smiled. "One that Ottosen will not like. It removes the incentive for your death since Seppa would then own the majority of Nordmere clan freeholdings."

"I told you I wasn't weak," Saulia replied.

"You did," Lauma said. "And now you've shown me that you're not a child. Ottosen won't like that either."

NADEZ WATCHED AS the last of the goods were stacked in the warehouse. Once the doors were shut and locked, she sighed and turned to look out over the harbour. Lights dotted the *Atlaine*, the only lights in what should have been a busy harbour.

"You need anything else, Master Intelligencer?"

She turned to find Sture, the warehouse manager, looking at

her.

"No, thank you," Nadez said. "The *Tazeyar* should arrive some time tomorrow. We'll have to load them up and send them out to deliver food north and south along the coast."

"You said that," Sture replied. "I already had the workers divide the goods up for each trip. Lots of room in the warehouse to do that."

"Good." Not that there was lots of room in the warehouse: that was not good. In fact, it was frightening at this time of year. "And thank you. Can you send word when the *Tazeyar* is spotted?"

"Will do," Sture said. "Good night."

"Same to you." Nadez turned and headed towards the Hall. Her tasks were not finished, not yet.

A dozen minutes later, she was at the door to Lauma's office. Lauma and Dagrun Lund looked up at her when she knocked on the open door.

"Nadez," Lauma said. "Good. The rest of our business has been dealt with. I was just giving Dagrun the most important news."

"Where's Saulia Holt?" Nadez asked.

"Clan Freeholder Holt left half an hour ago," Lauma said. "Accompanied by her uncle and heir, Clan Freeholder Karl Seppa."

"Her heir?" Nadez felt the tension in her shoulders ease. "She already named an heir?"

"She did," Lauma replied. "Her uncle inherits it all." She grinned and Nadez couldn't stop the laugh that bubbled up. She met Dag's puzzled look.

"You don't know how worried we've been," Nadez said. "Not knowing who would control the Holt Freeholdings. But this must mean that Tarmo Holt is dead?"

"Yes," Dag said. "I can confirm that both he and his wife are dead. We suspect at the hands of Fihaldo Pinho."

"And it's as we thought," Lauma said. "Ottosen sold Holt's debts to Pinho, who likely wanted to use Saulia as a way to gain a foothold in the Pale Sea."

"What will Pinho do now?" Nadez asked as she sat down.

"I'm not sure he will be a problem," Dagrun said. She sent a worried look Lauma's way. "There's an assassin after him. A Resolute. Pinho may not have long to live."

"A Resolute?" Nadez asked. "They really exist?" She'd never spoken to anyone who had first-hand knowledge of the legendary assassins.

"They exist," Dagrun said, still looking at Lauma. "I met someone who admitted to being a Resolute. It's Rahm."

"Of course it is," Lauma said. "I can't even say I'm surprised." She shook her head. "He always was secretive. How foolish I was to be taken in by him."

"Not foolish," Dagrun said. "I'd know if he was lying about this: he *still* cares about you. But to keep you and your children safe, he had to keep you a secret from everyone who might know who and what he is. And that led to him keeping secrets *from* you."

"If he kills Fihaldo Pinho, I will thank him if I ever meet him," Nadez said. "It will be one less threat to the Three."

"Pinho only became a threat because he was able to coerce a Resolute to do his bidding," Dagrun said. "Rahm was the one who forced Margit Ansdottir to betray Holt and destroy so many ships. Which makes Rahm partially responsible for the food shortages we face. Although he seemed remorseful when I told him it put Yakop and Berna at risk."

"Remorseful," Lauma said. "Not a word I'd ever use to describe my former husband." She sighed. "At any rate, he is far away from us, for which I am grateful."

"Is there more news?" Dagrun asked. "Now that I know the cargo has all been offloaded, I need to get back to the *Atlaine*. The shorter days mean we only have a few hours to get through the Teeth tomorrow."

"Yes," Lauma said. "The next time we meet we'll either have saved the Alliance or Byholt will have seceded from it."

"WHAT?" DAG DIDN'T even try to hide her shock. She'd thought the meeting was done and that she could head back to the *Atlaine*. "Why? I thought delivering Saulia would ensure that Nordmere was no longer a threat?"

"That's likely true," Lauma replied. "Of Nordmere. But Swyford's choice for the next Grand Freeholder looks to be no better than Tarmo Holt. I will not allow Byholt to be governed by such a self-serving, arrogant, callous person. Clan Freeholder Timonis has, along with his fellow Swyfordian and Nordmerian counterparts, allowed the people of Tarklee to live in squalor and hunger and desperation. They stopped funding orphanages to line their own pockets, throwing children who had lost everything into the hands of pirates. I will not sit back and let him do the same to Byholt."

"Your first mission was to observe Timonis," Nadez said. "Did you learn anything important?"

Dag sat back. Her assignment had only been a couple of months ago, but so much had happened since then, and she knew so much more now, that she had to re-think her report. "Joosep simply wanted me to confirm that Timonis would be Swyford's selection for Grand Freeholder," she said. "Other than that, I found out that Timonis was being cheated by a couple of business partners and his brother was having an affair."

"Nothing sounds too out of the ordinary," Lauma said.

"Tell me what your options are?" Dag had to leave soon if they wanted to get the *Atlaine* through the Teeth tomorrow but walking away from this conversation might mean walking away from the Alliance.

"Dissolve the Treaty or allow Swyford to elect Tavet Timonis," Lauma said.

"There has to be another way," Dag replied. "There *has* to be."

"We've looked at all the historical documents," Nadez replied. "We were only able to find something that allowed us to keep Nordmere from forcing a quick vote."

"What was it? Can you show me?" If she had more time, she would find something, she knew it. Calder would have to understand if she was late and they missed the window to get through the Teeth tomorrow. This was far too important. An extra day might not matter if there was no Alliance to return to.

"Here's the document we found," Lauma said, handing her a faded sheet of paper.

As soon as Dag grasped it, her Trait activated. "Something is here," she said. "Something that will help."

"*Only a meeting that includes every single council member,*" she read out loud. "*Either in person or by proxy, will be considered valid in the event that one or more member of the Alliance wishes to make a change to this agreement and a majority of each country must agree to any such change. In the event that a member country wishes to withdraw from the*

Treaty, the majority of the withdrawing country is all that is required."

"Yes," Lauma said. "That's what we used to force a full meeting: the threat of withdrawal."

"What if you used the other part of it?" Dag asked. "And changed the agreement?"

"Change it to what?" Nadez asked. "The Alliance is a trade agreement: what else could it be?"

"Keep the agreement," Dag said. "And change how it works. Change how the Grand Freeholder is elected. Or the powers the position has."

"Either one of those could satisfy me," Lauma replied. "Although we could still end up with Swyford and Nordmere abusing their own people."

"Then write it into the agreement that they can't," Dag said. "You have Byholt and Saulia and her uncle. How many Clan Freeholders are required to change the terms of the agreement?"

"A simple majority for each country based on land holdings," Lauma said. "Swyford will be a challenge but it's worth a try."

Dag felt her shoulders relax. "Thank you." That was all she could do for now. "I need to get back to the *Atlaine*," she said. "With Calder's Luck we should reach the Tceth with enough daylight to get through them tomorrow."

"All right," Lauma said. "Please say hello to my son. Nadez, we still have work to do tonight."

Dag left them and jogged back through the Hall towards the harbour. She'd talk to Calder and hope he could help dispel her fears. Because right now Dag had no confidence that Lauma Strauskas actually wanted the Fair Seas Treaty Alliance to continue.

Squinting against the morning sun, Gustav leaned over the prow of the *Tazeyar* and stared towards the mouth of Tarklee Harbour. He was looking forward to getting back to the Hall, not least because then he'd be able to relax and not try to force his Trait to work so much.

Swyford Clan Freeholder Tavet Timonis was the most stubborn person he'd ever met.

Gustav had assumed that someone so unreasonably convinced of his own exceptional abilities would be flattered and easily manipulated by Charisma.

How wrong he'd been. It wasn't that his Trait didn't work; it was just that Timonis so thoroughly thought he deserved the inflated compliments that nothing Gustav said affected the Clan Freeholder's opinions. The man considered himself so superior to every other person alive that no criticism from anyone *inferior* could dent his self-confidence. Praise was simply people recognizing his true brilliance.

All Gustav's Charisma had accomplished was to allow Timonis to believe that he was smart enough to understand who was superior.

It was exhausting.

But there was some friction between the Swyfordian Clan Leaders. Liina Nowack was following some of Lauma's directions and stockpiling food. He wasn't certain Koit Kozlow understood that they faced dangers from starving people, and even if he did, Gustav doubted the man would do anything other than keep himself and his family safe until the danger passed.

The city was coming into view now. Gustav left his perch to find Captain Eklund. The captain had agreed to send him ashore first, hopefully without the Clan Freeholders knowing, so he could report to Nadez and Lauma right away. He wasn't sure how much good a few minutes warning would do, but it wouldn't hurt.

"A dinghy is ready on portside," Eklund said when he approached him. "I'll give you as much time as I can."

"I appreciate that," Gustav said with a genuine grin. "Trust me, I know what that is going to cost you."

"Off with ye," Eklund said with a laugh. "It's a small price to pay considering what I've seen you put up with. How that windbag of a man ever came to be married is anyone's guess."

"It's not the getting married that surprises me," Gustav replied. "It's the staying married."

"Aye," Eklund agreed. "Maybe his wife encourages him to stay in Tarklee."

"I would." Gustav headed to the port side of the ship, where a dozen crew members were launching a dinghy. Once the boat was in the water, half of the sailors climbed down and settled behind oars.

Gustav took a seat in the prow just before one last sailor, Rolf, climbed into the dinghy.

"Captain says he can keep them all belowdecks for fifteen minutes," Rolf said to him as he headed to the stern.

"Sailors ready," Rolf said in a loud whisper. "Row."

In minutes, the dinghy was around the ship and pointed towards shore. Gustav took one last look back at the *Tazeyar* before turning to stare at the city. He waved when he recognized two figures standing on the pier. Nadez and Lauma were already waiting for him.

He jumped onto the dock as soon as the dinghy was close enough and ran to the two women.

"I have news," he said. "We don't have much time before the Swyfordians arrive."

"This way," Nadez said, and she led them into the city.

Gustav recognized the route. Nadez was taking them to her old stable, not the Hall.

Once inside, he waited impatiently while the Master Intelligencer lit a lamp.

"We thought it best to stay away from any potential prying eyes," Lauma said, sitting on a stone block.

"Is the Hall not secure?" Gustav sat down while Nadez paced the small space.

"Nordmerian Clan Freeholders are in the city," Nadez said. "We don't know what resources they have."

"Our assumption is that anyone they had in place to spy on Tarmo Holt would still be in position to watch me," Lauma said. "What news?"

"I'll start with the easiest," Gustav said. "I met with Berna and Kaja before we boarded in Lavais. The shipyard rebuild is progressing well and is on track to start building the first ship in a few weeks. Food gathering and preserving on the island is at capacity. Kaja left the Engen girls with a group that was planning on filling a warehouse with foraged food and dried fish. Some Byholt woodcutters had started foraging on the mainland with permission from the Clan Freeholder."

"Which one?" Lauma asked.

"Liina Nowack," Gustav replied. "She seems to understand the situation a little better than Timonis and Kozlow. At least, she gave permission to forage and has instructed her people to do the same."

"How much land does she hold?" Nadez asked.

Gustav looked up in confusion, but she wasn't looking at him.

"Eighteen percent," Lauma replied. "Does Kozlow understand the threat?"

"I'm not sure," Gustav said. "And even if he does, I doubt he'll do anything without Timonis's approval."

"*Skit karl*," Lauma said. "What about Skala? He holds almost as much land as Timonis."

"He was in the city when the food riots happened," Gustav said. "He must know that was real."

"So far, he hasn't done anything about it," Nadez said. "It's possible he will side with Timonis and simply head to his estate until spring, or summer, or whenever the worst of the food shortages are over."

"And what about Timonis?" Lauma asked. "Gustav? Any luck with him?"

"There is no convincing that man of anything," Gustav said, shaking his head. "All my Charisma couldn't change his mind on even the smallest thing. Don't waste your time."

"All right, thank you." Lauma stood up. "It must be time to greet our guests. Nadez? I'll leave you to deal with Timonis while I try to charm Melker Skala. If we can get him and Nowack to vote our way, we'll have the majority we need." She turned to Gustav. "And our news to you. Saulia Holt has returned and has been named Clan Freeholder. I would like you to attend the meeting when I introduce her to the rest of the Alliance council." She headed to the exit.

"Blow out the lamp when you leave," Nadez said. She flashed a smile before following Lauma out of the stable.

Gustav blew out the lamp, but he sat in the dark until his grin wore off. Saulia Holt was alive and had already been named Clan Freeholder. That changed everything, didn't it?

CHAPTER 2

CALDER STARED AHEAD: night had fallen and all he could do was hope that his and Dag's Traits worked together to get them safely out of the Teeth.

"Port five degrees," Darya called out, and he turned the wheel slightly. The ship rolled as it crested a wave, and he held his breath. He blew it out when he heard no warning calls or sounds of the *Atlaine*'s hull scraping against rock.

"Steady for a count of ten then hard starboard at fifteen degrees," Darya said.

Calder counted under his breath before sharply turning the wheel.

Dag had been late getting back to the ship, and he'd had them set sail for the Teeth immediately. The sun was already high in the sky when they arrived at the entry point, but he'd made the decision to keep going, assuming that they would have just enough time to make it through.

But the wind had died down and their momentum had eased. They hadn't been stranded, but their progress had been extremely slow.

As always, he wondered if his Trait was doing this on purpose: if there was a reason to be stuck navigating the most treacherous passage in the dark.

"Hold steady for a count of twenty then starboard another five degrees," Darya said. "Dagrun says that'll take us out."

"Thank *Jebris*," Calder replied. When he reached a count of twenty, he gently turned the wheel. Ten minutes later, Dag joined him, Rafael trailing her.

"That wasn't much fun," she said.

"No, it wasn't," he agreed. "Next time I think we'll make it through quickly, remind me of this. Darya, can you take the helm?"

"Aye, sir."

"Thank you. Rafael, take a break for an hour and then relieve Darya." He turned to Dag. "Come on, let's find something to eat."

He followed her below deck to the mess. A quick conversation with Cook and they were handed a tray with bowls of stew and bread with the promise of tea before they finished eating.

Calder carried the tray to the cabin. The whole time he'd been calling directions he'd been thinking about what Dag had told him: his mother was threatening to take Byholt out of the Fair Seas Treaty Alliance. Lauma Strauskas did not make idle threats.

Once the door was closed and their supper was on the table, he turned and gathered Dag in a hug.

"I can't tell you that she won't do it," Calder said into her hair.

"That's what I think too," Dag said. He felt her sigh, then she stepped away to meet his gaze. "It could even be the right thing for Byholt."

"But the wrong thing for the rest of the Alliance," he finished. "You gave her an option to try to save the Alliance. And our task hasn't changed: buy and deliver food so that people don't starve. My mother will do what she can to make sure that *all* the people of the Alliance have access to it, despite what their respective Clan Freeholders might try to do. Let's eat."

Dag sat down and pulled a bowl towards her. "I suppose we should focus on the immediate practical things we have control over," she said.

"Yes." Calder sat down and grabbed a spoon. "Like getting to Messanos and buying enough food to fill the hold."

"She won't do anything in anger, will she?" Dag asked. "Lauma?"

Calder took a bite of bread and chewed it slowly, thinking. "Nothing that will make things worse for Byholt," he said finally. His mother would never allow her emotions to cloud her judgment when it came to her responsibilities as a landowner.

Even if those same emotions ruled her dealings with her family.

Nadez stood by the side door; the one Lauma would enter the meeting room through.

The tables were all arranged, and all of the Clan Freeholders had already been seated. Except for Saulia Holt. There was an empty chair beside her uncle, one that placed her next to the Byholt contingent and kept her as far from Henrik Ottosen as possible.

Mykol was filling the water glasses in front of each Clan Freeholder, and she suppressed a grin when he started to fill Saulia's glass but then stopped halfway as though he had forgotten that there was no Holt Clan Freeholder.

Mykol finished with the water and hovered near the back of the room.

Nadez took a step forward. "Clan Freeholders, thank you for coming," she said.

"It's not by choice," Ottosen said. "The *Interim* Grand Freeholder threatened us."

"It's a bad time to be away from our holdings," Liina Nowack said. "What with the danger of food shortages."

"I told you not to believe that," Timonis said. "It's a trick; a made-up emergency that lets Lauma Strauskas seize power instead of allowing me to be voted in as Grand Freeholder."

"It's not a trick," Yakop Strauskas said. "It's the truth."

"Of course, you'd say that," Ottosen sneered. "You're only here because your mother lets you manage her holdings."

"Yes." All eyes turned to Lauma Strauskas as she entered the room. "My son is here because he has my support. All of us are here because of our families. Because those who came before us were able to obtain land and manage it to the benefit of future generations. I'm the closest to that since I personally bought most of the land that currently make up the Strauskas holdings. And my son manages those holdings for me, just as you, Henrik Ottosen, manage the holdings that were left to you by your family."

"As you say," Ottosen conceded. "We all are here because we inherited our holdings."

Lauma took a few steps and stopped behind her chair but she didn't sit down. She glanced back at Nadez and nodded.

Nadez edged close to the half-open door.

"Inheriting the lands and Clan Freeholder position within a family is our way," Lauma said. "As I'm sure you will agree."

"I do," Ottosen replied. "When there is family to inherit. Unlike the Holt—"

"Good," Lauma cut him off. "You agree." She flicked a hand signal, and Nadez opened the door wide to show Saulia Holt standing in the doorway.

"I am happy to announce," Lauma continued, "that the Holt Freeholdings have been inherited in accordance to our customs." She turned to the door, and Nadez stepped aside to allow Saulia to pass her and enter the meeting room.

"As you see, Saulia Holt has returned to claim her rightful place as Clan Freeholder," Lauma said. "She has already been confirmed by both myself and the Master Intelligencer. As well, Clan Freeholder Holt has designated an heir, as is her duty."

"No!" Ottosen was on his feet. "You cannot. I won't allow it!"

"I'm quite sure I don't require your permission," Lauma said.

Nadez edged past Saulia to stand in front of Ottosen. He was furious, as was Daina Heikki, although she at least was trying to hide her shock and anger. Gustav took a step towards Ottosen, and Nadez caught his gaze and shook her head. Ottosen wasn't the type to start a physical fight himself even though he'd shown himself more than willing to use assassins.

"You won't get away with this," Ottosen said. He looked around the room before finally sitting back down.

"Get away with what?" Lauma asked. She waved Saulia forward, and the young woman joined her uncle and sat down in the empty chair. "Are you contesting Saulia Holt's right of inheritance?"

"Where's the proof that Tarmo Holt is dead," Heikki asked. "And his wife. Saulia can't inherit if they're alive, and last I heard they'd fled to the Sapphire Sea."

"They did," Lauma replied. She finally sat down in her seat, facing the Nordmerians. "And the sad truth is that both Tarmo and Asla Holt are dead." She turned to Nadez. "Master Intelligencer?"

Nadez stepped forward. "One of my agents swore witness to the deaths of both Clan Freeholder Tarmo Holt and his wife Asla, to Interim Grand Freeholder Strauskas, as is required."

"I don't believe you," Ottosen said. "Where is this witness!"

"They are on assignment," Nadez replied. "Doing important work for the Alliance."

"I say they don't exist."

"Clan Freeholder Ottosen," Nadez said, stepping forward until she stood over him. "Are you accusing me of lying? Or are you accusing me of treason?"

Ottosen glared at her, but he didn't say anything.

"Clan Freeholder?" Lauma said. "I'm quite sure you did not mean to accuse the Master Intelligencer of either one of those things, so I suggest you retract your statement."

The room was quiet as Nadez stared down at Ottosen. He looked past her at Lauma before glancing around at the rest of the Clan Freeholders. Finally, he met her gaze.

"I retract the statement," he said.

"Thank you." Nadez turned and went to stand behind Lauma. She hadn't expected an actual apology, so a retraction would do.

"But I want to know," Ottosen said, "what proof you have that Saulia Holt was not involved with her father's treasonous schemes."

It took every ounce of willpower for Nadez to keep from rolling her eyes. Ottosen was so very predictable.

"Have you proof that Tarmo Holt committed treason?" Lauma asked. "I have none and wonder that you did not see fit to share yours with me."

Gustav grinned inwardly at Lauma's words. Ottosen could either produce his evidence and try to explain why he had not shared it with the Interim Grand Freeholder before now or he could back down.

Ottosen probably did have evidence: Nadez had said that he had sold Holt's debts to Pinho, so there must be some correspondence where Holt agreed to act on Pinho's behalf. Nadez and Lauma were counting on Ottosen keeping what he knew to himself, but that was before Ottosen had been forced to retract his comments about Nadez.

Would he back down twice in the same meeting? And just how much damage did Saulia's appearance cause to Ottosen's plans?

Gustav caught the look Heikki sent to Ottosen, who pursed his lips and tilted his head slightly. So, he would back down. What did that mean about their evidence: did it implicate more than just Holt? Or were they somehow expecting Pinho to come and save them from Lauma?

"I do not have proof that Tarmo Holt committed treason," Ottosen said. "But I have information that points in that direction."

"Yes, well," Lauma replied. "I have information that points to something as well, but *information is not proof.* Did you not tell me that yourself a few days ago?"

Gustav didn't know what Lauma was talking about, but Ottosen's eyes narrowed, and he frowned. "I did," he said finally.

"Indeed," Lauma said. "Unless anyone else has anything to offer, I formally declare Saulia Holt as Clan Freeholder of her late father's Freeholdings. As such, she is responsible for all of the duties of a Clan Freeholder, including voting. For the record, she has named her uncle, Karl Seppa as her heir." Lauma looked at each Clan Freeholder before nodding at Nadez.

"The next order of business," Nadez said. "Is why every Clan Freeholder's presence was required for this meeting."

"In accordance with the original Treaty documents," Lauma said. "Every single council member is required to attend in person or by proxy, in order to change the terms of the original agreement."

"You can't mean to change the Treaty," Timonis said. "It can't be done."

"It can," Nadez said. "It takes a vote based on the majority land ownership for each country to amend the agreement for all. But the majority of land ownership for only a single country is enough for that country to secede from the Treaty. Mykol? Can you please hand out copies of the document that lays out these terms?"

"The original document is fragile, and the writing is faint," Mykol said as he quickly handed papers out to each Clan Freeholder. "But I vouch that these copies are true to the original."

"I want to see the original," Ottosen said. "I don't trust this." He waved the piece of paper.

"Gustav?" Nadez motioned to him and he stepped forward.

The original document had been laid out flat on a piece of wood. Gustav held it out so that others could read it.

"It is faint," Gustav said as he stepped into the centre of the tables, "but the writing is still legible." He paused in front of Ottosen, who leaned forward to study the page.

"I can't read this," Ottosen said.

"I'll read it to you," Liina Nowack said. "My eyesight is excellent. Bring it to me." Gustav walked over and held the document out to her.

"*Only a meeting that includes every single council member,*" Nowack read. "*Either in person or by proxy, will be considered valid in the event that one or more member of the Alliance wishes to make a change to this agreement and a majority of each country must agree to any such change.*"

"I for one will never agree to any changes," Ottosen said, sitting back in his chair.

"Clan Freeholder Nowack," Lauma said. "Please read the last sentence for Clan Leader Ottosen."

"*In the event that a member country wishes to withdraw from the Treaty, the majority of the withdrawing country is all that is required.*" Nowack looked over at Lauma. "Are you coercing us? Are you threatening to break up the Treaty Alliance if we don't agree to whatever change you want to make to the agreement?"

Gustav backed away from the tables, watching as surprise and confusion along with some anger, rippled across the faces of everyone present except the Byholt contingent.

"Call it what you want," Lauma said. "But I will never again allow Byholters to be put in danger by a Grand Freeholder who only cares about their own power and fortune." She turned her gaze on Saulia Holt. "The way Tarmo Holt did." She pivoted her head to stare at Timonis. "And the way I think Tavet Timonis would."

"That is an outrageous accusation," Timonis said. "I demand that you retract that at once."

"No," Lauma said. "I will not retract it when even now, after being urged by me and my representatives, you still have not instructed your people to make extra efforts to forage and store food. We will be lucky if we get one more shipment of food before winter sets in. Do you expect my people, some of whom have even helped gather stores on Lavais Island, to share what we have when your people are starving? Or perhaps you are willing to let your own people starve? I will not allow such a person to oversee my people. I will take us out of the Alliance first."

"There is no coming threat of hunger," Timonis said. "I refuse to bend to your obvious reach for power."

"The threat is real," Gustav said. Nadez frowned at him, but he ignored her. "At least in Tarklee. I personally know where every single warehouse in the city is. They should be full, and they are not."

"That's because Lauma Strauskas has been giving the food away," Timonis said. "She's the cause of any food shortages."

"It's my father's fault," Saulia said. "He deliberately shipped in less food over the summer and early fall. I heard him and my mother arguing about it, after we had fled to the Sapphire Sea. His plan was to create food shortages that only he could solve once he owned most of the ships."

"The ships that were burned by the pirates," Gustav said. "Ships that never made it to the Sapphire Sea to purchase food for the winter."

"And now the growing season is over," Lauma said. "And we hope that our single ship can at least fill its hold and return here."

"Why didn't you send the *Tazeyar*?" Timonis asked. "Instead of having it ferry us to your pointless meeting?"

"The Frozen Gap is closed," Gustav said. "The *Tazeyar* barely made it through on its last trip."

"Then how did this other ship get out?" Ottosen asked. "And how will it get back here if it's such an impossible task?"

"Because it's going through the Teeth," Lauma said. "Because the Intelligencer who swore witness to the deaths of Tarmo and Asla Holt can navigate the ship through the Teeth." She stared at Ottosen. "That is the important mission she is on: bringing much needed food to us here on the Pale Sea. And I fear that will still not be enough." Lauma stood up. "I move that we reconvene in the morning, once you have had a chance to study the original terms of the Treaty and think about what you've heard here today."

Lauma left, followed by Nadez.

Gustav held the original document out, but no one bothered to look at it. Instead, all of the Clan Freeholders left in groups.

"STACK 'EM OVER there," Solvig said, and Pia, her arms full with a pile of rinsed and salted fish, headed to the rack Solvig was pointing at. Frida trailed behind her, carrying a single slab of fish.

After laying the fish out on the wooden rack, Pia placed another rack on top.

It was almost dark and the firelight and candles in the warehouse didn't quite reach to where she was working.

The double doors of the warehouse suddenly opened, banging against the inside wall. A group of people rushed in, a handful of pistols pointing at the group huddled near the fire.

Pia pushed her sister behind a stack of drying fish and crouched beside her.

"What's happening?" Frida asked in a quiet voice.

"Shh. I don't know, but I don't want us to be caught in it." Pia eased them both further into a shadow. She'd been working in this warehouse, amongst the racks, for two days now: she knew the best places to hide.

Quietly, she pulled Frida to the back of the warehouse. Once her sister was safely tucked into a space behind a rack of fish, she squeezed in beside her. And just in time—someone was coming.

"No one's back here," a woman called from close by. "Just a bunch of partially dried salt fish."

"I'd just as soon set fire to that as eat it," a man replied from closer to the fire pit.

"Such a *skit*," the woman muttered as she went past Pia's hiding spot. "Been hungry enough times that I'm never going to destroy food, no matter how much Benil might hate it."

Once the woman had rejoined her companions, Pia motioned Frida to stay where she was and edged out from their hiding place. Keeping to the shadows, she made her way to the rack of fish closest to the fire and peered out at the warehouse.

The light was much brighter than usual, and for a moment she worried that despite the woman saying she wouldn't destroy food, her companions had set the warehouse on fire. But although flames stretched towards the ceiling, the fire was still contained to the hearth.

Solvig stood facing three intruders while another half dozen of them were tying up her fellow food gatherers. Pia did a quick head count and smiled. Three woodcutters were missing, along with two of the local fishermen. Her smile fell; what if they were dead and not free outside of the warehouse planning to rescue them all?

"I got nothing else in the warehouse," Solvig said. "Just what you see."

"A place like this," a man facing her said. "Must have a cask or two of ale."

"Just the fish and those few preserves over there," Solvig said. "It's been a bad summer for shipments."

"Oh, we know." The man strolled right up to Solvig. "We're part of the reason why it's been so bad. Burned a few ships, we did. And more than one warehouse like this."

"Pirates." Solvig spat at his feet. "Worthless lot. Can't do anything useful so you destroy what others make. Thought those two Intelligencers fixed you lot for good."

"What do you know about Intelligencers?" a woman asked, and the man stepped back to allow her to confront Solvig.

"Know they caught that captain of yours," Solvig said. "Captain Margit Ansdottir was bested by them."

"And now I'm captain of the pirates," the woman replied. "And if you know where any Intelligencers are, you'd be wise to tell me."

"Captain of what?" Solvig asked. "A bunch of dinghies? Where's your ship?"

"How we came here doesn't matter," the woman said. "What matters is that you need to tell me who is here from the Alliance."

"No one here," Solvig replied. "We're just a bunch of fishermen and out-of-work woodcutters trying to put up enough food to get us through the winter."

"Salt fish?" the woman said. "That's your plan?" The woman looked over at the captives. "Check them all to see if anyone is carrying a patch. I don't want an agent of the Alliance to know anything about us."

Pia slipped back behind the stack of fish and crawled back to Frida.

"We need to get out of here," she whispered to her sister. "And find out if anyone else from our group is free."

"I know a way," Frida said. She led her to one of the back corners of the warehouse. The firelight didn't reach this far, and it was so dark that Pia grabbed her sister's hand to make sure they weren't separated.

When Frida stopped Pia felt cold air at her feet. She reached a hand out; the wooden wall was in front of them.

"I found this the other day," Frida said. "There's an opening along the floor."

Pia knelt down and ran her hand along the wall. There was a gap at the bottom: the sides had been cut straight so this was deliberate opening. It was less than a foot high and maybe twice that width.

"I'm not sure I'll fit through it," she said to Frida.

"I fit," her sister said. "I went through it already. I can go get help."

"Let me try first," Pia said. If there was any chance of keeping Frida from being out there alone, with pirates waving pistols around, she would take it. She got down on the ground and crawled to the opening. Her head made it through, but her shoulders were too wide. She could not go any farther no matter how much she tried.

Worried about getting stuck, she slid back into the warehouse and sat beside the opening. Ever since Frida had been rescued from Ottosen, Pia's greatest fear had been being separated from her sister: that she wouldn't be there to keep her safe. But Frida was the only one who could do this.

"You'll have to go," she said to her sister. "Three woodcutters were not captured in the warehouse. I think they're outside. Find them: they'll help you stay safe."

"I'll find them and then we'll come back and rescue everyone," Frida said.

"Find them and then do what they say," Pia replied, hoping that the woodcutters were alive and that Frida wouldn't end up out there all alone.

"Watch for us," Frida said. "I'll come here when I find them."

"All right." She didn't like her little sister out there alone. If she didn't find the woodcutters, Frida would be better off in here, with her and the pirates, wouldn't she?

Instead of thinking about all the ways her sister could be in danger, she thought about what she had seen at the fire. If her sister did bring help, they would need to know what they were up against.

The woman who said she was the new pirate captain was large, but to Pia's half-trained eye she hadn't carried herself like someone used to fighting. The rest of the pirates looked battle experienced but not very disciplined. The three who held pistols had been carelessly waving them around.

There were eight pirates, along with their captain. And any pirates who might be standing watch outside the double doors. Would they have someone guarding their ship? Except Solvig had implied that they hadn't arrived by ship. But they'd come in *something*. And they would need whatever it was to leave. She didn't think they were planning on staying here. Not if they were looking for anything other than dried fish.

She heard a noise at the opening.

"It's Bjorn," a man said. He was a Byholt woodcutter, although Pia hadn't had much to do with him. "Your sister found three of us. We have a plan to take back the warehouse, but we need your help from inside."

CHAPTER 3

NADEZ STIFLED A yawn. She'd slept badly: kept awake worrying about all the ways Tarklee would be worse off if Lauma pulled Byholt out of the Alliance. It could lead to higher prices for food, infighting amongst the Clan Freeholders, and the very real possibility of starvation when Clan Freeholders inevitably hoarded food. Because Lauma was right about that: Clan Freeholders in Swyford and Nordmere did not have a history of helping their own people, so they could not be counted on to help one another.

The longer-term consequences could be even more devastating. Without their own shipbuilding facilities, Byholt and Nordmere would need to trade for ships. What price would Tavet Timonis, who owned the only shipbuilding facility on the Pale Sea, extract? He would likely need to trade with Byholt for timber, but Nadez was under no illusion that he might decide to strand Nordmere without ships, which meant that country would have no way to control their own trade.

She had wanted to discuss that with Lauma last night, but the Interim Grand Freeholder had insisted that she had no time and had refused to hear her out.

Pausing in front of the door to the meeting room, Nadez gave in to the next yawn. She frowned as she pushed the door open and entered.

The Byholt and Swyford contingents were already seated.

Nadez stepped away from the door and Saulia Holt and her uncle entered and sat down.

Gustav slipped out of the small door and joined her along the back wall.

"Is she listening to reason today?" Nadez said, not bothering to hide her bitterness. When Lauma Strauskas had been appointed Interim Grand Freeholder: when *Nadez* had helped her secure that position, she had thought the two of them would always be on the same side.

"She's not being unreasonable," Gustav said. "And she promised to work at convincing them that her stance was the best for everyone."

"I wish I had your faith in her," Nadez replied. "Dissolving the Alliance is not an idle threat."

"No, but I don't think it's Lauma's first choice." He leaned closer. "Wanna know what she was doing last night?"

Ottosen and Heikki finally arrived. Without taking her eyes off them, Nadez lifted her chin. "What?"

"She visited both Liina Nowack and Melker Skala," Gustav said. "Do you think she looks like she's going to get her way?"

Nadez looked at Lauma, who was watching Ottosen and Heikki sit down, a small smile on her lips. "You're saying she already has the votes?"

"Yes," Gustav said. "At least, I think *she* thinks she does. Which is a different thing."

"Yes, it is." Nadez studied the Swyford contingent. With Lauma's son Yakop voting for Byholt and Saulia and her uncle with a majority for Nordmere, Swyford was the only open question.

"Thank you for coming for this second meeting," Lauma said. "I assume that you have all come to the conclusion that the document we showed you yesterday is a true account of the protocols that govern how to make changes to the Treaty agreement." Lauma paused, but no one spoke up to contest her statement.

"Good," Lauma continued. "Then I will make a proposal, after which others can comment or ask questions or even suggest their own changes. But make no mistake, I will not leave this room without some sort of modification to the Treaty."

"There's that threat again," Ottosen said. "Are we going to

stand for that? These are supposed to be negotiations, not coercion and intimidation."

"Negotiations are always based on the strength of your bargaining position," Yakop said. "Just because the Strauskas holdings carry weight under the terms of the Treaty does not make my mother's request a threat."

"Are you agreeing that one single person, Lauma Strauskas, has more power than the rest of us combined?" Heikki asked. "That doesn't sound like we have much choice."

"It's the way the Treaty was created," Yakop said. "A majority of holdings for each country is required to agree to any changes to the original agreement. The Strauskas holdings just happen to be the majority for Byholt. If it worked in your favour, you would not be contesting it."

"I want to hear the proposal," Saulia said. "I'll be the judge of whether I have a free choice to make or not."

"You shouldn't even be here," Ottosen said, glaring past Seppo at Saulia Holt. "It's ridiculous that a girl not even out of school should make such a decision."

"I may not be out of school," Saulia replied. "But I have been learning the duties and responsibilities of a Clan Freeholder all my life."

"From a traitor," Ottosen replied.

"Clan Freeholder Ottosen," Lauma interrupted. "As I said yesterday, if you have evidence, then share it. Otherwise, keep your opinions to yourself."

"I also want to hear the proposal," Clan Freeholder Nowack said, and Gustav nudged Nadez's arm.

"I will state it as plainly as I can," Lauma said, rising to her feet. "I propose that we change the way the Grand Freeholder is elected. Partly," she looked at Ottosen, "because I do not like Byholt being at the mercy of the Clan Freeholders of another country. Why should Byholter Clan Freeholders not have a say in who is to govern them and their people? I suggest that the Grand Freeholder be chosen by the majority for each country. That way we *all* will determine who rules the Three."

"Would each country still take a turn providing the Grand Freeholder?" Saulia asked. "Would the next Grand Freeholder be from Swyford?"

"I don't see any reason to change that," Lauma said. "Does

anyone else?"

"This would give you the power to veto any selection," Ottosen said. "Why would I allow you that kind of power?"

"Any one country could organize their own votes to block a candidate they disliked," Lauma said. "The fact that for Byholt it would just take the Strauskas vote does not invalidate the process."

"If each country can block the candidate," Melker Skala said, "what happens then? How are we to ever get to an agreement?"

"Another candidate would be put forward," Lauma said. "Until we find one we can all agree on."

"I will never submit to this," Ottosen said.

"But I will," Saulia said. She turned to Seppa. "Uncle?"

"I also agree," Karl Seppa said. "Grand Freeholder, that gives you a majority for Nordmere."

"I won't allow it!" Ottosen said. "You do not speak for me."

"He doesn't have to, Clan Freeholder Ottosen. The Holt and Seppa holdings comprise sixty percent of Nordmere's freeholdings. Based on the original agreement document that is more than enough for the motion to carry for Nordmere." She turned to face the Swyfordians. "Byholt also agrees to the change, so it's up to the Clan Freeholders from Swyford."

"If we don't agree, the voting remains as it has always been," Timonis said. "So of course, we vote no."

"*You* vote no," Nowack said. "I vote yes."

"You *skit*!" Timonis said. "How dare you repay my generosity by stabbing me in the back. You will pay for this betrayal. Kozlow!"

"I vote no," Koit Kozlow said. "Tavet Timonis will be the next Grand Freeholder, so I expect the rest of you will suffer the consequences."

"This kind of threat is exactly why we must change the election process," Lauma said. She was staring directly at Clan Freeholder Melker, who was scowling. Nadez could only hope that he was unhappy about the Swyford threat and not Lauma's proposed change.

"Of course, Melker votes no too," Timonis said.

"Does he?" Lauma asked. "We do need an answer, Clan Freeholder Melker."

"Ah *skit*," Melker said. "You are right, Interim Grand

Freeholder. I do not want to be at the mercy of a Grand Freeholder bent on vengeance. I vote yes."

"What! How dare you," Timonis screamed at his fellow Swyfordians. "I will make you pay for this. I will make you pay!"

"Swyford votes for the change to the Treaty agreement," Lauma called over Timonis' complaints. "I will have a copy of the text delivered to each of you. We will meet again in the morning to finalize the wording and discuss any additional issues."

Lauma ducked out of the door along the back wall, and Nadez stepped in front of the door just as Timonis rounded the table.

"She cannot do this!" he yelled at her. "I won't allow it."

"It's done, Clan Freeholder," Nadez replied. "Your issues are with your fellow countrymen, not the Grand Freeholder." She looked past him. "Clan Freeholder Melker is leaving. I suggest you take your concerns up with him."

"Melker!" Timonis yelled as he hurried after him. "Melker, we are not done."

GUSTAV RELAXED AGAINST the wall once Timonis rushed out of the council meeting. If he had not been so worried that the Fair Seas Treaty Alliance had almost been dismantled, he would have grinned.

Mykol was working as Lauma's assistant today, and he stood in the middle of the tables, trying to answer questions that were being shouted at him. He sent Gustav a pleading look, so he joined him.

"Clan Freeholder Holt," Gustav said when he noticed Saulia frowning at him. "I was saddened to hear about your parents but glad that you are well."

"Were you?" Saulia asked. "You were sent to spy on them, after all."

"I was," Gustav replied. "But that doesn't mean I wished them harm. Just that I wished your father to not damage the Alliance. Which he did."

"Which he did," Saulia said and sighed. "But my mother played no part in it and did not deserve her fate."

"I was poisoned while dining in your home," Gustav said. He doubted that could have happened without Asla Holt's knowledge. "But as I said, I was saddened to hear of your loss." He nodded and turned his attention to Mykol. Saulia Holt could pretend her mother was as betrayed by her husband as the rest of the Alliance had been, but he would not.

"Clan Freeholders," Mykol said. "One at a time, please."

"This is outrageous," Ottosen yelled.

"I agree," echoed Timonis. He was standing in the doorway. By the angry look on his face, Gustav assumed Timonis had not had any luck with Melker. "We will not stand for this. Once I am elected Grand Freeholder, I will reverse this decision, you have my word on that."

"*If* you are elected Grand Freeholder you can reopen this issue," Gustav said. "But the process for reverting back to the original rules will be the same one used here: a majority of each country's Freeholdings is required to make the change."

"Byholt will not agree," Yakop Strauskas said. "So, reopening this is futile."

"What do you mean *if* I become Grand Freeholder?" Timonis bellowed. He took a few steps into the room. "It's my turn. It's my right."

"It's not a right," Nowack said. "And I'm not voting for you, not when you've already threatened me."

"How dare you!" Timonis said. "I've been expecting to be elected for years. You gave me your backing already."

"And now I'm rescinding it," Nowack replied. "Recent events and lack of action by you have shown me that I don't dare subject my holdings or my people to your rule. If you get the votes you need, then I'm sure you will take your revenge, but as of now, I will back Skala for Grand Freeholder." She turned to him. "If he's interested in the position."

"You can't do that!" Timonis leaned over Nowack.

Gustav reached over the table to grab Timonis' arm. "Do I need to call the Guard?" Gustav asked. Timonis tried to shrug out of his grasp but stopped struggling when Nadez grabbed his other arm.

"No," Timonis said.

"Good," Gustav said. "Mykol? Do you need more time?" He let go of Timonis, who glared at him before he shook his arm free from Nadez's hold and left, followed by Kozlow.

"No," Mykol shook his head. "I understand the arguments for and against. I will include them in the records that I send to each Clan Freeholder. If you'll excuse me, I have a lot of copies to create by the end of the day."

"Yes, thank you," Gustav said. "I appreciate your hard work, as I'm sure the Interim Grand Freeholder and the Master Intelligencer do." He turned to Saulia. "And we are grateful to you for allowing Mykol to do this. I know he's working for you and as a new Clan Freeholder I'm sure his experience and expertise are missed."

"They are," Saulia said. "I appreciate that you understand how difficult it is for me to be without Mykol, but I do realize how much he is needed for this task."

Mykol beamed as he stacked some papers. "I'll be back outside your office as soon as I can, Clan Freeholder," he said to Saulia.

"I know you will," she replied. "Now, off you go. I know you have a busy day ahead."

Mykol left, and Gustav turned to find an angry Henrik Ottosen staring at him.

"Clan Freeholder," Gustav said. "Is there anything I can do for you?"

"No," Ottosen replied. "Lauma Strauskas may think she's won, but her reckoning is already in play." His smirk disappeared when Nadez stepped up and glared at him.

"We know about the Resolute," Nadez said. The smile she gave Ottosen chilled Gustav, as did the mention of a legendary assassin. "If you only knew who it was." Nadez took a step back from the Clan Freeholder. "Pinho will be lucky to save himself, never mind coming to save you."

Ottosen looked shaken, and when Gustav caught Nadez's eye and raised his brows, she shook her head and walked away.

Ottosen left the room with a lot less confidence than he had shown a moment ago, making Gustav wonder what other news Dagrun Lund had brought that hadn't been passed along to him.

Once the room was empty, he spent a few minutes gathering up glasses and the water pitcher. When there was nothing else to do, he left and headed out into the city. If Ottosen had some sort of agreement with someone named Pinho or a Resolute assassin, he hoped that someone would tell him because from her expression, it didn't seem like Nadez would.

PIA WAITED IMPATIENTLY by the opening. It was time, wasn't it? It had to be time. She lay down and tried to look out, but she couldn't see anything that would tell her the time of day. No moonlight, no signs of dawn arriving, nothing.

Bjorn the woodcutter had said they would be ready just before dawn. Then it would be Pia's turn. She already knew what she was going to do to create the distraction. She also knew that after that she was *not* going to follow Bjorn's order and hide. She was trained—well, half-trained which was more than most of the others, but the point was she could help. And even the little she could do from inside the warehouse would surprise the pirates. And that might be just enough to ensure success.

She hadn't come all this way; she hadn't brought her sister so far from home to lose her to pirates. She'd heard the stories of orphans being kidnapped only to show up later as part of the pirate crew. That would not be Frida's fate. Not as long as she was alive.

A bird sang nearby signalling that dawn had arrived. Pia stared out at the darkness.

"Good, you're here," a voice whispered.

She heard rustling sounds outside and then Bjorn's face appeared at the opening.

"Where's my sister?" Pia asked.

"Safe," Bjorn replied. "You have a way to get their attention?"

"Yes. I'm going to topple some fish racks."

"Good. We'll use that to take out the guards out front." His teeth shone as he grinned. "After that we're setting fire to some of their boats. That'll bring most of them outside right where we want them."

"Make sure my sister is safe," Pia said. "I'll be holding you responsible."

"She'll be safe," Bjorn said. "But only if we can defeat the pirates. Now, count to fifty and then start your distraction."

Bjorn left and counting under her breath, Pia stood and carefully made her way to the far corner.

By the time she reached thirty-five she was in place. She closed her eyes and continued to count. "Forty-nine, fifty," she whispered.

Pia placed her hands on a drying rack that was about chest high and then pushed. The wooden rack, weighted down by another half dozen racks of drying fish on top of it, slowly scraped across the rack underneath. The stack of racks swayed as the one she had pushed slid off the one below it. Slowly at first and then gaining speed, the half dozen racks fell onto the stack in front, the momentum causing that rack to cascade onto the next one until the whole section of stacked drying racks crashed to the floor of the warehouse.

Someone shouted in alarm and then Pia heard the sounds of running feet. She peered out to see people heading her way: pirates were coming to investigate. Three of the shadows raised arms and pointed pistols at the dark warehouse.

Pia made her way to the far end of the warehouse and crouched amongst the empty wooden racks.

"What in *Jebris'* name is going on?" yelled the captain of the pirates. "Edur? Go see what happened."

"Aye, Captain. Tilde, Benil, come with me."

Pia peered around a stack of racks. The fire flared when someone tossed another log onto it, sending light farther into the warehouse. A few lamps had been lit, illuminating the captain, who stood with her hands on her hips, staring out into the dark warehouse. The food gatherers huddled a few feet from the fire, their hands and feet tied together.

The other pirates—she counted six besides the captain—were scattered between the door and the fire. Including the three who held pistols.

A loud bang echoed across the warehouse when the double doors crashed open. Even from where she hid, Pia could see flames out beyond the door.

"The boats are on fire," the captain yelled. "We need to save them!"

Every single pirate rushed outside, including the three who had been sent farther into the warehouse to investigate the fallen racks.

Pia rose to her feet, ready to rush to the fire and untie the others. Suddenly, the pirate captain returned. She ran into Solvig's quarters and shut the door. A moment later, Bjorn stood in the warehouse doorway.

"Where'd she go?" he called out.

"In Solvig's quarters," someone called from the fire. "Said she was their captain."

"I'll get her." Axe in hand, Bjorn stopped in front of the door to Solvig's quarters. Another woodcutter entered the warehouse and hurried over and started untying the captives.

"Where's my sister?" Pia asked as she joined Bjorn.

"She's safe," he replied. The door didn't budge when he tried to open it. "Stay back."

The blade of his axe hit the door with a thud and sank into the wood. When Bjorn wiggled the axe head, wood groaned and shredded until he had created a hole in the door. Another swing of his axe and the hole was large enough for him to reach his hand in and unlock the door from the inside.

Pia followed him into the small space. The main room was empty, as was the sleeping chamber. The door to the privy was closed.

Bjorn wrenched the door open: the small room was empty.

The bucket that had been set into the floor was gone and Pia leaned over and looked down into the sea.

"She's in the water," Bjorn shouted. Pia scrambled out of his way and followed him as he raced out into the warehouse and then outside.

Smoke filled the dawn air, wafting up from the charred remains of a couple of boats.

"Ivar," Bjorn called to woodcutter who stood on the dock. "Did she get in one of the sailboats?"

"Someone did," he replied. "Swam out from under the dock too quick for me to nab 'em. The only seaworthy sailboat came back for 'em." He grinned. "It was riding so low in the water I thought they might capsize. Won't go far or fast in that."

"Good riddance," Bjorn said. "We didn't want to catch them: prisoners are nothing but work and we got enough of that. We saved the food stores and ourselves, that's what's important. Would be nice to know what they're doing here. And where their ship is. If they have one. It is possible they came all the way from Strongrock in those sailboats. Not smart, especially this time of year, but possible."

"Are you sure they're from Strongrock?" Pia asked as she followed Bjorn back into the warehouse.

"Yep," he replied. "I've dealt with Strongrock pirates before. That was them. Must be on the move because their captain is dead. There, see," he said, pointing across the warehouse. "Your sister is safe and sound."

"Frida!" Pia called and ran towards her sister, who grinned

and hugged her.

"We beat them!" Frida said. "The Byholt woodcutters and us! We helped them beat the pirates."

"We did," Pia replied.

"And look." Frida pointed to where a woodcutter was tying the hands of a woman she didn't recognize. "Lennart and I even caught one of them."

DAG STARED OUT across the water at Strongrock.

Calder had planned on giving the island a wide berth, but Dag's Trait had activated when he had mentioned that to her. She hadn't needed to convince him to visit the pirate settlement.

They'd lost half of a day of sailing in order to do it, but now it was night, and they were just off the Strongrock harbour. The itch between her shoulder blades intensified and she scratched it absently.

"My Trait definitely thinks there's something here I need to know about." She turned to face Calder, who stood beside her at the gunwale.

"It's quiet," Calder said. "We should be hearing sounds from the tavern."

"Maybe they ran out of ale," Dag replied. "Ansdottir's ship is missing. And weren't there a few sailboats?"

"There were at least three or four, from what I remember," Calder said. "But we did steal one of them. I doubt the *Vassan* towed any of them, but it is possible the pirates have taken them somewhere else on the island, like Teacher's beach for instance. Maybe they're looking for Ansdottir's treasure."

"Jaak seemed to think that was a well-kept secret," Dag replied. "And nothing about it triggered my Trait. I don't see any signs of life on shore and the tavern is dark." A gust of wind brought the smell of old smoke. "Which wouldn't make sense if some of them were off looking for treasure. Should we land and make sure?"

"I'll have a dinghy lowered," Calder replied. "We'll take Jaak: he knows Strongrock better than anyone else on board. Everyone going ashore should carry a pistol."

Dag sat in the bow, her pistol in her hands, as Jaak and another five sailors rowed them towards the dock. The silence was unnerving, as was the empty feel of the shore ahead. The smell of smoke was stronger now.

"The inn burned," Calder said from the stern. "It looks like the whole second floor is gone."

A few other smaller buildings near the inn had also been gutted by the fire. Dag jumped onto the dock and tied the boat up. Calder, lamp in hand, joined her.

"Pall offered to stay with the dinghy," Jaak said when the rest of the sailors had stepped onto the dock. "The rest of us should stick together."

"It looks like everything here was destroyed," Dag said. "My Trait is quiet."

"We'll check every building anyway," Calder said. He led the way up onto land.

They stopped in the small square. The pump was intact, and when Dag pumped the handle, water flowed from the spout. "They didn't run out of water." Food was a different matter, although the pirates would have been able to fish.

"Stay here," Jaak said to her and Calder. "I'll just make sure no one's in the inn."

"What do you think happened?" she asked Calder. She didn't think anyone was alive in the inn. At least, her Trait didn't activate.

"My guess?" Calder replied. "Without Ansdottir's discipline, Strongrock probably turned unruly. But was it simply drunken chaos, or were the pirates fighting each other?"

"No one's alive in there," Jaak said when he returned. "But I found a couple of dead pirates. I recognized them: they were some of the meaner ones. They were shot and probably dead before the fire was set."

"A fight between pirates then," Dag said, and her Trait twitched. "That's important. That there are at least two factions of pirates." She turned to Calder. "No one is left here, so I think we have to assume that the *Vassan* and the small sailboats went in separate directions."

"At this time of year, the *Vassan* could have only gone to the Sapphire Sea," Calder said. "And the sailboats must have gone south."

"Yes," Dag said. "My Trait has quieted. So, pirates ahead of us on the *Vassan* and pirates heading south."

"If they're lucky, they'll reach Swyford," Calder said. "And there's no way to warn them."

"No," Dag said. Her itch disappeared. "But at least we know. I doubt we'll find anyone alive here." She headed down the path towards the tavern.

The tavern was a shamble. There was no sign of Ursa or the cook, Espen. In the main room, tables were overturned and chairs broken, and it looked like both the kitchen and taps rooms had been searched. Dag didn't see one speck of food anywhere.

"No one upstairs," Jaak said when he and the rest of the men joined her and Calder in the main tavern.

"Is there anywhere else that might have food?" Dag asked. "I think they ran out. That might even be what caused the fighting."

"Just Ansdottir's cabin," Jaak said.

"We should look just to be sure that Strongrock really is deserted," Calder said, and they all followed Jaak out of the tavern to a narrow path.

"Would anyone have used her cabin after she died?" Calder asked.

Dag stared down the path, but nothing about it triggered her Trait.

"Maybe Ursa," Jaak said. "Rumour was the Captain set traps along the path to her cabin when she went to sea but that Ursa knew where they all were."

"I'll go first," Dag said. "In case there are any traps still active." She held out her hand and Calder passed her a lamp. Nothing looked out of place as she walked along the path. She paused: her Trait had not activated, not really, but there was something here. She lifted the lamp and studied a bush near the trail. Branches were broken, and when she peered in, she saw sharpened sticks tied into a ball. A thin line of rope dangled from it. She grabbed the end of the rope and pulled the ball of sticks out of the bush.

Someone had disabled this trap before it had been activated. Ursa? Was she hiding in Ansdottir's cabin? No. If Ursa was here, the trap would still be active.

She found one more disabled trap before she reached the cabin. The door was wide open, and when she swung the light inside, she found it in much the same state as the tavern. It looked like it had been searched but no one was inside.

"All clear," she called out and, in a few moments, Calder was at her side. "Nothing left. At least nothing that has triggered my

Trait," she said to him.

"I'll take a quick look," he said and stepped inside. "For Luck."

"Hard to believe they're all gone," Jaak said. "Pirates have been on Strongrock for decades and now it's empty."

"I'm sure some will return," Dag replied. "Once they get supplies and figure out who's going to lead them." Some of the pirates likely had nowhere else to go. "Who do you think took over for Ansdottir? Ursa?"

"I don't know," Jaak said. "Some would never follow her because she's never been a sailor; they'd say she's not a real pirate."

"But some would?"

"Sure, some would. Ursa was always trusted by the captain. And she's smart. A pirate could do worse."

"So, who would oppose Ursa?" Dag asked. She thought that Ursa was in charge of at least some of the pirates. But which ones? The ones that went to Lavais or the ones on the *Vassan*?

"That's easy," Jaak replied. "Nils and probably the new man Steen. Nils has been with Ansdottir for years, but I think both of them would rather answer to a man instead of a woman. I can't see either of them following Ursa."

"Nothing in here," Calder said from just inside the cabin. "If there was anything of value, it's been taken."

"By Ursa," Dag said. "Probably coin. I think she's gone to Lavais on the small sailboats. And Steen is on the *Vassan*."

"Steen," Calder said. "He was always ugly, even with Ansdottir's Trait influencing him." He sighed. "I suppose it's better that Steen isn't in Swyford. At least we can deal with him if we cross paths. Villagers wouldn't do as well. Come on, let's get back to the ship. Nothing we discovered changes our mission."

"Except that we know that pirates are likely ahead of us," Dag said.

CHAPTER 4

NADEZ WALKED THROUGH the empty corridors to her office. It was too early for many people to be about. She stopped beside the desk reserved for an assistant. Mykol had been busy. A sealed document was on the desk, a copy of the agreement from yesterday's meeting.

She picked up the document, broke the seal, and unlocked her office.

A few minutes later, she'd finished reading it. The new agreement was exactly what she had expected. Mykol might not have Kaja's Trait, but he hadn't left out a thing. Except for the animosity that some of the Clan Freeholders, notably Timonis, had shown during the meeting.

She had a few hours until the final meeting. At least she hoped it was the final meeting. She heard a noise in the outer office, and a moment later, Gustav poked his head through the door.

"Is that the agreement?" he asked.

"Yes. Come in. I just read through it, and I think it reflects what was discussed." She pushed the document across the desk to him. "I wouldn't mind another opinion."

"You don't trust Mykol." Gustav started reading.

"I don't trust anyone," Nadez replied, more to herself than to Gustav. She stared over his head, silent while he read.

"This is what I remember," Gustav said, looking up at her. "Will this end Lauma's talk of dissolving the Alliance?"

"It should," Nadez replied. "She basically has the ability to veto every single Grand Freeholder choice for as long as this agreement stands."

"You think it gives her too much power," Gustav said. "But won't the Grand Freeholder be independent once they're elected?"

"In theory, yes," Nadez said. "But what will Lauma do if the Grand Freeholder makes a decision she doesn't agree with? And what about those who are vying for the position? By now every Clan Freeholder in Nordmere and Swyford understands that in order to get elected, they must have Lauma Strauskas' approval. What kind of promises will they be willing to make?"

"Lauma seems to only be interested in what's fair for her people," Gustav replied.

"Yes," Nadez agreed. "And I believe her. But what about her son? Will he act in the same way when he inherits her land? Or his children? In my experience, power has a way of changing people; it has a way of making them believe they are right, just because they have the power to make decisions. And it certainly has an effect on the people around them."

"I guess," Gustav said. "I'm just happy that the Alliance still exists and I can still be an Intelligencer. I can, can't I?"

"Of course," Nadez replied. "We'll even get the school back up and running. But not until we have the shipyards operational and shipping is almost back to normal."

"Janni and Jarri are doing great work," Gustav said.

"So you told me." Nadez sighed. "It's too important a task to not worry about. I'd go and see for myself if I thought everything was sorted out here."

"You want me to go back to Lavais?" Gustav asked. "I've been told the road is tricky when the snow hits so I'll need to go soon."

"As much as I want you to stay here and assist either me or Lauma, I think it's best if you go," Nadez said.

"I can send Kaja back," Gustav said. "She's a much better assistant than I am anyway."

"That's a good idea. Thank you."

Gustav left, and Nadez continued to stare at the door.

She was afraid that there was little she could do about the unhappy Clan Freeholders in Swyford and Nordmere.

Nervous, Pia watched Solvig, who stared at the jumbled mass of racks and partially dried fish.

"I didn't ruin them, did I?" she asked. Knocking over the stacks of drying fish had been her best way to create a distraction for the pirates, but she and Frida had gone hungry enough times that she was worried she had destroyed desperately needed food.

"Nah," Solvig said. She reached down and grabbed a large filet. "It's hard to ruin these once they're dry. We'll need to give them a good wash and another coat of salt, but there's no permanent harm done." She handed the filet to Frida. "The bucket by the door has fresh water." Frida wobbled as she took her burden out of the warehouse.

"We'll fix them all," Pia said. "Frida and me." She leaned over and picked up a slab of fish. "I'm sure you have more important things to do."

"Not today," Solvig replied. "I want to keep busy so I don't have to look at that pirate and get mad all over again. Can't stand thieves. Too lazy to work hard and instead try to steal from honest folk."

"I heard one say that he'd burn the salt fish rather than eat it," Pia said. "But a woman, I think the one we caught, said she'd never destroy food."

"So, the other one was stupid as well as lazy." Solvig picked up a few pieces of fish and headed to the open warehouse doors. Pia followed her outside.

"That's good, Frida," Solvig said. "Just put it in the salt. Once they're washed and re-salted, we'll pile all the ones that fell out here. I need to inspect the racks in case any of them were too damaged to hold the weight. Once I do that, you both can help me get the fish back inside and on the racks."

Pia took a turn at the bucket and washed the dirt off her slab of fish before laying it on top of the others. She was about to follow Frida and Solvig back inside when she saw Bjorn heading towards the prisoner.

Curious, she followed him.

The dark-skinned pirate looked to be middle-aged. She didn't look as dark as a Pilalian, or even an Arressan, but she was darker than anyone from the Pale Sea got even after being out in the sun all summer.

"Gonna talk today?" Bjorn asked. He stopped a few feet from

the pier the pirate was tied up to. "Maybe tell me your name?"

The pirate looked up at him and shook her head.

"That's what I thought," Bjorn said. He turned to leave and bumped into Pia, who had crept up behind him.

"Hey, are you all right?" Bjorn asked.

"Fine," Pia replied. "It was my fault for sneaking up on you." She looked past him to see the pirate staring at her. "What are you going to do with her?"

"Dunno," Bjorn said. He looked over his shoulder at the pirate. "Can't let her go, not when she came here pointing a pistol. Can't keep her tied up here forever, neither."

"Can we send her to Lavais?" Pia asked.

"Can't spare anyone to row her there," Bjorn said.

"Can't you get to Lavais Port by land?" She tried to remember what she'd been taught about the island. It was flat with natural harbours, but did they only travel by sea?

"Dunno," Bjorn replied. "Doesn't matter. Still can't spare anyone to take her." He shrugged. "If she won't tell us who she is, I'm not sure I want to do anything for her. And I certainly won't let her get in the way of preparing for winter." He nodded and headed back towards the warehouse.

Pia took a couple of steps towards the prisoner.

"They're not coming back for you," she said. "So, you might as well talk to us."

The woman shrugged and looked away but didn't say anything.

"Maybe your old captain wouldn't leave you behind," Pia continued. "Ansdottir had that reputation." Pia didn't know a lot about the dead pirate captain, but she had heard that she was loyal to her crew and they to her. "Are you so sure about the new captain?"

The pirate didn't say anything, but her brow furrowed so Pia knew she was worried.

"I'll get you some water," Pia said. She went inside the warehouse and grabbed a dipper of water. The prisoner drank without saying a word.

"You should think about what Bjorn said," Pia said to the pirate. "If we can't keep you and we can't let you go, what do you think his solution will be?" She wasn't sure Bjorn meant to kill the woman, but she wasn't sure he didn't mean that either.

She left the dipper where she had found it and rejoined Solvig and Frida.

And the whole time it took to get the fish washed, salted, and placed back on the drying racks she kept thinking about that prisoner. So much so that her Trait triggered, and she Concentrated on the situation.

The pirate had information that might make the difference between life and death for more than a few people. She could not get past the one pirate who had been willing to burn the dried fish. They *had* burned other food stores, so she had to believe that was a real threat.

Intelligencers could probably extract any important information the prisoner knew.

She sighed. It looked like her plan to keep herself and Frida anonymous would not necessarily keep them safe. No one would be safe from hunger. Not when pirates were around, willing to steal food, or worse, destroy it.

She watched her little sister place the last filet on the rack and then smile up at Solvig.

Keeping Frida safe was her priority. Except now she didn't think she could keep her sister safe without ensuring the safety of everyone along this coast. Pirates on the loose were too big a threat.

Which meant that she would have to take the prisoner to Lavais Port and hope that at least one Intelligencer was there who could find out what the pirate knew.

GUSTAV PULLED HIS jacket tighter before shoving his hands into his pockets. The bitter wind whipped at the few leaves that remained on the deciduous trees, shaking some of them loose. They swirled above his head before drifting down onto the road.

He had been walking for hours, trying to stay warm and make good time to Pavil Barda's house. He shook his head: the exact same journey he'd undergone not even two weeks ago. He had assumed that it would be easy again, but the weather had turned, and now it was all he could do to keep putting one foot in front of the other.

He pulled his waterskin from inside his jacket and took a sip. It was still cold, but at least it was no longer frozen. He'd been at the Hall for so long that he'd forgotten that if you carried your waterskin outside of your coat, you'd be left with nothing but ice.

The sound of waves crashing against the shore drew him from the road. The sea was dark and cloud cover meant there was no moonlight, but he thought dawn was close. Whitecaps were visible in the dim light as they pounded the rocks below.

Another couple of hours should see him at Pavil's house, where he could finally get warm and have a meal. Even dried fish stew would be welcome.

Heavy snow started to fall, so he headed back to the road. For the most part, trees sheltered him from the worst of the storm, but snow blanketed the ground where there were breaks in the canopy.

Finally, he turned a corner and saw Pavil's house. He was halfway to the door when he realized that he didn't smell smoke.

He took a step back. There was no fire burning. It was still early in the morning, but wouldn't Pavil keep a fire going on a cold night?

Frowning, he went to the front door. There were no lights or sounds, but that didn't mean anything was wrong necessarily.

Rather than knock or try the door, he went around to the back. The shed was empty: neither the wagon nor the horse was here. Which meant that Pavil was not home.

The man would just have to understand. Gustav tried the back door and thankfully it opened into the kitchen. He stepped inside and exhaled: even just being out of the wind was a relief. He didn't want to think what would have happened if he hadn't been able to get inside. It was a long way to anywhere else along this road.

Wishing he had Kaja's memory, he tried to remember the layout of the room. He shuffled around until he found the hearth. Wood was stacked beside it and he ran his hands across the stones of the fireplace and up to the wooden mantel, where he found a flint. In moments he had a couple of lamps lit and a fire kindled in the hearth.

With one lamp in hand, he left the kitchen.

"Pavil?" he called as he went from room to room. But there was no answer. The house was empty.

The kitchen was much warmer when he returned. The cold room was beside the back door. Not wanting to take too much, he grabbed a couple of potatoes and carrots, scraped the dirt off them, cut them up, and using the last of his water, put them to boil in a pot.

Once his vegetables were cooked, he ate them, drinking the last of the liquid while it was still warm. He would need to find Pavil's stream and refill his waterskin, but for now, at least he had something warm to fill his belly and a fire to chase away any chills.

He meant to get water and bring in some more wood after eating, but the warmth of the kitchen and his long night lulled him into a deep sleep.

"Who's here?"

Gustav bolted awake and almost fell off the chair he was slumped in. He looked up into a lamp so bright that he couldn't see past the flame.

"Ah, it's you." The lamp was lowered, and Gustav found himself facing a worried Pavil Barda. "I hope it's not bad news that brings you along the road again so soon." Pavil set the lamp on the table and sat down. "I have enough bad news of my own."

"Sorry about just coming inside," Gustav said. "I'll pay you for what I've taken."

"Don't worry about that," Pavil said. "I leave the door open on purpose. I'd rather come back and find that a stranger's made himself at home than find a body frozen to death outside a locked door."

"Oh, of course," Gustav replied. "I wasn't sure I should just come in. And there's no bad news from Tarklee." At least the Alliance was safe for now. "I've been sent to Lavais shipyards to make sure there's no trouble with the ship rebuilding."

"Not sure about ship rebuilding," Pavil said. "But there's trouble close by. I was getting supplies when they arrived in Nurmi. Come in with pistols drawn, they did. I think they knew what or who they were looking for. At least they didn't bother anyone who stayed out of their way. I packed up my wagon and left without even getting all my supplies, even though I already paid for them. That's why I was a little jumpy when I found you. Was worried you were one of them."

"One of who?" Gustav asked.

"Pirates," Pavil replied. "They didn't say they were pirates, but they weren't from around here. And who else would draw weapons before even asking a question?"

"Pirates? How would they get here?" But he knew how. Either they had been stranded in Tarklee when Ansdottir died and came south either by road or small boat, or they were from Strongrock. "Ansdottir left a ship in Strongrock Harbour. Maybe they came on that." It didn't make sense though. The Frozen Pass was too dangerous this late in the season. That's why Dagrun Lund had to leave on the *Atlaine*: she had to navigate the ship through the Teeth.

"I didn't see a ship in the Nurmi harbour or anywhere else along the coast," Pavil replied. "Maybe they came on smaller boats. Like the first two Intelligencers, Calder and Dagrun."

"They would have to go through the Teeth," Gustav said. He knew Calder and Dagrun had done that out of desperation. Had the pirates been that desperate too? That sounded like worse than trouble.

"Maybe they ran out of food," Pavil said. "From what I know, pirates aren't much for farming and fishing."

"They probably did," Gustav agreed. "But why come here? You said they seemed to know where they were going. What made you think that?"

"One of them seemed to know the town," Pavil replied. "And was leading them through it."

"Leading them where?"

"Don't know," Pavil said. "I was on the north road, and I didn't stay long enough to find out."

Gustav nodded. "Fair enough. Finding out who or what the pirates are looking for is my job."

NADEZ ENTERED THE meeting room and stopped at the sight that greeted her. She had arrived early and yet every single Clan Freeholder was already seated around the table. She had to assume that they had all come to the same conclusion as she had. Lauma Strauskas was the key to any of them ever becoming Grand Freeholder, so they better treat her with respect.

She and Lauma had hoped that yesterday's meeting was the last one, but each Clan Freeholder had been given the opportunity to comment on the new agreement and many of them had.

After a few minor quibbles about wording, Mykol had been tasked with making changes and creating more copies for everyone. Today, barring any other objections, the new Alliance agreement would be completed.

They were not having another vote: Lauma stated that the vote they'd had was binding and that this was simply paperwork. Nadez wondered if she was worried about anyone having second thoughts and changing their vote. She didn't expect Ottosen to have any luck convincing Saulia Holt or her uncle to reverse their decision, but it was possible Timonis could pressure Skala.

She caught a look that passed between Skala and Nowack and relaxed. Neither one of them had changed their minds.

"Good day," Lauma said as she entered the room. "I trust everyone had a chance to reread the document and confirm that the changes we agreed to yesterday have been made? Yes? Good."

Lauma sat down facing the rest of the Freeholders. "I do thank you for making this one last meeting," she continued. "It's vitally important that the Treaty survives." She placed her hands on top of the table. "Are there any other issues with the document?"

"I'm satisfied," Clan Freeholder Seppa said. He looked at Ottosen, who ignored him.

"Anyone else?" Lauma asked. She looked around the room, but no one spoke. "Good. I proclaim the Fair Seas Treaty revised as per this document. Thank you. That leaves one last piece of business. I think it best to wait until ships have been built before we elect a new Grand Freeholder. That means a vote won't happen until summer."

"That's more than six months late," Timonis said, making Nadez wonder if he actually realized that he'd never be Grand Freeholder without Lauma's approval.

"And these are extraordinary circumstances," Lauma replied. "Surely a change in leadership right now would cause anxiety amongst our countrymen and women. We face a steep challenge already; I think we should make every effort to not inflict harm on ourselves."

"The Interim Grand Freeholder is right," Ottosen said. "We can't afford to make anyone nervous, not now that winter has hit."

"Thank you, Clan Freeholder Ottosen," Lauma said. "Does anyone else wish to comment?"

Nadez looked around the table. Timonis was scowling, but no one else said anything.

"Then this meeting is over. Thank you all." Lauma rose and quickly exited the room.

Nadez waited and watched as the Clan Freeholders left. When it was just her and Mykol, she joined him to help clear away the water glasses.

"Gustav should be doing this, not you," Mykol said, taking a glass from her and placing it on a tray.

"Assistants are very hard to keep these days," she replied. "I believe Clan Freeholder Holt agreed to let you help us get through these negotiations, and you have done a beautiful job. But now that this is over, you'll need to return to her. I can let the Interim Grand Freeholder know if you wish." She paused. Lauma was the one who had agreed that Mykol should work for Saulia. "Unless you would rather stay working for the Interim Grand Freeholder?"

"Oh no," Mykol said. "I mean, it would be an honour, but I've worked for the Holts all my life. And Saulia—Clan Freeholder Holt—needs me."

"That she does," Nadez replied. "I'll tell the Interim Grand Freeholder that you've returned to your regular duties."

"Thank you." Mykol picked up the tray and left the room.

Nadez spent a few minutes straightening chairs before heading to the small door. She couldn't put off meeting with Lauma. Besides, she wanted her opinion on Ottosen's behaviour. He had been angry about the changes and yet today, he'd acted as though he was on Lauma's side.

She didn't trust that.

"You gave Mykol permission to go back to Saulia?" Lauma asked. "Without discussing it with me?"

"Wasn't that what you and Saulia agreed to?" Nadez asked. "That he would help with the Treaty negotiations and then he would return to her service."

"Yes, of course," Lauma said. "It's just that now I'm without an assistant. Can you spare Gustav?"

"Sorry, I've sent him back to Lavais. I'm worried that something will happen to delay the shipbuilding."

"Berna's there," Lauma said, frowning. "She speaks for me, as they all know by now."

"True, but because she speaks for you some may be reluctant

to speak *to* her." Nadez suppressed her own frown. She had not expected Lauma to take her to task for either Mykol or Gustav. Neither of them reported to the Interim Grand Freeholder. Did she see them as hers to assign?

"Gustav is a Lavaisian," Nadez continued. "I thought that fact coupled with his Trait would make it easier for anyone with doubts to approach him. We can't afford to have the shipbuilding interrupted or delayed."

"All right," Lauma said. "I suppose it's too late to bring him back anyway."

"He left two days ago," Nadez said. Should she remind her who Gustav reported to? "He said he would have Kaja return as soon as she could. And that she would be a much better assistant than him."

"That will have to do," Lauma replied. "What are your thoughts on how this meeting went?"

"Timonis is not very bright," she said and was rewarded when Lauma laughed. "He doesn't seem to realize that there is very little chance of him ever becoming Grand Freeholder, let alone the one right after a crisis."

"He can't see anything except his own brilliance," Lauma said. "Do you think it could be a negative Trait?"

"Maybe," Nadez replied. She met Lauma's gaze and shrugged. Who better to see an unacknowledged Trait than someone with one of her own? "It would certainly explain his self-confidence in, well, everything he does."

"Can we find out for certain?" Lauma asked.

"Joosep was the one who picked up on Traits," Nadez said. "Because of his Trait. He never mentioned to me that he had come across Traits in any of the Clan Freeholders."

"Would he have looked for them?"

"No," Nadez said. "Probably not. And if he ever suspected anyone, he never recorded it. At least not in any of the notes I've read." She paused. "Dagrun would be able to tell. She figured out every Intelligencer and student's Trait on her own. Why?"

"Because if I knew it was a Trait, I would know that he can't help it," Lauma said. "And that it's not a simple matter of changing his mind. All right. Timonis is pig-headed but probably not dangerous. So, who is?"

"Ottosen," Nadez replied. "He even argued in your favour."

"He did," Lauma said. "And I agree that is not in character for him. What do you suggest?"

"You or I will make up some excuse that allows me access to his office and household and every single person associated with him."

"Wouldn't it be better if you sent someone he doesn't know to spy on him?"

"Of course, it would," Nadez said. "But I'm currently the only Intelligencer in the city. It's me, who he knows, or no one. I'm not comfortable just letting him scheme alone. At the very least I need to make him try to do it under my watch."

"All right," Lauma said. "I'll think of a reason for you to snoop around. He won't want to make me angry."

"No, he won't," Nadez agreed. She smiled but not from pleasure. Lauma knew the power she had over the Clan Freeholders. Would she wield it with compassion or with oppression?

CHAPTER 5

CALDER LOWERED THE spyglass. "It's a local trade ship," he said. He passed the glass to Rafael. "Do you know it?"

"I do." Rafael grinned. "It's my uncle's ship. Although it's worrying that it's so far from the coast."

They were still a day out from Messanos and almost as far from the coast of Pilalia, where Rafael's uncle generally plied his trade. Calder squinted at the ship. It was not more than a white smudge on the horizon, but they were catching up to it fast.

"Dag," he said, turning to her. "Do you sense anything wrong?"

"Nothing hidden," she said. "Can we signal them? A response might trigger my Trait."

"We'll be close enough in an hour," Calder said. "Rafael, I assume that you have a code you can use. Will you signal?"

"Aye, Captain, I do have a code," the Second Mate said. "It's out of date, but Uncle Adao will recognize it."

"Let us know how they respond," Calder said. "We can't take any chances that the *Spice Runner* has been boarded by Pinho's men." Rafael saluted and headed to the mainsail. A few minutes later a string of coloured flags was hoisted up to the top of the mast.

"Now we wait," Calder said.

"Let's hope it's your Luck working," Dag replied. "Like the last time when we met your father."

"My father," Calder said. "The Resolute. Sometimes I wish I didn't know. Then I could just dislike him for the way he treated my mother and not for being a dangerous assassin."

"Do you think he has killed Pinho?"

"Maybe." Calder sighed. Rumours said that Resolutes were extremely efficient. It was surprising that he had lost his token to Pinho, his target. "I hate that it solves a problem."

"A major problem," Dag said. "Unless someone else takes up Pinho's plan to control the Pale Sea."

"You still don't think the threat will die with him." They'd had this conversation before. "But it's not your Trait?"

"Not my Trait," she said. "My training. And I suppose my Trait in that I *always* expect hidden dangers."

"Because you usually find them."

"Because I usually find them," Dag agreed.

The wind was behind them, and soon Calder could make out the individual sails on the other ship. A line of flags was run up the single mast: no doubt a response to Rafael's message.

"My uncle requests a meeting," Rafael said as he joined them. "They're shortening their sails."

"Good, let's do the same." The other ship had slowed down, and he could see men up in the rigging, taking in the topsail.

He and Dag joined Darya at the wheel.

"We'll be alongside them in about fifteen minutes," Darya said. "Do you want to speak to them from the deck or will you take out a dinghy?"

"I think a dinghy," he said. "Dag, you're with me and Rafael." He didn't want to risk Dag: she was the only one who could get the *Atlaine* back through the Teeth. But she was also the only one who could determine what, if anything, was being hidden.

"Jaak," Calder called out. "Can you ready a portside dinghy?"

"Aye, Captain." The former pirate whistled and pointed at half a dozen sailors, who then all scurried to the port side.

The *Atlaine* hid the dinghy from view of the smaller vessel. Dag climbed down into it and sat in the bow while Calder settled himself at the oars. Rafael joined them, tossing the painter to Dag.

"I should row," Rafael said.

"I'll row," Calder replied. "You need to speak with your uncle. Dag will let us know if there's anything hidden about what he says and does."

"Aye, Captain." Rafael edged past him and settled in the stern, and Calder picked up the oars.

A few hard strokes took the boat out from behind the *Atlaine*.

"Ahoy, *Spice Runner*," Rafael called. "Greetings from the *Atlaine*. I'm Second Mate Rafael Machado looking to speak with my Uncle, Adao Machado."

The dinghy was now between the *Atlaine* and the *Spice Runner*. Calder stopped rowing, using the oars to keep them in place a few yards from the other ship.

"Rafael," came a shout from the smaller ship. "That *is* you. When I saw the signal, I hoped it was you, but these are dangerous times."

"Uncle, it is good to see you," Rafael replied. "I was worried when I saw your ship so far from a coast. Can we come aboard to speak of our worries?"

"Who is with you?"

"My captain and one other I trust."

"Permission to come aboard."

"I hope that's what you wanted," Rafael said.

"Yes," Calder replied. "Dag?"

"He's not hiding anything," she replied. "Not even his worry."

It took them a few moments to climb aboard the *Spice Runner*. Calder let Rafael greet his uncle and some of the crew before stepping forward.

"Captain Machado," he said. "I'm Calder Rahmson, Captain of the *Atlaine*. We should speak in private."

"Yes. In my cabin." He led the way through a hatch and along a short corridor.

"Please sit down." Adao gestured to a table. He rolled up a map before sitting. "It's late in the year for a ship from the Pale Sea to be here. Did you miscalculate and find the Frozen Gap closed?"

"It is late in the season," Calder said. "But the Fair Seas Treaty Alliance is facing a desperate situation. We're trying to help."

"I heard about the ships that were destroyed," Adao said. "I know more than one merchant who lost part of their fleet. It makes good work for the shipyards, though."

"Does that work benefit any one person more than others?" Dag asked.

"This is Dagrun Lund," Calder said. "One of my crew. And it is a good question. Does the loss and replacement of ships particularly benefit anyone?"

"I suppose it benefits whoever owns the shipyards," Adao said. "Pinho owned one of the two in the Sapphire Sea, but I can assure you that neither he nor his family are benefiting. The Messanos council stripped him of his property, including his shipyard, and rumour has it that he's either dead or soon will be at the hands of a Resolute."

"We've heard the rumour of a Resolute as well," Calder said. "But there's no proof that Pinho is dead?"

"There's no proof that Resolutes even exist," Adao replied. "At least I've never spoken to anyone who has ever seen one."

"So, the Arressan Council will benefit from the shipyard?" Dag asked. "Or has it been sold or given to someone else to manage?"

"I don't know," Adao said. "I've been staying away from the coastline as much as possible. Pinho's departure has created opportunities for those with even less morals than he had."

"What do you mean?" Calder asked.

"I mean pirates," Adao said. "Strongrock pirates are here, looting and murdering up and down the coast. And without the bigger ships that were lost to fire, and without a strong presence, even from a tyrant like Pinho, no one is even trying to stop them."

Calder looked over at Dag, who nodded. He sighed. Were the Strongrock pirates their responsibility? Or was Luck simply giving him notice to stay out of the pirates' way? They still had their mission: they still needed to buy and deliver food to the Three.

PIA HANDED A bowl to Frida before grabbing one for herself and leading the way to the far side of the fire.

It was snowing out and the wind was bitterly cold. Someone, probably Bjorn since he seemed to be in charge of the woodcutters, had brought the pirate inside. She was leaning against the wall, just barely within the circle of warmth from the fire, her hands and feet tied in front of her.

"They'd move you closer if you told them what they wanted," Pia said to the woman.

She sat down half a dozen feet from the prisoner and spooned up a mouthful of stew.

"Why do we have to sit near her?" Frida asked quietly.

"Because I want her to trust me," Pia said. "And she's more likely to if she realizes that we're outsiders too."

"I don't like her."

"Good," Pia said. "And don't trust her, either. I won't." She ate another spoonful of stew, chewed the salt fish, and swallowed. "Don't you feel good about eating food we helped prepare?"

"Yes." Frida smiled. "I especially like that no one can say I don't deserve it, because I do, after helping Solvig and you with the salting and drying."

"You always deserve to eat," Pia replied. "Everyone does, don't you think?"

"Being hungry is bad," Frida said.

"Being hungry is bad," Pia echoed her sister, hiding her anger. She despised Ottosen for starving her sister, for making her suffer in order to force Pia's compliance. She wanted Ottosen to suffer consequences for what he had done, and she wanted to be the one to inflict them.

But what she knew was the right thing to do would take her and Frida away from that path and onto a different, probably more dangerous one. At least for her. She planned on keeping Frida safe.

She'd thought of nothing else for the past few days: had tried to talk herself out of it more times than she could count. And even though she was completely disgusted with the decision she'd made, she knew she couldn't make a different one.

Gustav Gunnarson had told her that she was *one of us*, and at the time she'd felt in her bones that it wasn't true. Yet here she was, planning on working as an Intelligencer.

Because she couldn't escape the feeling that whatever this pirate knew was vital to keeping the Three safe. And if the Three weren't safe, there was no chance of keeping her sister safe.

She finished her stew and turned back to the pirate.

"I can get you a bowl," she said. "If you're hungry?" As far as she knew the pirate had still not said a word, not even to ask to go to the privy, so she wasn't surprised when all she got in response was a nod.

"Come on," she said to Frida. "I'll leave you with Solvig while I feed the prisoner."

"All right." Frida stood up and picked up her empty bowl. "Being hungry is bad, even for pirates."

"That's right." Pia led the way across the warehouse floor and knocked on the door to Solvig's quarters.

"Come in," Solvig yelled. "No need to ask my permission to use the privy."

"It's Pia and Frida," Pia said. She headed down the short hall to the main room, Frida behind her. "I was hoping Frida could keep you company for a few minutes."

"She's going to give the pirate some stew," Frida said. "Because being hungry is bad."

Solvig was at the table, an assortment of half-finished projects in front of her. She dropped a net that she seemed to be fixing and smiled.

"You have that right, little Frida," she said. "No one deserves to be hungry. Do you want me to teach you how to mend a fishing net?"

Frida nodded and climbed up on the bench beside Solvig.

"Thanks," Pia said. "I'll be back as soon as I can."

She left and headed to the big stew pot at the fire. Bjorn had his back to her, ladling some stew into a bowl.

"I'm going to feed the prisoner," she said to him. He turned and nodded.

"Don't untie her," he said and sat down with the other woodcutters.

"I won't," she said under her breath.

The pirate ate whatever Pia spooned into her mouth, but she remained silent. When the bowl was empty, Pia stood up. "If you need the privy you'll have to deal with Bjorn." She left and dropped the bowl off with the rest of the dirty ones and headed back to Solvig's quarters.

She stood in the hallway watching Solvig with her sister. She was kind and patient with her: exactly the type of person Frida deserved to be mentored by. Not her half-grown sister who kept changing her mind about who and what she wanted to be.

"Something wrong?"

Solvig was looking at her with a worried expression.

"Yes." Pia sighed. Like the pirate, she had to trust someone. "Can I tell you a secret?"

"Come sit."

Pia sat down and closed her eyes. She could trust Solvig, she was sure of that. If she wasn't, there was no way she could possibly tell her this.

"Frida and I aren't just orphans. I mean, we are orphans. Our parents are dead, but the Clan Freeholder," she paused and took a deep breath. "The Clan Freeholder locked Frida up and sometimes starved her in order to force me to do things."

"You poor dears," Solvig said. "That's why the little one worries about food, isn't it? I thought it was because you were poor. You're safe now. And no one here will force you to do things."

"I know," Pia said. "And I am grateful because it has allowed me to decide what I want to do. You see, the Clan Freeholder wanted me to go to school so I could become his personal spy. And I did go to school, but now I want to use what I learned to help everyone." She sighed and looked at the floor for a moment before raising her eyes to meet Solvig's gaze. "I think that the pirate has information that could be important to the Three."

"She won't talk to anyone," Solvig said. "And I won't allow torture under my roof."

"Good." Pia had wondered why Bjorn or one of the others hadn't tried beating information out of the prisoner. It made her next request easier.

"I'd like to have Frida stay with you, if that's all right," she said. "There's something I need to do. Something maybe only I can do. I need to take the prisoner to Lavais Port, or maybe even to Tarklee. Someone will be able to get her to talk."

"Frida is welcome to stay here," Solvig said. "But why is it up to you?"

"Because the school I went to was for Intelligencers," Pia said. "And there's another Intelligencer student in Lavais Port." At least she hoped there was. "And if not, then I need to get the pirate to Master Intelligencer Nadez Norup in Tarklee. And I can't drag Frida across the Three and keep her safe."

"Intelligencers," Solvig replied. "You don't need to say anything more. I'd be happy to keep Frida with me here while you go find Intelligencers to help figure out what the pirates are planning. Because it's nothing good, I can tell you that."

WHEN GUSTAV REACHED Nurmi, the town was quiet. He had spent the night at Pavil's, and early in the morning they'd left in the wagon. The trader had yesterday's abandoned supplies to pick up, so he was able to drop Gustav off at the edge of the town. Thankfully there had been no signs of pirates either along the road or at the merchant where Pavil stopped.

Now after ten minutes of walking he was in the town. And it was too quiet, even for a cold winter day: there was not a single person on the road.

His footprints were the only ones in the dusting of snow on the road until he reached a turnoff that he recognized. He'd been down this lane not long ago, collecting Tavet Timonis for the meeting with Lauma. Multiple sets of footprints led from the lane toward the centre of the town and the harbour.

He paused: should he find whoever had made the footprints or confirm that they had come from Timonis' estate?

He turned up the lane. If pirates were openly working with the Clan Freeholder, he—and every Intelligencer—needed to know.

As expected, the tracks led him directly to the gate to Clan Freeholder Timonis' estate and beyond, up to the house.

It was entirely possible that pirates had not made these footprints and that Timonis' men had gone to take care of the pirate threat. But he wasn't sure they would do that without directions from their Clan Freeholder.

Gustav had left before the negotiations had been finalized, and Timonis had still been in Tarklee. He'd made good time on the road despite the weather, but it was possible a log hauler or the *Tazeyar* could have delivered Timonis home already.

And if the Clan Leader *wasn't* at his estate and pirates *were*, did that mean they were already working together? This might be critical information, so he had to find out.

Gustav hurried back to the main road. Other than a few faces at the windows of houses, he didn't see anyone.

"Careful with that barrel," someone called from up ahead. "We'll have to roll it back."

"Never thought I'd be grateful for snow," came the reply. "Smooths out the bumps in the road. Can't stand the thought of ruining good ale."

Three people were in the road up ahead. Two carried sacks, and the third was pushing a barrel. Gustav slowed. Were they pirates? Who else would be moving a barrel of ale this way?

"I hate snow," one man said. "Means I have to wear shoes."

A fourth person, a woman, ran up and joined the others.

"Be grateful we have supplies," the woman said. "Benil, I said you could bring ale, but that doesn't mean you don't have to carry food. Here." She shoved a sack at him, and he grabbed it and tossed it over his shoulder.

"Heya!" Gustav called out and the four people turned to look at him. "Anyone know where I can get a drink?"

"Not any longer," the man with the barrel said. "Tavern keeper ran off when he saw me coming."

"Who are you?" the woman asked.

"Just a traveller," Gustav replied, smiling and trying to infuse Charisma into every word. "I came down from Tarklee and let me tell you, taking the road this time of year was a mistake. Winter came in fast and here I am, late."

"Late for where?" the woman asked.

"Home to Lavais Port," Gustav replied. "I'd hoped to borrow a dinghy or sailboat to get over there. Know anyone with a boat to lend? I have some coin."

"We'll take your coin," the woman said. "Edur."

One of them men dropped his sack and stepped forward. "Don't make me hurt you."

"Hey!" Gustav complained but he held still as Edur searched his pockets. He seemed satisfied with the purse he found and the few coins it held and didn't check Gustav's boots, where he'd hidden the bulk of his money.

"Here you go, Captain." Edur handed the purse to the woman, who looked in it before opening her coat. As she shoved the purse into a pocket, she exposed the butt of a pistol. She smirked when she saw where Gustav's eyes were.

"That's right," she said. "We have pistols, so don't make trouble."

"Can we get him to carry this stuff back to the house?" the man with the barrel asked. "That way we could maybe take another barrel."

"Shut up, Benil," the captain said. "I told you you'd get no help from anyone with your ale. And that includes any prisoners."

"Am I a prisoner?" Gustav asked. "I just want to go home."

"Quit whining," the captain said. She stared at him. "And let me think this through."

"Captain Ozlinch," the third man said. "If we take him, we'll need to watch him."

"Don't tell me something I already know," Captain Ozlinch said.

Gustav recognized the name. The tavern owner from Strongrock was named Ozlinch. She had tried to imprison Dagrun Lund.

"I won't cause trouble," he said. "I'll just find a boat and be off home." When he'd approached them, he'd only been thinking about confirming that they were pirates from Strongrock. Now that he knew they were, he was reminded that they were dangerous.

"Go on then," Ozlinch said. "Get out of my sight before I change my mind."

"Thank you." Gustav didn't waste any time hurrying past them and rounding a building. He broke into a run and didn't stop until he was at the dock.

He hid behind a building for a while, in case one of the pirates followed him. When he felt safe, he walked over to stare out at the shore.

Like the rest of the town, the dock area was deserted. A single, small sailboat was tied up at the pier, a light layer of snow covering it. It had been used recently, so he assumed that was how the pirates got to Nurmi from Strongrock. It wasn't a trip he'd want to make, especially in winter, and he had to admire their sailing skills even as he wondered just how desperate—and dangerous—they must be to even attempt it.

With a quick look over his shoulder, he stepped into the boat and nudged a lump. It was the sail, left unpacked and now half frozen to the bottom of the boat.

Had the pirates abandoned the boat? How did they expect to get back to Strongrock? Or were they planning on staying here all winter?

Then he had another, worse thought. What if the pirates no longer needed the smaller boat because they were planning on getting a ship? The pirates were staying at Timonis' estate: that only made sense if they were working together. Would Timonis help them steal a ship?

Gustav frowned. Of course, he would. Timonis, a man who felt superior to everyone else, was on his way back from meetings that had all but destroyed his chance of being the next Grand Freeholder. He would feel justified doing anything that gave him the power he felt was his due. The power and prestige he felt he was owed. That would include working with pirates and stealing one of the few ships that remained in the Pale Sea.

And if that ship was the *Tazeyar*, then Timonis and the pirates could sail to the Sapphire Sea and either buy food and charge exorbitant prices or simply leave the Three with a worse chance of surviving next summer and winter.

Gustav pulled at the sail, careful to not rip the cloth as he lifted it up off the boat. He had to get this sailboat seaworthy because he had to meet whatever ship was bringing Timonis home.

And he had to make sure no one else, especially pirates, could reach the ship.

DAG SHADED HER eyes and stared ahead. She'd noticed the sails an hour ago, and the *Atlaine* had been staying back, trying to stay just out of sight from anyone on board the ship she'd spotted. There was no sign that they'd been seen.

She was confident that they were following the pirates in Ansdottir's ship, the *Vassan*, but Calder wanted to confirm that by taking them in closer.

"We've left Pilalian waters," Calder said as he joined her in the prow. "And are now off the coast of Arressa."

Dag scanned the coastline. She'd been along here in Rahm's little sailboat, first with Jaak and later with her sister and Charis. Nothing looked familiar though, at least not from this distance. "We didn't come across any villages along here," she said. "Is that ship headed to Messanos?"

"Most likely," Calder replied. "If they were heading farther south, they'd keep to open water instead of sailing so close to land."

The ship surged ahead, and Dag looked above her to see sailors tying off the sail they'd just unfurled. "Are we going to pass them?" she asked.

"If we can do it without getting too close, yes," Calder said. "Darya will keep the sun to our backs. It will make it more difficult for that ship to spot us and even harder to identify us."

"You think they'll know the *Atlaine*?" She was getting better at recognizing ships but wasn't sure she'd ever be as good as Calder, even with her Trait.

"Someone will," he replied. "If it is the pirates. Even a

Messanos crew might."

They were close enough to the other ship that Dag could distinguish individual sails.

"That's her," Calder said. "The *Vassan*. I'll go let Darya know. Meet me in the cabin. We need to decide where we want to land in Messanos."

Calder left and Dag stared at the *Vassan*. Who was captain of the ship now? Was it Ursa? Even though the woman wasn't a sailor, she'd had some authority in Strongrock as the owner of the Crooked Mast. But that was before Ansdottir had hung Ursa's spy, Hanne. What had that meant for Ursa? And how had the pirates treated her once Ansdottir was dead and her influence had ended?

Calls echoed across the ship, and above her, sailors scrambled to take in a sail.

Now the *Vassan* was farther way, between them and the coast as the *Atlaine* headed out to sea.

Dag left the bow and went to the cabin she was sharing with Calder. A few moments later, Calder and Rafael joined her.

"The pirates won't attack Messanos," he said, sitting down at the table. "But they might be low on supplies and coin."

"Would they steal what they need?" Dag asked. She took the chair across from Calder while Rafael sat closest to the door. "If they've heard that Pinho has been chased out of the city?"

"I doubt they would steal in Messanos," Calder replied. "The council could send guards and take their ship next time they anchor. But I don't think they would head to the city unless they knew that Pinho was gone."

"Why not just resupply by looting the villages along Pilalia?" Dag asked. "If they're planning on heading back to Strongrock?"

"The villages would have food," Rafael said. "And a small quantity of ale or wine, but if they're looking to stock a tavern for the winter, they won't find enough along the coast."

"Or maybe they aren't planning on going back to Strongrock," Dag said. "Maybe they're hoping to fill the void left by Pinho. Your uncle said no one along the coast was challenging the pirates."

"And no one in Messanos will either," Rafael said. "The Arressan council won't interfere in what they'll see as a Pilalian issue."

"*Skit*," Dag swore. "So, they'll just let pirates come and purchase supplies with coin stolen from their neighbours? No wonder Pinho was able to conquer the whole coastline so easily." The Fair Seas Treaty Alliance wasn't perfect, but at least the Three helped each other instead of letting any one country fall to despots.

"Pilalia wouldn't appreciate it if the Arressan council intervened," Calder said. "There's too much competition for resources in the Sapphire Sea. Which is one reason why Pinho wants a foothold in the Three."

"It still seems short-sighted," Dag said. "People working together usually do better than when everyone is working for themselves."

"Or working at cross purposes," Rafael said. "Sadly, I don't see Pinho's rule changing how things are managed in Arressa."

"Especially since they were saved from Pinho in a way that makes the council responsible for his defeat," Calder said.

"I did that," Dag said. "*I* saved them by reuniting the Resolute with his token."

"But the council had originally contracted the Resolute to deal with Pinho," Calder said. "I don't know anyone on the Arressan council, but in my experience, people will take credit for whatever they can. Nor will they want to share credit."

"My uncle said something similar to me," Rafael said. "Before we left his ship. He said that we shouldn't trust the Arressan council to recognize that we're their saviours. And that they won't like being reminded that they had been defeated until we intervened."

"What about Charis?" Dag had a hard time believing that Charis, a man whose life she saved when she agreed to allow him in the *Hakon*, would forget that.

"He's not on the council," Calder said. "Who knows how much influence he has with them?" He sighed. "Whatever we find in Messanos, we need to decide if we want to get there before the pirates arrive or after."

"If possible, before," Dag said. "I do not want the pirates to find Inger before we can protect her."

CHAPTER 6

Nadez frowned as she followed Ottosen down a hallway.

She was visiting his Clan Holdings and he had offered to show her around his estate and introduce her to his manager. So she could spy on him.

She shook her head. Lauma hadn't even bothered to come up with a plausible excuse: she'd simply said that the Master Intelligencer was visiting each Clan Freeholder to see if there was anything that the Interim Grand Freeholder needed to be concerned about.

Nadez had been a little more specific and said that she was making sure that food supplies were being safely stored and that there were clear instructions on how and when and to whom the food would be distributed.

But those weren't the normal tasks of the Master Intelligencer. She had to assume that Ottosen realized what Nadez was doing and had advised his staff to not disclose any secrets.

She sighed again, wishing for Dagrun's Unseen Trait or even the weaker one Joosep had. Instead, she would have to rely on her training and gut instinct.

"The shipping records are all here," Ottosen said. "And meet my Provisions Manager, Rein Chebek. Rein, this is Master Intelligencer Norup. The Interim Grand Freeholder has instructed me to give her access to any records she wants to see."

"It's very nice to meet you." Rein Chebek was a middle-aged

man whose blond hair was peppered with grey. "Call me Rein. Are there specific records you wish to see first?"

"I have other work to attend to," Ottosen said. "Unless you need anything more from me, Master Intelligencer?"

"If I do, I will ask Rein to contact you," Nadez replied. She turned to Rein. "And please, call me Nadez. And yes, I would like to see every delivery of food that came in this year, no matter the source, and where it was sent either for consumption or storage."

She knew the name of the ship the suicide assassin had arrived on and the date it had anchored in Tarklee Harbour, but she didn't want Ottosen or his staff to know that she knew even that much. But she wanted to check the records in case any passengers were named. She didn't believe the assassin would be identified, but there might be someone else she could question. Confirming that the ship had bought goods in Messanos wouldn't prove that a suicide assassin had boarded, but it would mean it was possible.

Rein left her in a room with what he claimed were all of the ledgers used to document shipments for the past summer.

Nadez flipped through each ledger, making notes on what arrived and was signed for by Ottosen's people, as well as what ships the goods arrived on. Some of the ship names she recognized as ones lost to fire and pirates, but others were not familiar.

The records from the Merchant Adventurer's office had already been delivered to her office. Later she'd see if they recorded who owned the ships from the Sapphire Sea. She assumed that Fihaldo Pinho would be listed for a few of them.

Two hours later, the door opened, and Rein poked his head in.

"I've brought tea if you're ready for a break."

"Thank you." Nadez was touched. "I hope you are joining me." She hadn't expected anyone to show her warmth or kindness during her visit. Part of her was suspicious, but even if he wasn't simply being thoughtful, it would give her a chance to ask Ottosen's Provisions Manager some questions.

"I brought two cups." Rein shouldered the door open and entered with a tray. Nadez stacked the ledgers she'd been working on and her notes to one side, leaving room on the table for the tray. Rein sat down across from her and poured into two cups.

"I never met your predecessor," Rein said. "But I was sorry to hear of his passing." He added sugar to his tea. "So many terrible changes this summer."

"Thank you," Nadez replied. "I knew Joosep Sepp for many years, and his death was a blow to me personally as well as to the organization." She took a sip of tea hoping that Ottosen wouldn't try to poison her. Rein Chebek was exactly the type of charming person she would send with poison. In fact, he made her wonder if he didn't have a touch of a Charisma Trait.

"And yes," she continued. "It has been an eventful summer." Rein drank his own tea and Nadez took another sip. If the tea was poisoned, her host was going to feel it too. "I don't see anything in your records that identifies who owns the ships that goods arrive on, just who sold the goods to the Freeholder. Do you have that information?"

"Oh, I am sorry," Rein said, standing up. "I didn't realize you would want that as well. I'll be back in a moment." He slipped out of the room before she could tell him it could wait.

"It's all here." Rein returned with another book and set it on the table.

"Thank you." Nadez picked the book up and moved it to one side. "Have you been with Clan Freeholder Ottosen long?"

"Ever since he inherited the freeholdings," Rein replied. "I started working for his Uncle Tollack. That was a tragic death."

"I thought he died in his sleep," Nadez said. "He was well on in years, wasn't he?"

"Over seventy when he died," Rein said. "But in good health, from what I remember, although I was young, and my junior position meant I didn't interact directly with him. But yes, Tollack died in his sleep and although he was old, it was unexpected."

"And since he had no children, his brother Otto inherited?" She knew that the elder Clan Freeholder had been married at one time, but more than that, she didn't know.

"There was a son," Rein said, shaking his head. "Roald died a few months after his father passed away. His mother, the widow of Clan Freeholder Tollack, died within weeks, from a broken heart, it was said. I remember such sadness in the house."

"That is a sad story," Nadez said, thinking it a suspicious story. "And Henrik's father was the younger brother to the Clan

Freeholder Tollack?"

"Younger by two decades," Rein said. "And a half-brother: the two had different mothers."

"So, Otto inherited and passed the Clan Freeholdership down to Henrik," Nadez said.

"That's how it all worked out," he said in a casual voice that didn't match the intense look he gave her.

Nadez drained her tea and set the mug on the table. "Thank you for the tea, Rein," she said.

"Don't forget the book that lists ship owners." He gathered up the cups and put them on the tray. With a nod, he left the room.

Nadez stared at the closed door. Was Rein Chebek, a trusted member of Henrik Ottosen's staff, trying to tell her that his Clan Freeholder had gained his inheritance through murder? That the deaths of Henrik's uncle, aunt, and cousin were not unfortunate events and were instead deliberately caused?

She picked up the book and flipped it open. Had he left her proof? This book was older than anything else she had been looking at. In fact, some of the entries looked to be around the time when Rein would have been a young man.

She had no idea what could be done even if Ottosen, or more likely his mother and father, had murdered to ensure their line inherited the freeholdings. But she would find out what she could and then speak to Lauma. She knew more about the Clan Freeholders than anyone else Nadez could discuss this with. She might know what rumours had been whispered at that time.

"No. You're just a child."

"I'm fifteen," Pia said, angry. When she'd asked Bjorn to step outside for a talk, she'd expected him to be grateful, and maybe even helpful. She certainly hadn't expected him to try to tell her what to do.

"And I've never been *just a child*," she continued. Snow whipped around her head and she shook a few flakes from her eyes. "I'm a trained Intelligencer." She wasn't fully trained, but she had more skills than Bjorn was giving her credit for. "It's my duty to do what I can to protect the Three. Which means I need to take the pirate to someone who can get her to talk."

"She doesn't know anything," Bjorn said.

"I say she does," Pia replied. "Besides, I don't need your

approval. This is Solvig's warehouse: she makes the decisions, and she agrees with me. I'm simply letting you know that the pirate will no longer be your responsibility." She glared at him, balled fists at her sides.

Bjorn frowned. "Solvig may make the decisions for her people, but I make them for me and mine. I'm making this decision in the best interests of my Clan Freeholder, who is also the Interim Grand Freeholder."

The door to the warehouse opened and a frowning Solvig stood in the doorway. She turned her gaze from Pia to Bjorn.

"Is that the way of it, Bjorn?" Solvig asked. "You deciding that you can override my authority in the name of a Clan Freeholder from up north? I was happy to help train you to fish and forage and grateful for all of the help in putting away supplies for the winter. But no one said anything about *me* working for *you*. You'll let Pia leave with that pirate. Unless you're planning on taking over my warehouse?"

"No," Bjorn said. "That's not what I meant."

"Except it was," Solvig said. "Here I was hoping you'd assign someone to take the two of them to Lavais Port, where that pirate can be interrogated by someone who knows what questions to ask and how to get answers." She shook her head and then sighed. "I suppose it's time for you and your people to leave anyway because none of us want you to be stuck here all winter. You can take some of the supplies with you. I suggest you head to Lavais Port and try to find a ship that'll take you home."

"I'm sorry, Solvig," Bjorn said. "I didn't mean it."

"Maybe," Solvig said. "But next time you might. Tell your crew that I'm grateful but that it's time to leave." She stepped aside to allow Bjorn room to enter the warehouse.

"I'm sorry, Solvig," Pia said. "I know that there's still more work to be done here."

"Not your fault," Solvig said. "Bjorn made that comment, and now I don't think I can trust him. Asides, now that the snow's here there won't be as much to do. Firewood's all collected, and the warehouse is over half full of food. We'll be fine here without the woodcutters, and it really is time they went home."

"Thanks. I didn't like thinking that I made things harder for you."

"Not to worry." Solvig grinned. "Besides, now you'll have

company getting that pirate to Lavais Port. Didn't like the idea of you going there alone in bad weather. Come on. I have supplies to sort out. I think you'll all be leaving early in the morning."

SOLVIG WAS RIGHT. Pia, the pirate, and Bjorn and his woodcutters left as soon as it was light out.

Bjorn was still angry at her so Pia and the pirate kept well back of the others. Solvig had given them directions for a little-used overland route to Lavais Port that would take them most of the day. Sailing there only took a few hours, but neither Pia nor the woodcutters knew how to sail.

It wasn't lost on Pia that the only person who *could* sail was her prisoner. Another skill she would learn because, like gathering and preserving food, it would make her more self-sufficient.

The sky was overcast but the wind was light, making it feel warmer than Pia had expected. And walking behind the woodcutters had an unexpected benefit: the trail through the snowy woods was well-trodden by the time she and the pirate travelled it. It made for easy walking, although at times it looked like the men ahead of her struggled.

The woodcutters talked to themselves and a few times they broke into song, but no one spoke to her. Which suited Pia just fine.

After a quick stop to eat and heat some water for tea, they were on the move again.

The sun came out in the afternoon and although welcome, the reflection on the snow made Pia's eyes water. Soon though, the sun dipped down below the trees.

"There's the town," Bjorn called out, and a couple of the woodcutters whooped.

Pia looked past them to a huddle of buildings, most of which had light streaming from windows.

Bjorn stopped and let her catch up to him while his men filed towards the town.

"You're on your own now," he said. "I wish you luck. We're heading to the dock to find out when the next ship is due."

"I wish you luck as well," Pia said. She checked to make sure her prisoner's hands were still tied tight. "Come on," she said to the pirate. "If you want to get warm, you'll do as I say."

A few minutes later they were on a road that curved around the empty harbour. Buildings lined one side and a couple who exited one stared at Pia and her prisoner.

"Which way to the main office for the shipyards?" she asked them. That was where Kaja had been heading. She'd explained that it was the centre of the effort to rebuild the shipyards.

"I haven't seen you before," a man replied.

"I just arrived from Solvig Madsen's warehouse," Pia said. "I was helping her fill the warehouse with food. She has a good amount of dried fish stored now."

"I know Solvig," the man replied. "You one of her volunteers?"

"Yes, along with some Byholt woodcutters. But now I need to hand this person over to the Intelligencers in Lavais Port," she replied.

"Intelligencers been doing grand work around here," the man said. "Do you know the twins?"

"No, sorry," Pia replied. "I'm looking for a woman named Kaja. Is she still here?"

"Sure. Follow me." The man led them down a street that sloped down towards the sea. "She and the Interim Grand Freeholder's daughter are in charge of the town now." He looked back at her. "Some don't like that they're young and aye, that they're women. Me? I'm just happy that someone's taking charge. Not like our Clan Freeholder's even set foot in the port for weeks."

"That's Clan Freeholder Timonis?" Pia asked. He was Solvig's Clan Freeholder and she had nothing good to say about him.

"That be the one. Here we are." He stepped up to a door and knocked.

"Someone for Intelligencer Kaja," he said.

"Who is it?" A head peered out the door. "Pia, is that you?"

"It's me," Pia replied. "With a pirate that someone needs to interrogate."

"A pirate!" the man who had escorted them said. "You didn't say she was a pirate. They burned the shipyards. I wish—"

"We'll handle it from here." A second young woman pushed open the door. "Thank you for your help," she said to the man. "Can I count on your discretion until we know what this is about?"

"Yes, of course, Freeholder Strauskas. I can see that the pirate is already a prisoner. Good night to you." He hurried off before

Pia could thank him.

"Pia Engen," the woman, Freeholder Strauskas, said. "I'm Berna Strauskas. I believe you've met my mother."

The look she gave Pia made it clear that she knew about the assassination attempt.

Pia sighed. "I have. But my most pressing business is this pirate. She was caught when she and almost a dozen other pirates tried to raid Solvig Madsen's warehouse. I believe that she knows important information."

"Then bring her inside."

The pirate shrugged and stepped inside, followed by Pia. As soon as the door was closed, Kaja turned to her.

"We haven't heard anything about pirates. Let me get this one locked up and then you can tell us what happened."

GUSTAV HUDDLED IN the bow of the sailboat, rubbing his hands together against the cold. The winter wind had found a way under the sail he was hiding under, and whenever he peered out at the harbour, whitecaps sent spray into his face.

It was dark now, and just when he was contemplating finding a warm place to spend the night, he saw lights out in the harbour. A ship had arrived.

He carefully eased out from under the sail, untied the boat from the pier, and shoved off. As soon as he was a few feet from the dock, he raised the sail and steered towards the ship. When he was halfway to it, he recognized the *Tazeyar*.

He heard a whistle from behind him and when he turned to look, half a dozen dark figures spilled onto the dock. The wind carried muffled curses to him and he grinned.

He had hated to do it, hated to damage boats that the settlement would need, but he'd reasoned that with this weather, the harbour would freeze soon. The holes in the hulls of sailboats wouldn't matter once they were fitted with blades.

The dinghies were a different matter, but their owners would have all winter to repair them.

The ship was just past the mouth of the harbour, and he was close enough to see a couple of figures standing in the bow. They waved a lamp in his direction: they must be expecting someone and had seen him. Gustav dropped his sail, picked up an oar, and paddled towards them.

He was alongside the bow when one of the men whistled softly, the same melody as the pirates on shore. Gustav did his best to imitate it and a rope was lowered to him. He caught it and pulled his little boat in tight to the hull.

"Where are the rest?" someone asked from above.

"I was sent alone in case of a trap," Gustav said. "Now I know it's not, I'll signal them."

"We don't have time for this," came the reply. "We can't keep the crew in the mess forever."

"It won't take long," Gustav said, using Charisma. "I was told you'd have a weapon for me."

"*Skit*," the man said. "That was not part of the plan."

"Can't trust pirates to follow directions," a second man said.

"Do you want this to happen or not?" Gustav asked.

"All right, here's a pistol. Don't lose it. I'll want it back." He handed the gun down to Gustav, who suppressed a grin.

"I need to go back closer to shore to give the signal," Gustav said to the men. "We'll come back and board here, all right?"

"We'll be waiting."

Gustav loosened the line and pushed off from the hull. Once he was out into darkness and was sure that the two he'd spoken to could no longer see him, he fit the oars into the oarlocks. He rowed in a wide arc, staying away from any lamplight, to the ship's stern. There he grabbed a hanging line and with the pistol tucked into his waistband, pulled himself up onto the ship.

The deck and the rigging were empty: he didn't see a single sailor. He had to hope that Timonis and his men were holding all of the crew in the mess and they hadn't already killed them or Captain Eklund. Would they wait and let the pirates do that? It would be easy enough to set sail and throw prisoners overboard.

Then Timonis could make up any story he wanted; he could say the ship was lost at sea, and he was in the only dinghy that was launched. If his men lied for him, it would be seen as a tragic loss and not the traitorous act that it was. The pirates would have a ship, and if they stayed at Strongrock or in the Sapphire Sea, it might be years before anyone recognized the *Tazeyar*. Especially since there would be one less captain and crew from Tarklee to come across her.

He didn't see anyone, so he crept forward, keeping in shadows as much as possible. He made his way to the hatch that led below without any alarms sounding but then he stopped: someone was guarding the hatch.

With the pistol behind his back, Gustav stepped out of a shadow and sauntered up to a man wearing freeholder clothing.

"They need you at the bow," he said quietly, calling on his Trait. "To help the rest of my crew get aboard. I'll stand watch here."

"Are you sure?" the man asked. "I was told to make sure this door stays locked."

"I'll do that," Gustav said. "You know the layout of the ship. That's why they need your help and not mine."

"All right. I don't want to be part of the fighting though; I already told the Clan Freeholder and he agreed."

"Fine," Gustav said. "Just help them all get aboard." He had his proof that Timonis was part of this. Once the sentry was gone, Gustav flicked the lock on the door and entered. A short flight of stairs led down to a well-lit hallway.

He paused. The mess was halfway along the hall and Captain Eklund's cabin was at the stern. How many people did Timonis have working with him? Five, six? More than that?

Where would they have the most men stationed? Guarding the captain or guarding the crew in the mess?

Decision made, he hurried down the hall to the very end. He pressed an ear against the door to the captain's cabin, but he didn't hear anything. Was anyone there or had they taken the captain to the mess along with the crew?

He tried opening the door but it was locked. He rapped on the wood once and whistled.

"Is it done?" The door was wrenched open, and Gustav pointed the pistol at the chest of a man he recognized as one of Timonis' freeholders.

"Is what done?" Gustav asked. He backed the freeholder into the room, closed the door, and leaned against it. Three people sat in the middle of the room, their hands and feet tied together and gags stuffed into their mouths.

"Untie them," Gustav said, nodding at the prisoners. "Captain Eklund? Are you hurt?"

The freeholder didn't move, so Gustav levelled the pistol at him. "I said untie them." He crowded into the man, forcing him to back away. "It's Leif, right?" Gustav asked. "Leif Stendhal. You were with Clan Freeholder Timonis at the council meeting. I will shoot you if I have to. *Untie them.*"

Leif must have realized that he meant it. A moment later, the gag was out of the mouth of one of the prisoners.

"Gustav Gunnarson," Eklund said. "I am happy to see you. We're not hurt, but I am embarrassed." His hands were free, and he quickly untied his feet and stood up. When all three of the crew were free, Eklund turned to the woman. "First Mate, secure the prisoner."

"Timonis is working with Strongrock pirates," Gustav said once Leif was bound. "They had plans to board the ship and steal it." He looked over at Leif. "I scuttled all the boats on shore. Timonis' men thought I was with the pirates and let me on board." He grinned. "They were even kind enough to give me this pistol. I heard one say that your crew is in the mess."

"Vieno," Eklund said. "Pistols are below the maps."

The man, Vieno, opened a lower cupboard and pulled out four pistols. He loaded each one and handed two to the woman. "Judit and I will take care of them," he said.

"I want Timonis alive, if possible," Eklund said.

The two officers left and Eklund locked the door from the inside.

"Will the two of them be enough?" Gustav asked.

Eklund smiled. "This from a man who single-handedly stopped this vessel from being pirated?" He shrugged. "They both will feel responsible for what happened and will do whatever they have to—"

Three muffled shots rang out and then silence. A few moments later, a bell was rung.

"It's done," Eklund said. He turned to Leif. "Now all we have to do is wait for your master to be delivered to me so he can learn his fate."

"You have no legal right to pass judgement over a Clan Freeholder," Leif said.

"We are still at sea," Eklund said. "As the captain of this ship, I *am* the law."

Footsteps sounded outside, and there was a knock on the door.

"First Mate Judit reporting, Captain."

Eklund opened the door, and Judit stepped into the room.

"The crew has been released unharmed and three of the conspirators are dead." She paused. "I am sorry to say that Clan Freeholder Timonis was able to escape." She looked at Gustav. "He and a couple of his men found the boat you came in."

"No doubt we'll hear more bad news about him soon enough," Eklund said. "And well done in regaining control of the ship."

"Thank you, sir. What are your orders?"

"Gustav Gunnarson, I hope you weren't planning on remaining in Nurmi because we will be making all haste to Lavais Port. There's a representative of the Interim Grand Freeholder there who needs to know about Clan Freeholder Timonis' actions."

"Lavais Port is where I'm headed," Gustav replied. "And might I suggest you keep this one alive? I'm sure Berna will want to speak to him personally."

"If you think she'll find him valuable," Eklund said.

"I'll put him in the brig," Judit said. She grabbed Leif and pushed him out of the room ahead of her.

"I must see to the ship," Eklund said to Gustav. "Feel free to stay here or come with me to the bridge."

THE WHITE BUILDINGS of Messanos shone in the morning sun. Inger was there somewhere. Would she recognize the *Atlaine* and come to greet them?

Or . . . Dag stared at the ships in the harbour, trying to see if the *Vassan* was at anchor. Would her sister be hiding from the pirates?

"I think we arrived before the *Vassan*," Calder said as he joined her at the gunwale.

"Or they've already been and gone," Dag said. They had made good time getting here, but they hadn't seen the pirates since they first spotted them. They were counting on Luck, and she wasn't comfortable trusting Inger's safety to something so unpredictable.

"Maybe they went somewhere else," Calder replied.

"Maybe," Dag agreed.

"Come on," he said. "The dinghies will be launched soon. Let's get ashore and find out for sure."

"And find Inger." She followed him to where a dozen sailors were lifting a dinghy off the deck. She waved to Jaak, who was among the crew launching the dinghy.

"Rafael, with me," Calder said.

"Jaak," the Second Mate said as he met up with Calder. "You come along with those three." He pointed to three sailors nearby.

Jaak helped steady Dag as she stepped into the dinghy. She made her way to the bow and stared at Messanos as Calder and Rafael and the rowers got settled. In moments, the boat was heading toward the dock.

She closed her eyes and re-opened them quickly, hoping her Trait would guide her gaze to something she needed to see, but her Trait was quiet. Too quiet.

Would Inger have heard that a ship from the Pale Sea had arrived? Dag scanned the shoreline: her sister's blonde hair should stand out amongst the darker haired Arressans and Pilalians. So, where was she?

The dinghy reached the dock, and she climbed out, impatiently waiting for Calder to join her.

"She's not here," she said. "Inger should be here and she's not."

"Did your Trait activate?" Calder asked.

She shook her head. "No. Come on." She headed along the dock towards the office of the Merchant Adventurers.

"I'll go in first," Calder said when she stopped across the road from the small building. "In case Luck is needed."

Dag nodded and closed her eyes. Inger wasn't here. It wasn't her Trait telling her that; maybe it was because they were twins. But in her heart, she knew her sister wasn't here: not in the office or in the city.

Calder slowly approached the office and opened the door.

"Hello?" he called. "Is anyone here?" A woman met him and he turned and waved Dag forward.

She ran across the road. "Where is she? Esma," she said. "I wasn't expecting you." She entered the small office, joining Calder and his sister.

"I've been helping Inger," Esma said. "We've been purchasing goods for you. Then yesterday she didn't show up even though we had meetings planned." She shook her head. "I've searched everywhere for her. I checked her rooms this morning; it looked like she didn't make it back there last night."

"Have the pirates landed?" Dag asked. "The Strongrock

pirates?" Had they arrived already and done something to her sister?

"I haven't heard of any pirates," Esma said. "At least none that arrived by ship."

"Did you talk to Charis?" Calder asked. "Or the council?"

"I tried to find Charis," Esma said. "But he's gone too."

"Would they be together?" Dag asked. "Esma? Can you take us to Inger's rooms?" She hoped there was a clue to where her sister had gone, otherwise she would have to search the entire city.

"Sure," Esma replied. "It's close." She led the way out of the office, Dag and Calder behind her.

A block away, Esma turned down a narrow lane. At the third door, she gestured to Dag.

Dag opened the door and stepped inside. She suppressed a grin. It was Inger's room all right. Clothing was draped over the two chairs and the bedding was a tangled mess.

Her humour faded as she stared around, looking for a clue to help her find her sister. The itch started between her shoulder blades and she closed her eyes in relief. Finally, her Trait had activated.

When she opened her eyes, her gaze landed on a piece of paper half-covered by a vest. She picked up the paper. It was a note addressed to her sister.

"*The council has been betrayed and both of you are in danger,*" she read out loud. "Both of you," she repeated. "A warning to Inger and who else? And why would the Arressan Council want to harm them?"

Esma peered over her shoulder at the note. "It must mean Charis," she said. "He's been urging the council to sanction Pinho even though he's left the city and assumed dead at the hands of—" she paused and looked at Calder, "the Resolute. Although why they would threaten him over that, I don't know."

"We need to talk to Charis then," Calder said.

"I'll see if I can find him," Dag replied. "You get the *Atlaine* loaded."

"All right," he said. "Stay safe."

"I'll do my best," Dag replied. She stayed behind after Calder and his sister left, searching every inch of Inger's rooms, but nothing else triggered her Trait.

The state of the room made her believe that Inger had left on her own: that she hadn't been kidnapped, at least not from her rooms. It was a small comfort, but at least it was something to give her hope.

As was the fact that Inger's Trait had changed enough that she should be able to hide. Although her pale skin and hair would make it harder in a land where few people shared that colouring.

She stepped back out into the city. She knew one place to look for Charis. A small hiding spot that she and Calder had visited last time they were in Messanos.

Hoping that there would at least be a clue there, she headed out into the city.

Chapter 7

"HMMM," LAUMA SAID. "I'm not sure I can help you. My family had a very small Freeholding, and I never had much to do with the Clan Freeholders from Swyford or Nordmere. At least not until I bought enough land to make them notice me."

Nadez leaned back in her chair. She was in Lauma's office, trying to uncover the circumstances surrounding Henrik Ottosen's rise to Clan Freeholder.

"It was worth a try," Nadez said. In truth, because it was such a rare thing, she'd forgotten that Lauma was a self-made Clan Freeholder. "I did find evidence that the Suicide Assassin arrived on a ship owned by Fihaldo Pinho." The Merchant Adventurers' records had listed him as the owner of the ship. "I'm not sure we can assume there is no longer a threat from the Sapphire Sea, but Ottosen might not have any other contacts."

"Well, we know no one's arriving from the Sapphire Sea any time soon," Lauma said. "So, if there is still a threat, we don't have to worry about it until the spring. There are plenty of other issues that need my attention. And yours."

"You're right," Nadez said. "I should let you get back to them." She wasn't about to drop this even though Lauma didn't see it as urgent.

Nadez left Lauma's office and headed back to her own. Once there, she pulled out the ship ownership records. Most of the ships that sailed between here and the Sapphire Sea had been lost, but there were still a handful owned by people other than Fihaldo Pinho. What she didn't know was whether the owners were friends or foes of the Fair Seas Treaty Alliance. And whether they would even bother travelling this far to sell goods in the spring. With so many ships from the Sapphire Sea lost, there would no doubt be plenty of coin to be made closer to home.

She sighed and locked the ledger away in a cabinet.

It meant that getting the shipyard up and running was still the best way to ensure they could feed themselves for the next few years.

With a thought to food, she left her office and headed out into the city.

The cold winds blew fat snowflakes in off the Pale Sea, and drifts were piling up against the sides of buildings. Nadez shivered and pulled her coat tighter around her, wishing she had thought to bring gloves.

Most of the people she passed seemed intent on getting to their destinations, although a few food vendors were still selling hot pies and rolls.

She entered the warehouse and stood near the door. She didn't want to be recognized, not when all she wanted was to take the pulse of the city.

A family stood near a big pot, each child holding out a bowl as a man ladled out either soup or stew. Cots lined the far wall, and a group of children were chasing each other amongst them.

Boxes and barrels were stacked along the floor: proof that this warehouse had plenty of food, at least for now. But it wasn't enough to get them through to spring. They needed Calder and Dagrun to come back with more supplies, and even that was no guarantee against food shortages and possible starvation.

At least people had a warm place to stay and plain but filling food.

She visited three more warehouses before midnight. All of them were open and welcoming people with food and warm places to sleep, and even better, not once did she see anyone begging on the street.

The snow had stopped by the time she made her way back to the Hall.

It was late and she was due at Melker Skala's Tarklee residence early in the morning. He wasn't someone she thought would cause trouble, after all, he had voted with Lauma and against Ottosen, but she had to be seen visiting every Clan Freeholder. Besides, someone there might know more about how Ottosen had inherited the freeholding.

PIA OPENED THE door of her sleeping chamber. It was early, but she could hear people moving around in the house. She tiptoed along the hall and stopped just outside the doorway that led to the kitchen.

"You're certain it's Timonis' man?" Pia recognized Berna's voice.

She wasn't sure what to make of the Interim Grand Freeholder's daughter. She was both afraid and in awe of the mother, but she didn't trust her, so she wasn't planning on trusting the daughter either. Except she didn't see a way not to if she really was going to be an Intelligencer.

"I'm sure," a male voice said. "But Timonis got away."

It took Pia a moment to recognize the voice, and when she did, she burst into the room.

"Gustav, you're here!" Here was someone she *did* trust, partly because he had claimed her as one of his own.

"Pia," Gustav said with a grin. "I heard that you caught yourself a pirate."

"I had help," she replied. "But what's this about Timonis?"

"He was working with pirates," Gustav said with a scowl. "They were planning on taking the *Tazeyar*—stealing it." His face brightened. "But I scuttled all the boats and snuck aboard and saved Captain Eklund and his crew."

"You did not," she said but returned his grin because she was certain that he had. Her trek across the island paled in comparison, but at least she'd had an adventure of her own to talk about. "We were attacked," she said. "Pirates tried to take Solvig's warehouse, but we chased them off. And caught one. I brought her here because I think she knows something."

"I'm sure she does." He turned to Berna. "I'd like to question her, if you don't mind."

"I think we all should be there," Berna said. "You, me in case I have questions about Timonis, and Kaja, so she can tell my mother."

"And me," Pia said. "She's my prisoner."

"You brought her here because you couldn't get her to talk to you," Berna said.

"Pia comes too," Gustav replied.

"We should make sure the pirate knows we have one of Timonis' men here," Pia said. "So that she understands no one is going to rescue her."

"Pirates have a reputation of never leaving one of their own behind," Gustav said.

"That was the old pirate captain," Pia replied. "I'm not sure about the new one. I don't think she's been in a lot of fights, and the crew didn't seem very disciplined."

"I came across the pirates in Nurmi," Gustav said. "There was a large woman one of them called Captain Ozlinch."

"Ursa Ozlinch," Kaja said. "According to Dagrun and Calder, she had quite a bit of authority on Strongrock even though she wasn't a sailor."

"They don't have a ship," Gustav said. "Which is why they are trying to steal one. I only saw a single small sailboat."

"We burned the other boats," Pia said. "When we retook the warehouse."

"That means they're probably even more desperate than they were," Gustav said. "With no way to get them all back to Strongrock."

"They'll have to depend even more on Timonis," Berna replied. "We know what the pirates want, but why is Timonis helping them? Our pirate must know. Maybe she'll tell us if she thinks she's been left behind. And my guess is Clan Freeholder Timonis has already sent word that he was shocked to find Leif Stendhal working against him."

Pia nodded. She still didn't quite trust Berna, but she was smart and seemed to know how the Clan Freeholders thought. At least a bad one like Timonis.

"I'll make tea and porridge," Pia said. "There's no reason we should do this on empty stomachs."

PIA WAITED FOR Gustav's nod before opening the door wide enough to ease inside with the tray. She saw the pirate look over her head and knew the moment she had seen the other prisoner. They would eventually have to put him in this same room, but Pia had wanted to see the pirate's reaction first.

She set the tray down on the floor, closed the door, and carefully untied one of the pirate's hands.

"Don't try anything," she said. She stepped back and leaned against the door. She had promised to signal if the pirate did anything other than eat her porridge.

Berna hadn't wanted to let her do this, but she'd argued that the pirate would trust her more than anyone else. For days Pia had been making sure she was fed. If the pirate was going to believe anyone, it would be her.

The pirate picked up the bowl, lifted it to her mouth, and let the porridge slide in. After she'd finished, she carefully placed the bowl back on the tray and picked up the mug of tea.

Pia stared at her while she drank.

"You're not our only prisoner, you know," she said conversationally. "We have someone who works for the local Clan Freeholder. Maybe you know him? His name is Leif Stendhal."

The pirate's expression didn't change.

"It seems he was trying to steal a ship," Pia continued. "For Captain Ursa Ozlinch." The pirate paused while drinking her tea.

"Yeah, we know who the new pirate captain is," Pia said. "I don't think anyone is getting back to Strongrock any time soon."

The prisoner put down the teacup and backed away. She waited patiently while Pia retied her hands.

She picked up the tray and opened the door. "We don't think Clan Freeholder Timonis will help his freeholder, so I hope you weren't hoping he would help your captain save you." She left the room, making sure the door was locked before heading to the main room.

"She didn't recognize Leif Stendhal," she said. Berna and Gustav sat at a table while Kaja stood near the window. "But I'm pretty sure she believes no one is coming for her."

"So, we wait to see if she feels abandoned and is willing to talk to us," Gustav said. "Should we question Leif or wait until the pirate says something?"

"We should hold off until tomorrow," Berna said. "To allow Timonis time to send a message. Kaja, please let Captain Eklund know he'll need to wait a day or two until you're ready to leave with him."

"I'll go see him now," Kaja said and headed out of the kitchen.

"If that's everything," Berna said. "I have work to do."

"Sure," Gustav replied. "I'm going to say hello to the twins."

"Just don't take up too much of their time," Berna said as she left the kitchen.

"Pia, come with me," Gustav said, standing up. "And meet some fellow Intelligencers."

DAG WATCHED THE entrance to Charis' safe house for half an hour, but there were no signs that anyone was inside. The key was still in the hiding spot above the door, and in moments she was inside with the door to the alley closed behind her.

The curtain on the small window let in a narrow beam of sun that was enough for her to see that the place was empty. She ran a finger across the table, leaving a track in the dust.

No one had been here for a while—days certainly, maybe even weeks. She scanned the small room: maybe not since she and Calder came here after she had found Saulia Holt and Rahm's token.

She frowned, wondering if Rahm had returned from assassinating Pinho. She couldn't imagine him not being successful, and she supposed she should be worried that he could be killed, but that didn't seem possible. Maybe the magic of the token made him invincible.

She sighed. Nothing in the small room triggered her Trait. She sat in a chair and closed her eyes. She would look for Charis at the council offices. She had no idea what she might be walking into, but she had no other leads. Someone there might know where he was, and if for some reason they had imprisoned him, she had to trust her Trait to keep her from walking into hidden dangers.

She knocked on the door to the council building. The only time she'd been here was when Charis had asked the council to allow Inger to take over the Merchant Adventurers on behalf of the Fair Seas Treaty Alliance. She hadn't been introduced to the council members, and now she hoped her lack of knowledge didn't prove to be dangerous.

A woman answered the door. Her eyes narrowed, and without saying a word, she led Dag to a waiting room. Dag nodded but didn't speak. This woman obviously thought she was her sister. Did that mean the council wasn't responsible for Inger's disappearance?

"I'll tell the council that you're here," the woman said. She frowned and exited through a door, leaving Dag alone in the room. What had Inger wanted from the Messanos Council?

"Inger Lund, I told you it was too dangerous to come back here."

Dag turned to find an older man peering at her from an open doorway.

"You're not Inger," he said. "You must leave. Hurry, before it's too late." He backed away and was about to shut the door when Dag lunged at it, grabbing the door and keeping it open.

She squeezed past the man, and he quickly closed the door. It was dark, but enough light filtered in for her to see that they were in a closet. Her Trait triggered when her eyes fell on the back wall: there was something there, behind the coats and hats that hung from pegs.

"You're going to help me leave," Dag said. "Hurry. I can find the mechanism, but you know where it is." He didn't move. "I know there's a secret passage. Come on, I doubt you want to be found trying to warn Inger Lund."

Dag heard raised voices from the waiting room, and with a worried look at the door, the man reached up and pulled on a hook.

"But you're not Inger Lund," he said as the back wall of the closet swept out, revealing an opening.

Dag hurried through it, followed by the man. He pulled a latch and the wall moved back in place, plunging them into darkness.

"Keep quiet," he whispered in her ear.

A moment later, she heard the closet door open.

"No one's here," a woman said. "Where did she go?"

"I'm not sure, Councilwoman." Dag thought she recognized the voice of the woman who had ushered her into the waiting room. "Perhaps she had more urgent business to attend to?"

"Send someone to the Merchant Adventurers office and see if Inger Lund is there," the councilwoman said.

"Yes, Councilwoman. I will go myself."

After a few minutes of silence, Dag's companion put a hand on her arm and tugged her forward. As silently as she could, she followed him through the dark passageway. Eventually he stopped, and she heard a soft scraping sound and felt cool air flow across her face.

She followed the man into a dimly lit room. It was some sort of storage room: dusty furniture was pushed up against two of the walls, and wooden crates were stacked at one end.

"Thank you," Dag said, turning to look at her companion. "For saving me. As you guessed, I'm not Inger Lund. I'm her sister Dagrun, and I'm looking for her and Charis Diakos."

"My name is Nilus," he said. "I am, or at least I was, a Messanos councilmember. Until Thekla Floros took control and disbanded the council." He sighed. "I warned the others, but they wouldn't listen."

"What did you warn them about?"

"That Floros was working with Pinho," he replied. "I thought she would simply take over his empire. I didn't realize that she would change the contract with the Resolute."

"What! I returned his token. What happened with the Resolute?" If her sister was Rahm's target, Dag would do her best to kill him before he could hurt Inger. Even if it caused a rift between her and Calder.

"Somehow Councilwoman Floros got a hold of the Resolute's token. She changed the contract, sparing Pinho and instead targeting Charis Diakos." He sighed. "Charis is the one who told me that Floros was working with Pinho. I didn't believe him until it was already too late."

"What about Inger? Has she been targeted?"

"Not by the Resolute," Nilus said. "There was a one-for-one substitution. But Floros wants your sister." He looked at her. "I don't know why, but I assume she hopes to use her to force the Fair Seas Treaty Alliance to do something."

"Inger is in hiding," Dag nodded, relieved that Rahm wasn't planning on assassinating her sister. She should be safe, and Dag's Trait meant that she would find her, eventually.

"Yes," Nilus said. "And no. She told me she was going to protect Charis. The two of them had become very close. Inger told me that she knew who the Resolute was and that she could make him listen to her."

"*Skit.*" Dag didn't know what Rahm would do. Inger and Esma were obviously friends, but did that mean Rahm could ignore his contract and token? "I have to leave," she said. "Does Floros have guards?" Calder and Esma were at the Merchant Adventurers office. What would the councilwoman do to them?

"Not Council guards. That's the only reason I haven't been detained. The council was disbanded without observing the proper procedures, so the Messanos Guard has chosen to stay neutral, for now. But outside of this building she is accompanied by some of Pinho's men. Here, there is a rarely used exit through the garden."

CALDER SCANNED THE street in front of the Merchant Adventurers office. It was late afternoon and Dag hadn't returned, and he was wondering if he should go looking for her.

Inger, with Esma's help, had procured enough to almost fill the *Atlaine*'s hold, and it had been quick work loading the ship. The *Atlaine* was now ready to sail.

He noticed a woman standing at the side of the building, and he paused in the street, just across from the Merchant Adventurers office. He watched her. And because she kept looking behind her, he saw the three men who were loitering a little farther down the street. Guards, he thought, but to protect the woman or to help her detain someone else? He didn't like either option.

"Everything is out of the warehouse."

He turned to find Esma at his side. "Do you recognize that woman?" he asked, turning to face his sister, blocking her from the woman's view and forcing her to look over his shoulder. "She has three men with her."

"She was here yesterday looking for Inger," Esma said. "Come on." She dodged around him and walked towards the woman.

"I told you yesterday I haven't seen Inger Lund," Esma called out. "Nothing's changed."

"Something has," the woman replied. "I saw her at the council office earlier today, but she left before Councilwoman Floros could speak to her. Who's that?" She nodded at Calder.

"My brother," Esma replied. "He's just picking up some supplies."

"A brother the council doesn't know about?" the woman asked.

"Have you met our father?" Calder asked. The woman paled, so he assumed she knew who and what Rahm was. "It was a surprise to us too. Why are you looking for Inger Lund?"

"Oh, the councilwoman just wanted to clarify something with

her," the woman said. "I'm sure it's not that important."

"Then why come here two days in a row?" Calder asked. "And bring three men with you?"

"The docks can be dangerous," she said and nervously looked over at her companions, who were now heading towards them.

Calder sighed. "Do you think this is a wise plan?" he asked. "After all, we are Rahm's children. Even if you successfully take us here, which I very much doubt you can, you will have to face our father." He looked at Esma, who rolled her eyes.

The woman looked from Esma to Calder. She frowned at them but made a hand signal. The three men stopped a dozen paces up the street. One of them leaned against a wall, but they all kept their eyes on Calder, Esma, and the woman.

"What am I to tell the councilwoman?" the woman asked.

"That you felt that a physical confrontation with Rahm's children was a risk you could not undertake on her behalf," Calder said. "And that Rahm would know that *she* had given the orders you were trying to carry out." He stared at her. "I promise, whatever his faults are as a father, Rahm cares deeply about his children. I'm certain that neither you nor the councilwoman you work for would care to be a target for his vengeance."

"I don't suppose we would," the woman said. "But don't think you've won anything." She turned and headed up the street to join her companions.

"I don't think I've won anything," Calder said as he watched the four turn a corner and disappear from view.

"Did she come looking for my sister?"

He turned. Dag leaned out of the open door to the Merchant Adventurers office. Rafael hovered behind her.

"Yes," Calder said. "She said she'd seen Inger earlier today. I take it that was you?"

"It was." She backed away from the door and into the office.

Calder followed his sister inside and with a last look at the now empty streets, closed the door. He joined Dag, Esma, and Rafael at the main desk.

"I saw you stop in the street," Dag said. "And then I recognized the woman from the council office. I ran into Rafael as I was climbing in the back window." She frowned. "That woman and a councilwoman named Floros were planning on detaining me. A former council member helped me escape."

"Floros is head of the council," Esma said. "But why would she want to detain Inger? Or tangle with me?"

"I was told that she somehow got her hands on Rahm's token and changed the contract," Dag said. "Pinho is no longer the target—Charis is."

"*Skit*," Calder swore. "Why can't Rahm keep possession of his token? This means that Pinho will continue to be a threat to the Three. What's Inger's part in all of this?"

"She must be helping Charis," Esma said. "Trying to keep him alive. I wish she'd come to me. I could have spoken to Father."

"Maybe she didn't have time," Dag said. "It's even possible she spoke to Rahm and he refused to cancel the contract." She looked over at him. "I know that if Calder was in danger, I'd act first and ask questions later."

Calder nodded. *That* was why Inger was involved. She and Charis were a couple. "I'll find them," Calder said. "And talk Rahm down from killing Charis." He had to listen to his son, didn't he?

"I'll go with you," Esma said. "He won't want to be disowned by both of his families."

"I should be able to discover if they're still in the city," Dag said. "And if they're not, I'll be able to find out where they left from and where they were heading."

"All right," Calder agreed. If Inger and Charis had left the city, then he and Esma would track them down. Dag was the only one who could navigate the *Atlaine* back through the Teeth to Tarklee. The supplies they had just loaded into the hold were still desperately needed.

"So, WHAT DID you think about the twins?" Gustav asked Pia. They were alone in the kitchen of the house where Berna Strauskas was headquartered. He'd taken her to meet Janni and Jarri yesterday, but he'd wanted to give her some time to think about what they were accomplishing as Intelligencers.

"They seemed nice," Pia replied. "Too nice and too, I don't know, gentle to be effective Intelligencers."

"But they *are* being effective." Gustav still wasn't sure what to think about Pia. He had thought that her only concern was for her sister's wellbeing. And yet she had delivered the pirate to Berna and Kaja because she felt, what? Duty bound? Obligated to the Intelligencers?

"But not as Intelligencers," Pia said. She glanced over at him. "And I do recognize the enormous benefit they are to the Alliance. But they're not acting as Intelligencers."

"No," he agreed. "They're not." Although they didn't have the right mental outlook to be Intelligencers, the Breck twins had useful Traits. It would be a shame for the Alliance to miss out on their talents; or the talents of anyone else with a Trait who lacked the right temperament.

"You are," Pia said. "And I am too, even though neither of us has finished our training."

"Yes. And I'm a little surprised about you. Since it wasn't your choice." He held her gaze, but she didn't comment on being forced into Intelligencer training by Henrik Ottosen.

"There you are," Berna said as she entered the kitchen, followed by Kaja. "I just received a message from Clan Freeholder Timonis." She waved a piece of paper in the air. "As expected, he placed the entire blame on Freeholder Stendhal, claiming that he had no idea what was happening on the ship and that it was only by chance that he was able to escape the *Tazeyar* unharmed. It's time to let Leif Stendhal know how his loyalty is being rewarded."

"And the pirate too?" Gustav asked.

"Well. I won't tell her," Berna said. "But she is locked up in the same room, so it would be hard for her to not overhear what we talk about." She left the kitchen, and Gustav followed with Pia right behind him.

The two prisoners were being held in the shipbuilding office, a space that belonged to Clan Freeholder Timonis but that, to Gustav's knowledge, had always been used by the senior ship builders. The main room was filled with tables stacked with plans and half-built models of ships.

The smaller room in the back was usually used as storage, but now it was empty of everything except the two prisoners, who were tied up and tethered in separate corners. Leif Stendhal stood up when Berna led the small group into the room. The pirate remained seated on the floor, although she watched them closely.

"Leif Stendhal," Berna said. "Clan Freeholder Timonis claims that you acted alone. Do you have anything to say?"

Leif closed his eyes and bowed his head, but Gustav thought

that was just for show. The man had known he would be disowned; it was possible it had already been discussed in the event any of Timonis' men were captured.

"I am filled with regret at the shame I have visited on my Clan Freeholder," Leif said. He lifted his head. "Might I see the message he sent you?"

"No, but shall I read it to you?" Berna asked.

"No," Gustav and Pia said at the same time.

"There could be a coded message," Pia added.

"Kaja already warned me." Berna smiled at Leif. "See, none of us trust your Clan Freeholder or the note he sent. But now, since you asked to see it, I am certain that Timonis' note has an embedded message meant just for you." She glanced over at the pirate. "Or perhaps it was for your pirate friend."

Leif's eyes never left the note as Berna folded it into a small square.

"Nothing more to say?" Berna asked.

"The pirate is not my friend," Leif said.

Gustav looked over at the pirate. Did she look more despondent than before?

"But you must have been working together," Berna replied. "If your Clan Freeholder is to be believed. Or do you say he was lying? That you were not working with the pirates that attempted to take control of the *Tazeyar*?"

Leif Stendhal stared over Berna's head, and the young woman shrugged.

"All right. You'll both be handed over to Captain Eklund tomorrow morning and transported to my mother in Tarklee."

"And then what?" Leif asked.

"Well, there is a jail there," Berna replied. "I'm sure you'll see the inside of that." She turned and left, followed by Kaja. Gustav was about to follow them, but Pia stepped close to Leif.

"That's if you even make it to Tarklee," Pia said. "A ship's captain is the law. If it were me, I wouldn't want someone on board who had just tried to kill me and my crew. It's winter, and there are bound to be rough seas between here and Tarklee. Accidents happen in rough seas."

Pia nodded at Gustav as she left. He followed, locking the door and hurrying after her.

She grinned when he caught up to her. "You should try talking to the pirate," she said. "Use your Charisma on her."

"Not Leif?"

"He won't talk," Pia said. "When I warned him that he might not make it to Tarklee, I could tell that he's prepared to die. Timonis' message might even instruct him to make sure he dies before he can be forced to tell the truth. But the pirate? She wants to live."

"You don't think you're the better option?" Gustav asked. "She knows you."

"And has never said a single word to me," Pia replied. "I think it'll take a Trait, and so far, mine hasn't worked."

"All right," Gustav said. "I'll let her worry for a few hours, and then I'll see what Charisma can get out of her."

CHAPTER 8

"MASTER INTELLIGENCER, IT is so nice to see you again." Melker Skala's smile seemed genuine to Nadez.

She'd been here a few days ago, and he and his people had been very accommodating, but she hadn't found anything unusual. She was hoping that a surprise visit would uncover a secret or two. They might not have anything to do with what she was looking for, but she had a hard time believing that any Clan Freeholder had no secrets. Even Lauma had one: her former husband was a Resolute assassin.

"Clan Freeholder Skala," Nadez replied. "I appreciate you giving me access to your records again." He led her to the same room she had worked in before. She paused and scanned the room. It looked like little had changed since she had been here.

"It's no trouble," Skala said. "I'm happy to help. Let me know if there's anything you need."

"Can I ask if your grandmother is in residence?" Nadez asked. "I would very much like to speak with her if she is interested in having a visitor." At almost ninety years old, Valda Skala was one of the few people still alive who would have known Ottosen's uncle.

"You wish to speak with my grandmother?" Skala asked. "She doesn't get many outside visitors anymore, but she loves meeting new people. I'll go see if she's prepared for company."

"Thank you," Nadez said. Skala nodded and left, and she walked around the room.

A ledger was out on the desk, the most recent account dated yesterday. She flipped the page and scanned more—inconsequential—entries.

"My grandmother asks that you join her for tea," Skala said when he returned. "I am afraid she won't be much help with the details of managing the freeholdings. It's been decades since she's been involved in the day-to-day operations."

"Oh, I realize that," Nadez replied. "Lauma mentioned her the other day, and I thought it would be nice to pay my respects."

"Then come this way." Skala led her to a room at the end of a hallway and opened the door. "Grandmother, this is Nadez Norup, Master Intelligencer for the Fair Seas Treaty Alliance. Master Intelligencer, meet Valda Skala."

"Freeholder Skala, it's an honour to meet you," Nadez said.

"I haven't been a Freeholder in ages," the older woman said. "Call me Valda, and I shall call you Nadez." Valda didn't get up, but she patted the arm of the chair next to her. "Come and sit. I have no idea why you want to talk to me, but I am delighted. I need to know all about how you came to be the master spy."

"I'll leave you two," Skala said. "Grandmother, be nice." He left just as a woman came in with a tray with tea and cups.

"I'm old enough that I don't have to be nice," Valda said as Nadez sat down beside her. "Though I usually am. The older I get the more I realize just how important things like being nice are. Madara, this is Nadez Norup, the Master Intelligencer. Madara looks after me," Valda said to Nadez. "We've known each other for decades. What do you think the Master Intelligencer wants with an old woman like me?"

Madara poured tea for each of them before pulling up a chair and joining them.

"She knows that old women know things," Madara said finally. "And that no one comes to visit anymore, so you'll be more likely to reveal secrets."

"What do you say, Master Intelligencer?" Valda asked. "Is Madara right?"

"I also know that the people who care for old women know things," Nadez said. "And that you might tell me secrets because everyone that can be hurt by them is already dead."

Valda laughed, and Nadez smiled and picked up her tea. She waited while Valda and Madara exchanged a look.

"I like you," Valda said. "So yes, I might be willing to tell you secrets. What do you want to know about?"

"Henrik Ottosen's mother and the death of his uncle Tollack and cousin Roald," Nadez said.

Valda's eyes widened. "Really? After all these years?"

"Recent events have made me wonder about Henrik Ottosen's mother," Nadez said. "I believe she was from the Sapphire Sea?"

"She was," Valda said. "Grete, Henrik's mother, was a beautiful woman who caught the eye of old Otto when he went to Messanos on business. I have no idea what she saw in him, but she married him anyway."

"Messanos, you say. Is there still family there?" Nadez didn't know enough about suicide assassins to know where they were trained, but the Arressan council had targeted Pinho with an assassin. Perhaps assassins were simply part of their culture.

"Probably," Valda replied. "I remember a cousin or aunt or some female relative visiting when Henrik was young."

"A young woman?" Nadez asked. "Was that around the time that the Clan Freeholder died?"

"Such a sad event," Valda said. "Madara would know more about that than I would."

"My father went to school with Tollack," Madara said. "And yes, you have the right of it. He died during the cousin's visit. A very sad coincidence."

"Did everyone feel the same?" Nadez asked. "That it was a coincidence?"

Valda and Madara exchanged a look.

"You are bringing up very old history," Valda said.

"Some would say it's dangerous history," Madara added.

"As Master Intelligencer," Nadez replied, "dealing with danger is part of my job. Can you tell me who thought it was *not* a coincidence?"

"Everyone with a brain in their head," Valda said with a chuckle. "Grete was never subtle about her desire for Henrik to inherit." She lowered her voice. "The rumours were that the young visitor was not a relative at all, that instead she was an assassin." She shrugged. "I always thought she was both."

"Was there a price paid?" Nadez asked.

"I'll say." Valda and Madara shared another look. "I see no harm in telling the Master Intelligencer," Valda said to her companion. "I have enough secrets to take to my grave; this doesn't need to be one of them."

"I would like to know *why* the Master Intelligencer is asking these questions," Madara said.

Valda turned to Nadez. "That does seem a reasonable question. Perhaps I'll tell you my secret if I like your answer."

Nadez hid a smile and sipped her tea. These two could certainly keep a confidence when they wanted. She set her teacup down and nodded.

"A suicide assassin recently failed in an attempt on the Interim Grand Freeholder's life," she said. "A young woman who we cannot identify but who arrived on a ship full of goods claimed by Henrik Ottosen."

"That doesn't mean Ottosen brought in the assassin," Valda said.

"No, but a subsequent assassination attempt by a person in Ottosen's household leads me to believe that he was."

"The Engen girl," Madara said.

"Yes," Nadez replied.

"*You* saved them," Valda said and grinned. "When Madara told me that they'd been taken from Ottosen's household, I was just so happy. Are they safe? They deserve better, those two."

"They're safe," Nadez replied. "The younger one had been locked up to make the older one do Ottosen's bidding. Everyone deserves better than how they were being treated."

"But those two in particular," Valda said.

"Another secret?"

"Of course." Valda smiled. "What does an old woman like me have except for forgotten memories and secrets?" She leaned back in her chair. "If Roald had not been killed, those girls would be in line to become Clan Freeholders."

"What?" Nadez was shocked. "Tollack's son had a child? I didn't realize he'd been married."

"A girl child," Valda said. "And he wasn't married, but he had a child nonetheless. The mother was a caregiver to Tollack. She left the household as soon as Clan Freeholder Tollack was buried and returned to her parents' house along the coast. Shortly after that, Roald died and then his mother. What woman would then admit to having given birth to a child of that line?"

"No one smart," Nadez replied, shaken. How many deaths had it taken for Otto and his son Henrik to inherit?

"That girl grew up and married and had two girl children of her own before she and her husband died," Valda said. "Pia and Frida Engen."

"Does Henrik Ottosen know this?"

"Of course not," Madara said. "They would be dead if he knew. And if his mother had known, they would never have been born."

"So, Ottosen *wasn't* responsible for the deaths of Pia and Frida's parents," Nadez said.

Valda and Madara exchanged a long glance.

"Perhaps not," Madara said. "And definitely not for that reason."

Nadez raised her eyebrows. Was Madara implying that Ottosen murdered two people in order to gain control over a child with a Trait?

"Of course, there's no proof of any of this," Madara continued.

"But if murder is the way this family solves problems . . ." Nadez trailed off.

"Precisely," Valda said. "And that brings us back to my other secret. One I will trust you with. Henrik Ottosen's mother set sail for the Sapphire Sea and was never heard from again. Another rumour had it that she was fulfilling an obligation to her cousin's family: an assassination to repay the two that were carried out on her behalf. And that she completed the task but was unable to escape and killed herself."

"Rumours," Nadez said. "Not proof." But it made perfect sense. If Grete was an assassin, she wouldn't kill in her own home, that would be too risky. Instead, she would rely on her connections and have someone else carry out the assassinations. But there would be a cost for that, likely a debt owed. One that she repaid with an assassination of her own but lost her life in the process.

Would a successful assassination combined with a suicide leave yet another debt that Grete's son had collected on? Did that mean Henrik Ottosen knew about his mother's past and how he had inherited the freehold?

"There is no proof of any of this," Valda agreed. "It's simply the ramblings of an old woman."

THE ITCH BETWEEN her shoulder blades intensified, and Dag sighed.

"One or all of them left the city from this dock." She turned to Calder and Esma. They were on one of the smaller docks that sat at the edge of Messanos' main anchorage. "If we can find out what ship docked here, we might be able to find out who left on it. Then we'll have a better idea of where they were heading."

"I'll ask around," Esma said. She headed along the dock towards the shore.

"We'll go after her," Calder said. "And bring her back safe."

"Alive," Dag said. "I just need Inger alive. And we'll *all* go. You won't find her without me."

"You need to get the *Atlaine* through the Teeth," Calder said. "Esma and I will find Rahm *before* he catches up to Inger and Charis. Once you've unloaded in Tarklee, you can come back and meet up with me."

"No. Yes." Much as she hated it, she knew that Inger was not more important than their mission. And if saving Inger meant people starved in the Three, neither she nor her sister would forgive her.

She sighed. "Rahm's contract is for Charis. He won't hurt Inger." Unless her sister got in the way.

"He won't," Calder agreed. "And if Charis truly cares for Inger, he won't allow her to put herself in harm's way for him." He gave her a sad smile. "I know I wouldn't."

"But we Lund women are stubborn." She was rewarded with a laugh. If she was in Inger's position, she would do everything in her power to save Calder, including putting her own life at risk. She had to assume her sister would do the same for a man she loved: she *had* already left her life behind for him. A life Inger had been grateful to have after falling in with pirates.

"Zelesso and then Yedris," Esma said as she rejoined them. "The only ship that sailed from here—and it was a ship, not a kog—in the past day was heading to Zelesso to pick up goods that are destined for Wekesa, the major city in Yedris. That should make our task a lot easier."

"Will it?" Dag asked. "We have two cities to search." Zelesso was the second largest Arressan city. "Is it possible that Charis has friends or family in Zelesso?"

"I didn't hear him talk about knowing anyone in Zelesso," Esma said. "But I do. And they'll know if Rahm is there."

"Do you think Rahm has followed them?" Calder asked. "You said there was only one ship that left in the last day."

"You may have Luck working for you," Esma said. "But Rahm leaves nothing to chance. He wouldn't set foot on a ship with a captain he didn't control."

"Of course," Calder said. "On board, the captain is the law. Our father wouldn't put himself at someone else's mercy."

"Not mercy," Dag said. "Justice. So, Rahm left on his own ship. We came across him in a smaller boat, a kog. Does he have anything larger? Anything that could catch up to this ship?"

"If he doesn't, he'll just steal one," Esma said. "We have to assume that he's on the trail."

"Come on," Dag said. "Only one ship sailed from here. Rahm must have left from somewhere else."

There were only a few places where a ship larger than a kog could anchor. Dag's Trait activated when she stepped onto a small dock at the edge of the city. Half a dozen older men and women were patching sails and fishing nets.

"What ship was anchored here?" she asked a weathered man folding his nets.

"No ship," was the reply, but he looked over his shoulder.

Dag followed his gaze to a stack of wood. Her Trait activated, and she walked over and nudged a few pieces of wood aside.

"Of course," she said to herself.

"Of course, what?" Esma asked from her side.

Calder lifted up the exposed length of wood that Dag had exposed. He turned it around so that the name that was carved into it was visible. *Vassan.*

"Rahm has teamed up with the Strongrock pirates."

PIA CROSSED HER arms and returned Leif Stendhal's stare until he looked away. She suppressed a snort of disgust. He was so loyal to Timonis that he wouldn't even fight for his own life. In her experience, people who were so dedicated that they were prepared to die for their Clan Freeholder were also willing to do terrible things to others in their name. Like lock children up and starve them.

She pushed off from the wall and went to stand in front of the pirate.

"Supper time for you," she said as she carefully untied her tether from the wall and wrapped it around her ankles to hobble her. "Just you," she said, glancing at Leif. "No sense wasting food on someone who acts like he's already dead."

She pushed the pirate to the door and out into the main storage room. All of the clutter had been taken out, and now there was just a table and two chairs that had been placed across from each other. A single bowl of stew sat in front of one.

"That's for you." Pia untied one of the pirate's hands and tied it to the table leg before guiding her into the chair.

The pirate ate quickly, and as soon as the bowl was empty, Pia tied the pirate's hands behind her back, securing them to the chair. She set the bowl on the floor near the door and leaned against the wall.

Gustav sat down across from the pirate and smiled.

"That's what we ate for supper too," he said. "I thought it could have used a little more seasoning, but spices, like everything else, are in short supply."

Pia Concentrated on the pirate, trying to see if Gustav's Trait was working on her. She flashed a hand signal to Gustav to keep talking about food.

"I imagine everything was in short supply on Strongrock," Gustav said. "And that's why you came to Lavais Island." He shook his head and grinned. "Sailing one of those little boats all that way from Strongrock took some skill. I grew up on the water, and that's not a journey I'd take lightly." He leaned across the table. "What was it like? Did you sail along the coast? What's the Blighted Wood like up close?"

"Cold and depressing," the pirate said, then she clamped her mouth shut.

"I bet," Gustav continued. "Those little boats are so much better on ice than the open water once winter hits. I'm Gustav, born and bred right here in Lavais Port. You know we want to help you, right? Kinda hard to do that when I don't even know your name."

Pia held her breath. Her Trait was showing her that the pirate's resolve was weakening ever so slightly.

"Name's Tilde," the pirate said finally. She sighed and seemed to collapse in on herself. "And it was rough going on Strongrock at the end, and we were desperate and running out of food."

"Well, you made it here," Gustav said. "Along with your captain. The only pirate captain I ever heard of was Margit Ansdottir. I saw her in Tarklee Harbour. Ansdottir, not your new one. Captain Ozlinch, is it?"

"She's not really a captain," Tilde said. "But she was willing to take charge."

"I suppose that's because she was in charge of the tavern and inn," Gustav said. "Ursa Ozlinch doesn't put up with fools, is what I heard."

"She does not," Tilde said. "Which is why I took up with her and not Steen."

Pia followed Gustav's eyes as he glanced at his hands. She nodded at his signal and quietly picked up the bowl and retreated from the room.

She found Kaja and Berna in the main room.

"Her name is Tilde, and she said that the pirates she's with are following Ursa Ozlinch," she said. "They came directly from Strongrock not long ago."

"It's good to know for sure," Kaja said.

"At least we know pirates haven't been hiding out somewhere for months," Berna added. "With help from locals."

"What about a pirate named Steen?" Pia asked.

"Calder reported a few issues with a man named Steen, but I wasn't aware he was a pirate." Kaja shrugged. "But from what Calder said, he is unpleasant. It's interesting that Ursa Ozlinch's Trait didn't work on him."

"Maybe he has an opposite trait," Berna said. "How did they get to Lavais?"

"They came in small sailboats," Pia said. "Along the shores of the Blighted Wood. They ran out of food on Strongrock."

"So, this Steen has Ansdottir's ship?" Berna turned to Kaja. "What was the name of it?"

"The *Vassan*," Kaja said.

"I'll have Gustav find out if Steen took the ship somewhere," Pia said. "After he learns how and why the pirates contacted Timonis. If the tea is ready, I'll take it in."

"It's right here." Berna gestured to a tray on a nearby table. "And thank you. This has already been helpful."

"Sure." Pia picked up the tray and headed back to the small

room.

Gustav and Tilde were smiling as if they had shared a joke, but the pirate quieted when Pia entered.

"Oh look, tea," Gustav gushed.

Pia suppressed the urge to roll her eyes, but Tilde was smiling again. Pia poured the tea and untied one of Tilde's arms so she could drink it.

"Thank you," Tilde said after taking a sip. "This is what I missed the most."

"Did you run out on Strongrock?" Gustav asked.

"Yeah," Tilde said. She seemed very relaxed now. "Ran out of tea before we ran out of ale. But *that* was when things got worse."

"So, you decided to come to Lavais," Gustav said. "Did Ursa Ozlinch know who to contact?"

"Ursa." Tilde shook her head. "Ursa didn't know anything except how to get some of us to work together. No, it was Edur. He always was one of Captain Ansdottir's favourites. She told him all her plans."

"So, Edur was the one who knew to contact Timonis," Gustav said.

Tilde laughed. "Turns out the captain was making deals with more than one Clan Freeholder. She was always smart, Captain Ansdottir." Tilde sighed. "I still miss her."

"She had a formidable reputation," Gustav said. "I suppose that's why both Holt and Timonis were willing to work with her."

"She was smarter than them," Tilde said. "It was Pinho that did her in. That was what the rift was about once the captain was gone. The question for those of us left was, do we make a new deal with Pinho or Timonis?"

"That's where the captain's ship went?" Gustav asked. "To the Sapphire Sea?"

"Yeah. But Steen," Tilde sneered, "has no idea who he's dealing with. Edur told me Pinho got the best of the captain; that he threatened her into betraying Holt. Steen's no match for Pinho no matter what he thinks."

"Then it sounds like Steen will not be someone you need to worry about ever again," Gustav said.

"You got that right," Tilde said. "A waste of a ship though. That's what we're here for. The ship that was promised."

"Promised by Timonis," Gustav said.

"Yeah. Edur even has the promise to pay note Timonis gave the captain. Once we collect on that, we can set back up on Strongrock."

"And that's what you want?"

"*Skit* yes," Tilde said. "I just want to go home."

CALDER WATCHED THE horizon. He didn't expect to see the *Vassan*, but with Luck, it was a possibility.

"I can take the tiller if you need a break," he said, turning to Esma.

"You might as well get some sleep," she replied. "We'll need to sail well into evening if we hope to catch up with Father."

"I'll try." Calder turned ahead again. Despite his training, he didn't think he could sleep right now.

He and Esma were in the *Hakon* on the trail of Rahm and the pirates. He had said goodbye to Dag and the crew of the *Atlaine* this morning, and there had been a knot in the pit of his stomach ever since. It wasn't his Trait; Luck wasn't warning him, and he had full confidence in Darya and Rafael, and Dag of course, to get them all back through the Teeth safely. But he was still on edge.

Esma was confident she could find Rahm in Zelesso if he'd followed Inger and Charis to the southern Arressan city. She wouldn't tell him how she knew, or *who* she knew, so he had to trust her.

And he was trying to, he really was. He wanted to be able to trust his sister, but he really didn't know her well, and as an Intelligencer, he knew how dangerous it could be to trust the wrong person.

He closed his eyes and concentrated on his fear and unease. He sighed. He wasn't really concerned about Dag's safety. It was more worry that he and Esma would fail: they either wouldn't find Rahm in time or Rahm wouldn't listen to them. That his father would kill Charis and Inger would get hurt or killed. That *he* would fail Dag by not saving her sister from his father.

And Dag would never trust him again.

It had only been a few months since they'd met: when Dag had definitely *not* trusted him. Losing that trust now, after they had been through so much together, would break his heart. Just as harm to her sister would break Dag's.

He sighed and opened his eyes, wishing with all his heart that he could force Luck to work for him, force his Trait to help him save Inger. But no matter how desperate he was, he knew that wasn't how his Trait worked.

At dusk, he and Esma traded places. The moon rose, casting enough light for him to keep the little sailboat safely following the shoreline. He had only been this far south a few times, and although he'd studied maps, he didn't know the currents and sandbars along this part of the Arressan coast.

They were counting on Luck to keep them safe; hoping that his hand on the tiller would provide some protection against any dangers lurking in the water. Sailing this fast at night, it would only take one submerged tree or unexpected rock to wreck the *Hakon* and destroy any chance of catching up with Rahm.

"Looks clear ahead," Esma said from the bow.

"Good." He looked as a cloud drifted past the moon. It was almost full, and if the sky remained clear, they could sail safely for hours.

"How far to Zelesso?" he asked.

"We should make it by midnight," Esma replied. "If the wind holds and the sky stays clear."

"Midnight," Calder replied. "Only the rough parts of town will still be awake. My guess is that the pirates will find a tavern. What about Rahm? Where will he start his search?"

"I know exactly where Father will go," Esma said. "And it won't be to start looking for Charis. Saba would never forgive him if he didn't visit the moment he set foot in port."

"Who's Saba?"

Esma turned to him, and her smile flashed in the moonlight. "My mother," she said. "You are about to meet the rest of my family: my mother and *our* younger brother Kasim."

"I am?" Calder asked, then he started to laugh. "If your mother is anything like mine, Rahm will not want to explain my existence." Was this Luck? Was his Trait doing its best to throw Rahm off balance and keep him from chasing after Charis?

"He might have already searched and left," Calder continued. "They are a day or so ahead of us."

"Maybe," Esma replied. "But Mother never complains about the amount of time Father is away travelling, but she does insist that once he's home, he's there for at least one full day. Nor will she let him leave in the middle of the night. If he arrived anytime last night, he'll be there until morning."

"Does she know what he does?" Calder asked. His own mother had not, and he didn't want to cause Esma unnecessary stress.

"Not that he's a Resolute," Esma said, all humour gone from her voice. "And I'd prefer we keep it that way."

"Of course." Calder nodded. He would do his best to honour Esma's wishes.

The moon was still high in the sky when they sighted lights lining Zelesso's harbour.

Calder followed Esma's directions and sailed the little boat to a small dock near the edge of the city. It wasn't as hidden as the dock in Messanos, but it was similar enough that Calder knew it was a regular spot for the *Hakon*.

His sister led the way along mostly dark streets to a house where light escaped from around a curtain in a window. Esma rapped on the door but instead of waiting, entered the house.

"Mother?" she called. "It's me."

Calder stepped inside, closed the front door, and stayed there while Esma headed down a hallway.

"Mother?"

"Esma!" An Arressan woman exited a door and swept Esma up in a hug. "Your father didn't tell me you were coming too! How lovely."

"Is he here?" Esma asked. "Is Father still here?"

A second door opened, and a shadow hovered just inside a dark room.

"Hello, Rahm," Calder said. "You can probably guess why I'm here."

"Esma," her mother said. "You brought company."

"Mother," Esma said. "This is Calder. A friend of mine and Father's. Calder, this is my mother Saba."

"Come in and be welcome," Saba said. She took Calder's arm and steered him towards the room she had been in. "Rahm, fetch us some mead, will you?"

Calder looked over Saba's head and met Rahm's angry glare.

"That would be nice," Calder said. "If it's not too much trouble."

"Nonsense," Saba replied. "Rahm will be happy to do that. Come sit and tell me how you and Esma came here? Did another ship enter the harbour and I missed the signal? Rahm?" She turned to her husband. "The mead?"

"I'll help you, Father," Esma said, and Calder nodded at her, grateful. Rahm did not look happy at his presence. He might be Rahm's son, but at the moment, Calder was not sure that meant that his father wouldn't hurt him. Especially if he threatened to expose him as a Resolute and ruin the happy family life he had built here.

CHAPTER 9

"ARE YOU SURE there's nothing you want me to do about Ottosen?" Nadez asked Lauma. They were both bundled up against the cold wind that whipped through the streets of Tarklee, on their way to visit Saulia Holt. Because it had better security than the apartment in the Hall, Saulia had decided to live in the city estate, forcing Nadez and Lauma out into the elements.

She was visiting Saulia because the other Clan Freeholders had been told they would all be visited. Lauma had decided to join her, and Nadez had welcomed the chance to talk, but it hadn't gone the way she'd expected. Lauma didn't seem to think her revelations about how Ottosen inherited, or his potential links to suicide assassins, was an urgent issue.

"There is nothing *to* do," Lauma repeated. "If there is a connection between Ottosen's mother and the suicide assassins, now that winter has hit, there is no way for him to contact anyone in the Sapphire Sea."

The pair turned a corner, and Nadez put her hand on Lauma's arm and forced her to stop.

"You said if," Nadez said. "Does that mean you don't believe what Valda Skala told me?"

Lauma sighed. "I believe what she told you, but I also believe that it's an internal Clan Ottosen concern and that even if it was provable, the Grand Freeholder should stay out of it." She shook her head. "If there was a murder during my tenure, I would investigate it, but this happened so long ago, and most of the people involved are dead."

"Because they were assassinated," Nadez said, but she let go of Lauma. "What about the attempt on your life? Pia is a witness that Ottosen tried to have you assassinated."

"Pia is not here," Lauma replied. "And since we stole her sister from Ottosen's household, I'm not sure we can assume any Clan Freeholders would believe her."

"I had every right to take that child," Nadez replied. "But yes, Ottosen could convince others that she is lying for us because we saved her sister." And many wouldn't even wonder why the sister *had* to be rescued. But as Master Intelligencer, it was her duty to investigate any assassination attempts—especially successful ones. Even if they were decades old. "I won't mention it again."

"Thank you," Lauma said. "Now let's focus on our visit with Saulia Holt."

They walked the rest of the way in silence. Nadez was still going to investigate Ottosen; she just wasn't going to discuss it with Lauma. The Interim Grand Freeholder was correct that right now Ottosen couldn't contact the suicide assassins in the Sapphire Sea. And the changes made to the Fair Seas Treaty probably meant Ottosen had nothing to gain by Lauma's death. But he had still tried to assassinate her twice. He might choose a different target, but Nadez thought it highly likely Ottosen would use assassins again.

Saulia Holt's housekeeper ushered them into a sitting room. The new Clan Freeholder joined them a few minutes later with Mykol.

"I hope the weather wasn't too horrible," Saulia said. "I admit I was a little surprised to get your message. I myself have just barely begun to grasp the freeholding situation, so I'm not sure I can be of any help in your examination. The records were not kept in good order."

"I'm sure Mykol can help me with whatever I need," Nadez said. She believed Saulia. No doubt Tarmo Holt had left a mess of secrecy and hidden agendas.

"Mykol is the only reason the freehold is even functioning," Saulia said. "But I can spare him for a few hours."

"Master Intelligencer," Mykol said. "If you'll follow me, the office is this way."

Mykol led Nadez to a smaller room that contained a substantial wooden desk and chair. Shelves flanked a window that looked out into a snowy garden. She crossed the room to a shelf of what looked like ledgers.

"Which ones document the food shipments?" she asked.

"I'm afraid there isn't a single set for that." Mykol joined her and pulled a ledger from the shelf and opened it. "The records I managed for the Grand Freeholder were kept in the standard way." He glanced at her. "I saw to that, but here?" He pointed to a line of script. "Here we have the purchase of wood from Byholt right above a note that three casks of mead were produced." He shook his head. "I have no idea how the former Grand Freeholder kept things straight."

"I suppose that was the point," Nadez replied. "I know you were loyal to him, and I can't fault you there." Except she could. Mykol knew Tarmo Holt had kidnapped and tortured Joosep Sepp. "But things were being hidden from everyone, including his own family. The records are at least done by date?"

"Yes. These here are all from this past spring." Mykol trailed a hand along the spines of a dozen ledgers. "Up to today." He turned to her. "I thought I might as well continue in the same vein. I am training an assistant to copy the whole year into a better format, but they haven't begun that task yet."

"This year is what I'm most interested in," Nadez said. "Food shipments and production."

"Yes, Clan Freeholder Holt told me that's what you were looking for."

It took Nadez a second to realize Mykol was referring to Saulia and not her father.

"This will take me some time." She pulled the first three ledgers from the shelf and placed them on the desk. She rather liked the idea of seeing the records of everything that had happened in the freehold during the time Holt was conspiring with the pirates in one place.

"That's what I thought," Mykol replied. "I take it that you don't need my help going through the records?"

"I'm sure Clan Freeholder Holt has more important things for you to do," she said and was rewarded with a smile.

"If you need anything, just ask for me." Mykol nodded and stepped out of the room.

Once the door was closed, Nadez opened the first book.

A few pages in, she wished every freeholding kept their records in this manner. As someone with little real knowledge of the business of freeholders, she was finding it fascinating to see all the different things that went on at one time.

There was no mention of pirates, although there was an entry about a trip Holt had taken on his ship. The record stated that he went to the Sapphire Sea, but the time between the day he left and the day he returned was far too short for that long a journey. And there were no transactions recorded. No goods were sold or bought on that short trip, which meant it wasn't for trade.

It wasn't proof that he'd visited the pirates on Strongrock, but it was the most likely explanation.

The winter sky outside was dark by the time she had read through the last ledger. Not bothering to light a lamp, she sat back and stared at the books on the desk.

As interesting as it had been to go through Tarmo Holt's records, she had no more information than she'd had before. She couldn't prove that he had been preparing his holding for a famine or that he was working with pirates. Or even that he had been secretly buying ships. All things she *knew* he'd been doing, but that his records didn't show.

She stood up and stretched. She hadn't actually expected to find anything incriminating, but she had *hoped* to. Not to punish the Holt clan: Tarmo and Asla were dead, and their treason was known. But finding proof might have given her confidence that none of the other Clan Freeholders were hiding anything she had to worry about. Because if Tarmo Holt could keep his actions out of his records, any of the others could too.

The Interim Grand Freeholder would be long gone by the time Nadez stepped out into the hallway. Hoping to find her way back to the room where she'd left Lauma, she went left.

But it didn't lead her to the sitting room. Instead, she found herself in an unfamiliar hallway. As she was turning to retrace her steps, she heard voices from the other side of a partially open door.

"Your father promised me," a man said. "Told me I'd be set up for life."

"I would like to." Nadez recognized Saulia Holt's voice. "But circumstances have changed."

"Mine haven't," the man replied. "So, if you can't honour the Clan Freeholder's commitment, I'll find someone who can."

"I need some time," Saulia said.

"I can't afford to feed all these children," was the reply. "Not with food so scarce and dear. Someone'll want them."

"How many?" Saulia asked. "How many children?"

"Seven. Two sets of twins and triplets. And all of them have abilities."

"But are they useful abilities?" Saulia asked.

"I was told to look for twins and triplets with abilities," was the reply. "And to fetch them here. Figuring out what they can do was not my task. Nor was keeping them once they were in the city."

"All right. Bring them here. I will honour my father's commitment as far as that goes."

"I'll bring them in the morning," was the reply. "Before I've fed them."

Nadez hurried down the hall and back into the office. She sat down at the desk and waited a few minutes before leaving again, going in the opposite direction.

The housekeeper found her wandering around the house and showed her to the front door.

During her walk back to the Hall, Nadez wondered what Saulia Holt was planning on doing with children from the Sapphire Sea. Children with Traits who had been either stolen by, or sold to, Tarmo Holt.

Should she wait and see if Saulia told her about the children herself? What if she didn't?

Because if Saulia Holt knew they had abilities—knew they had Traits—and didn't tell her, Nadez had to assume that she was more her father's daughter than she'd led them all to believe. And that Saulia Holt could not be trusted.

Gustav tugged at his hat, trying to shield his ears from the bitter wind that blew in off the Pale Sea. The *Tazeyar* was just barely visible through the blowing snow. He kicked at the edge of the dock. Ice was starting to form along the wood, and he wondered if the sea around Lavais Port was about to freeze.

"So that's it?" Pia asked from his side.

She'd joined him in seeing Kaja off, along with her prisoners:

Tilde the pirate and Timonis' freeholder, Leif Stendhal.

"That's it for the prisoners," Gustav replied. "We have more work to do. Come on."

He led her away from the shore, past the shipbuilder's hall towards the shipyards.

He didn't know how or why, but for some reason Pia had decided that he was the one she would trust. Or like, or whatever made him her favourite. Ever since he'd gotten the pirate to talk, Pia had been shadowing him. And he was actually fine with that. She was smart and useful, and what needed to be done would be better, and safer, done by two.

He stopped in front of a small work hut and knocked on the door. A moment later his da opened the door.

"Get in with ye," Gunnar said. "Don't want the heat to get out."

"Pia Engen this is my da, Gunnar Falk." He stepped inside the little space. "Da, Pia's another Intelligencer student."

The little workroom was crowded once the three of them were all inside. A wooden workbench filled most of the space, and a piece of something his father was working on sat on it.

"Intelligencer, huh?" his da said as he eyed Pia. "Not much to you. You got a Trait too? Those twins have been working miracles over at the shipyards." He gestured to the piece of wood on the table. "They saved this piece, and it hardly needs any fixing before it's ready to go back in."

"She has a Trait," Gustav said. "But you don't need to know what it is."

"It's nice to meet you," Pia said. "And my Trait isn't very useful."

"Jarri thought the same about his," Da said. "Turns out, he was wrong. You just need to find the right way to use yours, I expect." He turned back to Gustav. "You come here just for a friendly visit?"

Gustav shook his head, and his da snorted.

"Thought not. Too much to do, what with pirates around. What is it you need from me?"

"I need a boat fitted with runners," Gustav said. "And I need to know as soon as it's safe to use it." Ice boats could travel on both ice and water, but they were unwieldy in water, and moving between water and ice was tricky and dangerous.

"I can get you one and get it kitted out by tomorrow," Da said.

"Whether it's safe or not depends on where you're headed."

"Nurmi," Gustav said. "I'm heading to Nurmi. Freeholder Leif Stendhal claimed he knew nothing about pirates helping his Clan Freeholder to steal a ship. I want to see for myself if that's true." He knew it wasn't; he'd seen the pirates coming from Timonis' property, but he needed proof.

"Another night this cold and the ice should be solid," Da said. "I'll talk to Torsten and see what he thinks."

"Thanks, Da." Gustav turned to Pia. "I'd like to check on Janni and Jarri. Want to join me?"

"Sure."

"Tell that Jarri for me that he's doing great work," Da said. He winked at him. "It's true, but he needs to hear it."

"I will," Gustav replied. "I'll come by tomorrow and see what Torsten thinks."

Pia opened the door, and he shivered when a cold blast of air hit him.

"Close that door!" Da called, and Gustav hurried outside and shut the door.

"Who's Torsten?" Pia asked as they made their way down the hill to the shipyards.

"He used to be a ship's captain," Gustav said. "Worked a log hauler up and down the coast. He's got the best weather sense of anyone on Lavais."

"He has a Trait?"

"Most likely," Gustav replied. "Although he wouldn't call it that."

"But you would," Pia said.

"Not to his face," Gustav grinned at her. "Or to Da. Look, they've stopped work for the day. We might be able to get some tea."

Half a dozen people were milling around the piles of parts that had been salvaged. He spotted Jarri, smiling despite his face being red from the cold.

"Jarri," he called as he reached him. "My da said to tell you that you're doing great work. The piece he's working on needs hardly any fixing to make it usable."

"I'm glad to hear that," Jarri said. "Come on. I've been out here for hours, and Janni promised me a fire and some hot tea. Hi, Pia."

"Jarri," Pia said and nodded as they all headed to the main workroom.

Janni wheeled her chair over when she saw them come inside.

"Gustav, Pia, it's nice to see you," she said. "Kaja stopped by before she left and told us everything. But come on, I want to hear how you got the pirate to talk."

"Over tea," Gustav said. "Then I need an update from you for Berna." A few minutes later, he had his tea and Jarri had his seat by the fire. Gustav sighed and looked around at his fellow Intelligencers. This was what he valued most about being an Intelligencer. This feeling of working towards a common goal: using their skills and knowledge and Traits to benefit their community. It was worth living apart from his family. And worth the dangers they had to face. At least he thought so. He looked at Pia, who was talking to Janni. He hoped Pia did too.

He'd ask her before he left for Nurmi. She had her sister to think about, after all. And becoming an Intelligencer hadn't been her idea. Maybe she wouldn't want to put herself in danger. No matter how much he wanted her help, he wouldn't force her. Even if he wasn't sure he could do this alone.

CALDER SAT DOWN across from Rahm. They were the only two in the small front room and he was hoping to finally have a chance to talk.

They'd barely spoken since he and Esma had arrived. He'd left it to Esma and their father to explain who he was and why they'd followed Rahm instead of travelling with him.

Esma's brother Kasim, his half-brother, had seemed skeptical but Saba, Rahm's Arressan wife, had taken their story at face value.

"She doesn't know, does she?" he asked his father.

"About you? No, and I don't want you to tell her."

"I won't," he said. He didn't think he'd have to since Esma was going to tell Kasim. "I meant about what you do." He paused. "And why you're really here, sailing with pirates."

Rahm looked away in disgust. "Far too many people already know. She will not be one of them." He turned back and glared at him.

"She doesn't have to know," Calder said. "As long as you don't fulfil this contract. Leave Charis alone."

"I won't hurt *her*," Rahm replied. "Your Dagrun's twin. So, you don't have to worry."

"You will if she gets in the way. If she makes it impossible for you to not kill her." He shook his head. "Which she will. I am asking as your son to not do this."

"I must," Rahm said. "It's more than a contract. It's a compulsion. You have no idea what I went through when my token was lost."

"Not lost," Calder interrupted. "Hidden. And found and returned by Dag, who you will reward by murdering her sister."

"I won't, I promise, but I will not live with an unfulfilled contract again, I cannot."

"Even if you lose both of your families?"

Calder turned to see Esma enter the room. She walked over to Rahm and stared down at him.

"Because you will," she continued. "Calder will tell his family, and I will tell mine. And none of us will welcome you into our homes and lives ever again. Is it worth that?"

"You wouldn't cause your mother such pain," Rahm said.

"*I* wouldn't be the cause," Esma said. "You and your lifetime of secrets and lies would be." She sat down beside Calder. "You know she would never forgive you."

"I can't," Rahm repeated. "I can help save the woman, but the man is my target."

"Then you'll have to go through me to get him," Calder said. "And yes, I know that I am no match for you." He would risk his life to save Inger and saving Inger meant saving Charis. "If you kill me, Dag will come for you, and you will not be able to hide, not from her."

"No, you can't," Rahm said. "I told you, I have no choice."

"There's always a choice," Esma said. "And you've spent your life making the ones that keep you lying to the people you claim to care about the most. Make a different choice. We'll help." She met Calder's eyes, and he nodded.

"Give us the token," he said. "I'll take it away and have Dag hide it so that no one can ever find it again."

"You know I don't have it, and I have to fulfil this task in order to get it," Rahm said. "And just hiding it isn't good enough. The compulsion makes me weak, and I won't do that to myself again."

"That's it?" Esma asked. "You aren't even willing to try? I'm going to talk to mother." She stood up, glaring at Rahm. "I wouldn't go far if I were you."

"I'll give you some privacy," Calder said. He ignored Rahm's angry look and went to the door. "I'll be back later."

"Thank you," Esma said. "It will be better to deal with one secret at a time."

"That's what I thought," Calder said. "Good luck." He left the house and headed out into the city. He had wanted to give Esma some time to talk to her mother, but he also wanted to hunt down the pirates. It might take Rahm longer to find Inger and Charis if he couldn't use the *Vassan*.

He followed the street down to the sea. He recognized one of the two ships that were anchored just offshore. The *Vassan* was quiet, and he didn't see anyone on board, although someone must be there. Even pirates wouldn't be undisciplined enough to leave their ship unattended.

But he would bet that most of them had come ashore to visit a tavern.

He followed the shoreline to the end of the pier and the taverns he was certain he'd find. There were two, but he discounted one as too well-kept for Strongrock pirates. Besides, that one was shut tight.

A shout of laughter came from inside the second tavern, and he paused to stare out at the *Vassan*, wondering if he could steal the ship out from under the pirates' noses.

He shook his head. It took at least four to five experienced sailors to manage a ship that size. Esma would help, and if Rahm cooperated, they could probably manage to get it too far out to sea for dinghies to reach it. His father might even know a sailor or two in town who would be willing to ship out with them.

Or had that been Rahm's plan all along? Calder didn't see the Resolute tolerating an undisciplined pirate crew unless he absolutely had to.

"Lookit the *skit karl* that washed up."

Calder turned to find Steen staring at him from the side of the tavern.

"Heard you got away from Ansdottir," Steen said. "She was mad about that."

"She was the one who didn't manage to get away from me," Calder said and shrugged. "Didn't know you were part of her crew."

"I helped them take the *Bright Breeze*," Steen said. "So, the captain rewarded me by letting me live. Turned out better for me than for her."

"Looks that way," Calder said. He wasn't surprised Steen had turned on his own crew. The man didn't seem to care about keeping friends or being loyal.

"I'm captain of the *Vassan* now," Steen said. "And the Strongrock pirates."

"You're a long way from home," Calder replied. "And on another man's journey."

"Oh, you mean the real Rahm. Sure, I know you were using a false name. You might have chosen an easier going man to steal that name from though." Steen took a few steps closer to Calder, and he could smell the ale on his breath.

"I know a lot more about Rahm than you do," Calder said. "If you know my real name you might know what I'm talking about."

"Rahm*son*," Steen said and started to laugh. "That's why you're here. You're home. Did your da send you with a message?"

"That's right," Calder replied. "He said to tell you he's not coming back. That you can leave now and head back to Messanos or go somewhere else that's not here."

"Not without what was promised me," Steen said.

"Coin?" What else were the pirates after? "We found Ansdottir's treasure if that's what was promised you."

"Coin is only useful when you have a place to spend it," Steen replied. "You gonna let us come into Tarklee and buy food and drink? I didn't think so."

"So, he's promised access to Messanos," Calder said. "As well as coin." He wasn't sure how much influence his father still had with Pinho and the council, but considering the large amounts of coin he'd given his mother over the years, he likely had considerable funds hidden away.

"We'll get ships the way pirates always have," Steen said. "We'll steal them. From the Pale Sea probably, so you tell your people to take care." Steen laughed and scratched his chin. "I have a pitcher of ale waiting for me. Tell your da the *Vassan* is at his disposal." He mock saluted and walked past Calder into the tavern.

The noise level increased when the door opened and muted

again when Steen shut it behind him.

Calder turned and headed away from the shore. He'd find the market and break his fast before returning to Saba's house, hopefully giving Esma enough time to tell her mother and brother the truth about Rahm before they were forced to deal with his existence.

He'd like to give them all more time, but unless Rahm could be convinced to halt his mission, he didn't have it to spare.

PIA RUBBED HER hands together in an effort to keep them warm. It was another cold day, but this one had dawned clear. The sun was just rising, and clouds of smoke and steam rose from the collection of buildings that made up the shipyards.

She wandered down the hill and past the rebuilt cradle to the pier and stared out at the sea. She had completed the task she'd come here to do. She had delivered the pirate who had then given up some of her secrets to Gustav. Now she could return to her sister at Solvig's warehouse and work hard at keeping them all fed and safe over the winter.

Or she could go with Gustav to Nurmi and try to find proof of Clan Freeholder Timonis' deception.

She knew that's what Gustav wanted her to do. She'd used her Trait and Concentrated on him yesterday.

Gustav was heading to Nurmi, and he was hoping she would come with him.

And she wanted to. She'd never felt like she belonged the way she had in the past few days with Gustav and the Breck twins. Like they all knew that separately they didn't amount to much but put them all together and they were part of something that could accomplish big and important goals. And that made them a family of sorts.

Except she had family: a sister who was depending on her.

She sighed. Training to be an Intelligencer had not been her decision, and the constant threats against Frida had meant that she'd always kept herself apart from her training mates. Before this she would have told anyone who asked that she was *not* an Intelligencer. That *she* was spying on *them*.

But even though they knew her history, every single Intelligencer she'd dealt with had treated her like one of their own. Nadez Norup had saved her sister from Ottosen. And then, instead of expecting Pia to work for her, the Master Intelligencer had set her and her sister free. She'd even had Gustav and Kaja sneak them out of Tarklee to a safe place in Swyford.

And once she was safe and anonymous, Pia had surprised herself by acting like an Intelligencer. By *becoming* an Intelligencer.

The wind whipped off the sea, and she shivered. It was time to get back. Gustav was probably waiting for her. But she knew what she wanted.

GUSTAV LOOKED UP when Pia entered the main room of the ship building office. He was relieved to see her. When he got up this morning, she'd been gone from the house they were staying in, and when she wasn't here at the office, he'd been worried.

"Tea's made," he said before returning to the notes he was reading. They were the only ones here, so it would be a really good time to talk to her. He peeked at her as she found a mug and poured herself some tea. "It's a cold day out there," he said, putting as much Charisma into his words as he could.

She laughed as she sat at the table across from him. "Your Trait doesn't really work on me," she said. "But it does warn me that you want something."

"Oh, sorry." He'd known that when she used her Trait that his wasn't very effective but not that in general it didn't work. "Is it every time?" She didn't seem angry that he'd tried, so that was good, wasn't it?

"Pretty much," Pia replied. "You look so worried that now I wish I hadn't said anything."

"My Trait has failed in the past," he replied. That had led to him being poisoned by Saulia Holt's family, not something he wanted to repeat. "And it put me in danger. I wish I knew how to tell if it wasn't working."

"You can't tell?" Pia asked. "I thought we all had something that indicated when our Trait was working. I know mine is activated when I get a shiver even when it's not cold. Although, I can tell the difference between a shiver from cold and a shiver from my Trait activating."

"I never figured one out," Gustav said. "No matter how hard I tried."

She stared at him until he had to look away.

"I can't tell," she said.

"Me neither." He shrugged. No one really knew how or why Traits worked: maybe his just didn't warn him. "If the weather holds, I'm leaving tomorrow for Nurmi."

"I'll be ready," Pia replied. "But we're going to Solvig's warehouse first. I need to make sure Frida is all right," she paused. "And that Solvig will look after her even if I don't come back from Nurmi."

"You'll help me find proof of Timonis' treason?" he asked. "Even though it's a huge risk?"

"Less of a risk with the two of us," she replied, and his shoulders drooped in relief. "Besides, making sure the Swyford Freeholders do not make deals with pirates will help keep Frida and everyone else in Swyford safe."

"Yes," Gustav agreed. "Pirates and those who work with them tend not to care much about regular people." He nodded. "Thanks for agreeing to this. I was worried I was asking too much of you. I know that you're all that Frida has in the world and that she wasn't treated well by Ottosen."

"Yeah, well, you were part of her rescue," Pia said. "I will never forget that. Anyway, I'm heading over to watch the twins work. I find it incredible to see Jarri take what looks like burned debris and pull it apart and uncover useable parts. It's the closest thing to magic I've ever seen. Want to come with me?"

"Later," he replied. "I'm rereading the notes Kaja made for Berna and then I need to see Da to check if the iceboat and the weather are ready for us to leave tomorrow."

"All right. Thanks for the tea." Pia took her mug to the side table and with a nod, left the office. A cold gust of wind lifted the edge of the paper he was reading.

He sighed. He'd thought it would be hard to get her to agree to come with him to Nurmi, instead she'd already understood his need for her to accompany him.

He didn't think her perception was solely because of her training. She was only a year younger than him, but she *was* almost three years behind him in training. But she'd been on her own for a long time, responsible for her and her sister, all while trying to save them both from Henrik Ottosen. That had to make a person grow up faster than someone like him who had gone from an idyllic and sheltered home to a sheltered school.

But they did have something in common; they both understood and accepted that personal risks were necessary for the good of the Alliance.

Chapter 10

Rahm peeled away from the wall of a house and headed Calder's way. They were still two streets from Saba's house, and the cocky grin on his father's face made Calder falter.

"Don't worry," Rahm said when he reached him. "Esma and I agreed on terms. Saba hasn't been told about my current task, but I was allowed to tell her about you. And just you," he said. "You're my son from before I met Saba. If you say anything different, the deal is off, and I will live with whatever consequences I have to."

"Including killing me when I get in your way?" Calder didn't like that Esma had changed the plan without talking to him. She had different goals, and it looked like saving her mother from hurt and disappointment was more important to her than saving Inger and Charis' lives.

"I will not hurt you," Rahm said. "Or the woman. It's just Charis I need to kill. Then I'll get my token back, and to be honest, I'll retire. Too many people know what I am and how to make me dance to their tune."

"Probably for the best," Calder agreed. "You seem to have a hard time keeping track of your token. Pinho is still out in the world somewhere, a threat to the Alliance and probably to you and my new family, and you're chasing a man who has done nothing but put himself in harm's way to help save his country from that tyrant. I'd think that after the last time you would have been more careful with your belongings. And yet here we are."

Rahm's face clouded in anger, but Calder lifted his chin and met his glare. His father might be one of the most formidable killers on the Sapphire Sea but that didn't make him smart. Or careful.

Rahm shook his head and looked away. "I deserve that. You're right. Losing control of my token twice is shameful. They sent a girl child. I thought she was looking for food, but once she found my token, I knew what she was: a suicide assassin. Just starting out but smart and fearless and she got the better of me, but it was my fault." He grinned. "Which is one reason why I have agreed to stay here and allow you and Esma a week to return to Messanos and retrieve my token."

"Two weeks," Calder said automatically. "And you tell Steen and his pirates that they take directions from me." Not only would they travel faster and more safely, but it would also keep Rahm off the *Vassan*.

"I've already bargained with Esma," Rahm said.

"Sure, for her to not tell Saba what you are," Calder replied. "Now you're bargaining with me so that *I* don't tell her."

Rahm stared at him for a moment, then he laughed. "I could never win an argument with your mother," he said. "And you have a lot of her in you."

"Two weeks and Steen works under my direction," Calder said. It was interesting to think that Rahm lied to Lauma Strauskas because he could never persuade her; he could never win an argument. Not much to build a life on. No wonder they hadn't lasted as a couple.

"I'll let Steen know," Rahm replied. "Although how you always seem to know the worst rogues on every sea, I don't know."

"Luck," Calder said. "And probably because I am my father's son."

"That you are." Rahm slapped a hand on his shoulder. "Now come and be formally introduced as such."

Two weeks, Calder thought as he let Rahm lead him to his second wife's home. He'd need Luck working with him if he was to find the token and bring it back in that time.

Nadez stood in the doorway staring out at the empty alley wondering if she should just confront Saulia Holt.

It had been days since she'd visited the young Clan Freeholder. Days since she'd overheard the conversation about children with Traits and still Saulia had not contacted either her or Lauma about them.

There was no law that said that Traits must be reported to the Master Intelligencer, but Joosep had been very clear that it was expected. Not that it stopped Holt and Ottosen from keeping children with Traits a secret.

She closed the door and returned to her office.

The ledger on her desk was open: one of many from the Merchant Adventurers office. She was pretty sure that she had found the ship that had brought at least one set of children to Tarklee. Buried in the detailed list of goods had been a note about a satchel of children's clothing that was to be delivered to an address here in the city.

Based on the conversation she had overheard, the children were no longer there but the man who had brought them might be. If she visited him, would he tell Saulia Holt? If she knew that Nadez was aware of the children, would Saulia finally notify her?

Nadez worried that some or all of the children had been stolen, and if not, if they'd consented to this, did their parents know they had been taken so far from home?

Sometimes Intelligencer students were very young when they arrived at the Hall. Calder had only been six when he'd left home. But it was always with both the child's and the parents' consent, and the child always had the option to change their mind. More than one student had gone home after a few days or weeks. They often returned later, when they were older, but some never did. To take and keep them against their will would be cruel.

Besides, it was important that Intelligencer students wanted to be there, wanted to learn and wanted to be part of an organization that helped defend the Alliance. Look at poor Pia Engen, forced into it against her will. It had made the child bitter and resentful and someone Nadez couldn't trust.

She sighed and dug a second book out from the stack on her desk.

This was a census of the Nordmere Freeholders dating back to the time when Tollack was Clan Freeholder.

The year he died, or was murdered, as she suspected, there was a young woman listed as a servant who was not listed the following year. That year the same young woman was recorded as living with her parents, along with an infant that had neither mother nor father identified. She flipped through the pages. Every single year the census was taken it noted a child named Freya as being in the house but not part of the family.

Freya married and bore Pia and her twin brother Pertu and a few years later, Frida. The boy died when he was eleven, and soon after that Freya and her husband died too, orphaning the two girls. Then, for reasons she couldn't discover, they were then taken into Henrik Ottosen's household and Pia Engen was sent to the Hall.

The quickness with which everything happened made her believe that not only did Ottosen know that Pia had a Trait, he knew exactly how he wanted to use it.

Had the Clan Freeholder used murder to get what he wanted? Not that she thought he was to blame for the boy's death. But the parents had been healthy until a mysterious illness killed them. A young man and woman dead within hours of each other. It didn't often happen.

She shut the ledger. She couldn't prove her suspicions, and Lauma thought they should stay out of the affairs of the Clan Freeholders, but Nadez was finding that difficult.

How was the murder of two freeholders, one the Clan Freeholder and the other his heir, *not* be the Master Intelligencer's concern? Not to mention that the current Clan Freeholder seemed to be aware of what had taken place and might have committed murders of his own. And he had tried to have the Grand Freeholder assassinated: twice!

She sighed. Maybe Lauma was right but for the wrong reasons. What good would it do to accuse the Clan Freeholder and his dead parents? Short of having Henrik Ottosen confess, she couldn't help the Engen girls gain their birthright.

She might not be able to help those children, but she could help some others. She grabbed her coat and hat and headed back down the hall to the alley.

Saulia Holt had been allowed plenty of time to disclose that her father had collected children with Traits. Now Nadez was going to get some answers.

The house was in a working-class part of Tarklee and looked much like its neighbours. Smoke rose from the chimney and light glowed from the front window.

A dishevelled middle-aged woman answered her knock.

"Nadez Norup, Master Intelligencer," she said and stepped around the woman and inside before she could stop her. "I have questions about the children."

"There are no children here," the woman said. "And I don't care who you are, you can't just push your way into my home."

Nadez pulled out her patch and held it up. "The Master Intelligencer has the right to access any building or vessel when on Alliance business. I know that the children aren't here now, but they were."

"I'm not saying a word," the woman replied. "I have rights too."

"You do," Nadez said. "I'll give you time to secure your home: to bank the fire and extinguish the lamps before I take you in for questioning. Oh, and find something warm to wear. The jail cells are cold this time of year."

The woman glared at her for a moment before her shoulders slumped in defeat.

"It weren't my idea," she said. "So, I'll not pay the price. There were children here, seven of them. One pair lived here for three months. I treated them right, too."

"Did you?" Nadez asked. "Were they happy? Will your neighbours tell me that they were clean and well-tended?"

"Neighbours?" Now the woman looked terrified. "Why would you ask them about the children?"

"Because if they were kept locked inside," Nadez said, "the neighbours wouldn't have seen them. Seven children from the Sapphire Sea would be noticed in this part of Tarklee."

"It weren't my fault! Clan Freeholder Holt wanted them kept out of sight."

"So, you locked children up for him." Nadez frowned. She would take this woman to the jail and see how she liked being locked up. "I need names, ages, the countries they came from, and the date they arrived at your door. And whether or not they were stolen."

"Weren't none of them stolen," the woman said. "I would never do that to any child."

"Do you know that for sure?" Nadez asked. "Did the children tell you? Now get your house secured. You are coming with me."

PIA HUDDLED IN the prow of the sailboat, the collar on her coat pulled up to her eyes and a warm hat tugged down over her ears. She'd been sitting here for two hours, and while she was grateful that Gustav had found her a warmer coat and hat, she was still freezing.

"How much longer?" she shouted to Gustav. He had it worse than her. Not only was he buffeted and battered by the same cold winds, he had to keep one hand on the tiller to keep the little sailboat on solid ice and away from the open water that lined the shore.

"We're almost there," Gustav shouted his reply. "See?"

She followed his gaze as they rounded a point. Yes, there was the dock and Solvig's warehouse. The boat shifted when Gustav stood up and fumbled with the sail.

"My hands are too cold," he said. "We need the sail down now!"

She crawled to the mast and held onto it as she stood up. Her fingers grew cold and stiff in moments as she tried to untie the frozen knot Gustav pointed at.

"Hang on," he called and sat back down and pushed the tiller hard to one side.

The boat turned in a circle, heading them away from the warehouse.

Finally, she had the knot untied and was able to fold the stiff sail halfway down. She caught Gustav's eye, and he nodded and pushed the tiller to the opposite side, turning the boat back towards Solvig's dock.

"Take it all the way down now," Gustav said. "And then sit down and hold onto something."

Pia hurried to get the sail down. Once it was in the bottom of the boat, she sat down on top of it and clutched the mast. The boat lurched and bounced as the runners hit a ridge of ice and then it plunged into the open water. The weight of the wooden runners made the boat ride low enough that a wave swept over the gunwales, soaking the sail under her.

Their momentum carried them halfway to the pier before Gustav put an oar in the water and paddled them closer.

By that time, a crowd had gathered on the pier. Pia waved when she recognized Frida's small figure. Pia scrambled up to the prow and slowly unwound the painter. It was stiff with cold and wet from the sea, but she was able to toss the end up to Solvig, who grabbed it and pulled them in.

"Early for an ice boat," Solvig said as she tied the little boat up. "But you handled getting it off the ice well."

"Thanks," Gustav said. He tossed a second rope up to Solvig. "It's been years since I sailed one of these; I forgot how frozen the lines get."

Pia jumped onto the dock and pulled Frida into a hug. "Are you all right?" she asked, pulling back and looking her over. Frida nodded, and Pia relaxed. "Good. I need to help with the boat. I'll meet you inside."

"Sure," Frida said. She hugged Pia again before stepping away. "I'm glad you're all right too."

"So am I," Pia said, but her sister was already running along the dock towards the warehouse.

"We'll take care of everything," Solvig said. "You two come and warm up. There's fish stew."

"There's always fish stew," Knut said as he joined them. "I'll get Ragnar to help me get this iceboat out of the water. I think a freeze is on the way, and we don't want it to get frozen into place."

"Thanks," Gustav said. "The sails need to be brought inside to dry properly." He glanced at Pia. "I need to get the iceboat ready to leave tomorrow."

Pia nodded. She still had to talk to Frida and Solvig, but she planned to leave with Gustav. Finding proof that Timonis was working with the pirates was too important.

She felt warmer just being out of the wind, and when she reached the fire, she peeled off her hat and sat down. Gustav sat a little closer to the fire and held his hands out towards it, rubbing them together.

"Here's some stew." Frida handed her a bowl and went back to the pot that sat on a rock beside the fire.

By the time Frida filled another bowl and handed it to Gustav, Pia had eaten more than half her stew and finally felt warm enough to take off her coat.

"Did you get the pirate to talk?" Frida asked as she sat down at her side.

"Gustav did," Pia replied. "Then she was taken away to Tarklee."

A gust of wind kicked up sparks from the fire. Pia turned to see Solvig and Knut walking towards them. Knut carried the sail: he stopped a few feet away and shook it out before laying it flat on the warehouse floor.

"Glad to see ye back in one piece," Solvig said, "And you too, Gustav, although it sounds like you're not staying long."

"If the weather holds, I plan on leaving tomorrow," Gustav said.

"The woodcutters got you and the pirate to Lavais Port, did they?" Solvig asked Pia.

"They weren't happy about it," Pia replied. "But they did what was asked. I didn't see them board it, but a ship came in just after we parted." She glanced at Gustav. That was the ship he had saved from pirates.

"If they boarded it, they might just make it home," Solvig said. "Winter has hit hard and early even this far south. Up north, the Pale Sea might already be mostly frozen."

Solvig pulled a chair close to the fire. "And what about you, Pia? Are staying here or going with Gustav?"

"That depends on Frida," Pia said. "And you. She can't come with us." She looped an arm around Frida and pulled her close. "Sorry. If you need me to stay, I'll stay."

Frida looked up at her. "Are you doing something that will help people?"

"I think so," Pia replied. "Not in the same way that gathering food does, but it will help a lot of people. At least it could stop them from being hurt."

"It will," Gustav said. "I might be able to do it myself, but having another Intelligencer I trust with me increases the chances that we'll be successful."

"Then you should go," Frida said. "And help people."

"Frida will be fine here," Solvig said to her. "Now that winter's set in, I don't expect the pirates will come back. Soon enough we'll be fixing blades on a boat and taking some of that salt fish across to the mainland. And if the weather turns even worse and it looks like staying here is risky, we'll all move over there."

"Thank you." Pia turned to Gustav. "I'll be ready to leave in the morning."

"That's good," Gustav said and grinned.

Pia smiled back at him. Gustav said that he trusted her. She didn't really know when that had become so important, but it was. Gustav trusted her.

DAG STOOD AT the stern watching the Teeth recede. She was getting far better at navigating through the spires and had even begun translating her instructions into sailing terms herself. Another few times through and she wouldn't need Rafael watching over her.

"We should be in Tarklee by nightfall," Darya said, joining her. "Cook has the meal ready, if you're hungry."

"I'll eat later," Dag said. "Is this cold usual for this time of year?" She knew the Frozen Pass closed in winter, but there had been places amongst the Teeth where ice had started to form. Now she was worried that it could become impassable before she returned for Calder. And even if she could navigate them through it to the Sapphire Sea, it might be far too risky to try to return to Tarklee. Better to be stranded in the Sapphire Sea over the winter than to trap the *Atlaine* in ice in the Teeth. That would risk the ship and everyone on board. This was very likely the last shipment of food this fall. It did mean they would get an early start on shipping in the spring.

"The bitter cold does seem to have come earlier," Darya replied. "But it takes a long stretch of sustained cold for the surface of the Pale Sea to freeze. She'll be navigable for some time yet, although Woodlea Bay won't be reachable." She grinned. "Nothing up there except woods and loggers anyway. I hear the ice is so thick they cut holes in it and fish through them."

"Yes, I've heard that too," Dag replied. "Hopefully it gets them to spring since we can't ship more food their way." Lauma had explained the ice fishing to her when they'd planned their deliveries. They had assumed the ice would make it impossible to head north, which was why they'd sent food to Byholt first, but she hadn't realized it would be cold enough for the sea to freeze here in the south.

"We'll do our best to work with whatever the weather is," Darya said. "And make a return trip through the Teeth." She grinned. "And if we get stuck on the warm Sapphire Sea until spring, I won't complain. Unless there's anything else, I'll be off. Once I've eaten, I'll relieve Rafael so he can head to the mess before Cook closes it down."

"Enjoy your meal," Dag said. Darya left her still staring at the Teeth. Wintering in the Sapphire Sea wouldn't be the worst thing in the world, as long as Calder and Inger were safe.

Nadez and Lauma would just have to handle any issues that arose in the Three. If they'd been able to change the Treaty terms, some of the Clan Freeholders would no doubt be scheming, but the world wouldn't fall apart if she wasn't in Tarklee.

Dag smiled when, a few hours later, Tarklee Harbour came into view. They'd made good time and now that they were here, she wanted to unload the ship as quickly as possible and head back to Messanos. Worry about her sister was growing now that she was close to returning for her.

"Dagrun!"

She turned: Rafael was hurrying towards her.

"What is it?"

"The *Tazeyar* sailed into the harbour right behind us," Rafael said. "Captain Eklund signalled that he'd like to meet with you right away. He has a prisoner on board, a pirate."

"A pirate," Dag repeated. "Let him know I'm on my way over."

"Aye," Rafael said and headed back to the bridge.

Dag climbed down into the waiting dinghy. "Sorry, change of plans," she said to the two sailors waiting to row her ashore. "My presence has been requested on the *Tazeyar*."

"I saw it behind us," one sailor said. "We'll get you there in a few minutes."

When they reached the other ship, a rope ladder was dropped over the side.

"Dagrun Lund," Captain Eklund greeted her when she stepped over the gunwale. "I take it your journey was successful?" He frowned. "I was expecting Calder Rahmson as well. Is he not coming?"

"He's taking care of some issues in Messanos," she said, hoping that was the truth. "Getting the food back here was too important to delay. I plan on returning for him as soon as I can."

"Dag!"

She turned to see Kaja hurrying towards her.

"I am very glad to see you," Kaja said. "Gustav got some information out of her, but I'm sure she has more secrets."

"I'm happy to see you too," Dag said. "And who has more secrets?"

"The Strongrock pirate," Kaja said.

Dag looked past her at a woman whose hands and feet were bound.

"A Strongrock pirate? We stopped there on our way to the Sapphire Sea: the settlement had been abandoned. We thought they might have split into two groups and that some were headed to Swyford." She met Kaja's eyes. "We ran across some of them in the Sapphire Sea, on the *Vassan*."

"CAN'T YOU STAY longer?" Kasim asked. "I feel like I'm losing my brother after just learning of you."

"We have to go," Calder said. "But I'll be back, I promise." He had to agree with his new-found brother; he didn't want to leave, but Rahm's deadline started this morning. He and Esma had two weeks to recover Rahm's token and return it to him.

"Why can't I come with you?" Kasim asked. "Father says you're travelling on the ship he arrived on. Surely one more person can fit on it?"

"You can't come," Esma said as she joined Calder at the front door. "Quit pestering us." To soften her words, she hugged him. "We'll be back within two weeks." She turned to Calder. "Father is meeting us at the ship. Let's go."

"See you soon," Calder said as he followed Esma out the door and into the streets of Zelesso.

"Is he always like that?" Calder asked after they'd gone a few blocks. He hadn't been home enough to know if Berna, as the youngest, had felt left out while he was off on an adventure. Although Berna had another older brother at home: as their mother acquired the Freeholdings, Yakop had stayed and learned to manage them.

"Yes," Esma replied. "He's fourteen now, so he should be allowed to do things, but not this."

"Not this," Calder agreed. He'd stayed out of whatever conversations Esma and Rahm had had with Saba, so he didn't know what lie they'd told for their need to return to Messanos so soon after arriving. But he was certain they hadn't told her the truth.

"I'll make it up to him," Esma said. She turned to him and grinned. "Unless you want to. It would be a nice change to share the burden of being the older child."

"I can't make any promises," he replied. "But I would like to spend more time with him." And he did, but saving Charis and Inger from Rahm the Resolute was more pressing.

The *Vassan* was anchored offshore, so at least Steen hadn't tried to leave rather than set sail with him aboard.

"Just a reminder," he said to Esma. "No one on board this ship will like me. I killed the previous owner and captain."

"We'll share a cabin and take turns standing watch," Esma replied. "Oh look, there's Father. And is that angry man your friend Steen?"

"It is." And even from here, Calder could see that Steen was furious. And Rahm was amused.

"Captain Steen," Calder said. "I appreciate your help in this matter."

"I'm doing this against my will and my better judgement," Steen said. "But I promised Rahm here that I'd deliver you to Messanos and bring you back safe and sound."

"See?" Rahm said. "We're all getting along. Glad that's settled. Esma, don't do anything dangerous. And Calder." Rahm stared him in the eye. "Don't let anything happen to your sister."

"I can look after myself," Esma said.

Calder simply nodded at his father. He would do everything within his power to keep Esma safe anyway. Then he saw Steen's face and realized that Rahm's comment hadn't been meant for his children.

Rahm was making sure Steen knew that he expected both Esma *and* Calder to be safe on board the *Vassan*.

"Permission to come aboard, Captain," Calder said to Steen. He had already decided to be even more courteous and deferential to Steen than he would be to any other ship's captain. He knew full well that once at sea, the pirate captain was the only law that mattered. He was not about to insult or belittle a man with that kind of power. Especially not when he was already hated for killing the ship's previous captain.

No doubt every single pirate on board this ship would see Calder as the instrument of their reduced circumstances. And they weren't wrong: if Captain Ansdottir was still alive they'd probably still have their safe haven in Strongrock.

Steen frowned and looked from Esma to Rahm before settling on Calder.

"Don't make me regret this," Steen said. "Permission granted."

"Thank you, Captain," Calder said. "If you can spare a cabin, we'll stay out of everyone's way until we reach Messanos." He held up a satchel. "We have our own provisions. If you prefer to put me to work, you know I'm a good Cook's helper."

Steen didn't smile, but his frown wasn't nearly as deep. "I might take you up on that," he said. "If you promise to show Cook what you do to make stew taste so good. It could even make the crew feel a little less murderous."

"You're the captain," Calder replied.

"I am," Steen said. "And it's in your best interest to remember that. Dinghy is over this way. Let's get moving."

GUSTAV TURNED THE tiller, and the little boat skimmed across ice, parallel to the shoreline. He and Pia had left Solvig's as soon as it had been light enough to see.

They were now heading north along the coast, just past the Elorelle River and Setberg. They couldn't get much closer to Nurmi without risking being seen from shore.

"If we don't find a place to set ashore soon, we'll need to backtrack south to land," he said to Pia, who made a face. "I don't like the idea of a long walk in the cold any more than you do." But a worse choice was spending the night outside. He'd sail them back to Setberg if he had to. It was still abandoned, with plenty of cabins and workshops where they could be warm and out of the wind.

"There." Pia pointed. "I see a beach."

Gustav stared at the shore. There was a break in the rocks where a little beach sloped up to the forest. "I'll take us in." He steered towards the shore. The ice ended a dozen feet ahead and whitecaps dotted the open water.

"Get ready!" he shouted to Pia, who had crept away from the prow and now huddled against the mast.

The boat dropped from the ice into the water. It listed to port when a wave hit it, but then it settled. "Now!" he called out.

Pia nodded, stood up, and started working on loosening the knots in the lines.

The tiller bucked under his hand as he kept the boat pointed at the shore. Waves dragged at the runners and the boat spun until they were broadside of the beach.

"Take down the sail," he called to Pia.

She tugged at a few sheets and then folded the stiff canvas and pushed it down into the bottom of the boat. He scrambled to get the oars into place, then he rowed, working with the waves to keep the bow facing the beach.

When he thought they were close enough, he turned the boat so that he faced the beach. It would allow him to see where he was landing as well as make it easier to get the boat back out to sea when they left.

Waves sliced past the prow and gently pushed them to shore, making it easier for Gustav to handle the boat. He pulled up the tiller, and a moment later, sand scraped the bottom of the boat.

"Lift me up and I'll grab that tree branch," Pia said, pointing to a branch that stretched overhead. "Then I'll tie a rope to something solid. You can use that to get to shore so neither of us gets wet."

Pia stepped into his hands and reached up to grasp the tree. Once she was up on solid ground, he tossed her the painter, and she tied it around the tree trunk.

Gustav rolled up the sail and stowed the oars. Then he pulled on the painter, taking in any slack and dragging the sailboat as high up the beach as he could. Hanging onto the painter, he climbed up the bank to join Pia.

"We still have a few hours before dark," Pia said. "Do you think we'll make Nurmi by then?"

"Yes," he replied. "And more importantly we'll have time to find a warm place to spend the night."

The woods here were sparse and mostly bare of leaves, but there were enough evergreens to keep the worst of the wind off them. At first Gustav worried about leaving a trail to their boat, but when he looked behind him the wind had already partially obscured their tracks. In less than an hour their footprints would be gone.

He set off north. Because there was no road along this coast, they kept within sight of the shoreline. Nurmi was a seaside village, so there was no chance they would pass it.

Two hours later they came across two buildings that looked deserted. Gustav stopped. He smelled smoke, but it wasn't coming from these buildings.

"I think the town is close," he said. "We need to be careful."

"I don't think anyone is here," she said. "There's no smoke from a fire, and I don't see a cleared path through the snow."

"Let's take a look around to make sure," he said.

They both peered through a window of the closest buildings. It was some sort of workshop, and it was empty. Gustav moved to the second, larger building. There was a small window along the side.

"I think this one's a warehouse," he said. "But it's empty."

"Maybe it's supposed to be full of food," Pia replied, and he nodded grimly.

An empty warehouse wasn't a good thing for Nurmi, not if it should have been full of food, but it was good for them.

A second window at the back of the building hadn't been latched. Pia climbed through it, and he followed her. Inside, they found a fireplace with a stack of wood beside it.

The smell of smoke might draw someone to them, but they had to risk it. Even out of the wind it was very cold. Frostbitten fingers or toes would not only be dangerous for them, they could jeopardize their mission.

"Here's the last of the dried rabbit," Gustav said as he handed a chunk of meat to Pia. "Don't worry, we still have the fish."

"Thanks," Pia said. "I'll take first watch." She took a bite of rabbit.

"Sure." Gustav spent a few minutes eating. The rabbit was chewy and dry, but it still tasted better than the fish. "I'll get some snow for water." He grabbed the pot and ducked back to the window they had entered through. It only took a few minutes for the snow to melt over the fire. He and Pia took turns sipping hot water from the pot.

When he'd had a drink, he lay down near the fire and closed his eyes.

CHAPTER 11

NADEZ WATCHED THE two ships in the harbour. They'd arrived almost an hour ago and still no one had come ashore. What was wrong?

"Is one of them the *Atlaine*?" Lauma stopped beside her on the pier.

"Yes," Nadez replied. "And the *Tazeyar*. They seem to have had a conversation before sending anyone ashore. Oh there, finally." Two dinghies were on their way.

"You're worried," Lauma said.

"I am. The *Tazeyar* wasn't supposed to stop here on its way north."

"The good news is that whatever goods Calder and Dag have in the hold, the *Tazeyar* is already here and can distribute them."

"I suppose," Nadez replied. "There's Dagrun in the first dinghy."

"I don't see my son" Lauma said. "Now *I'm* worried."

As soon as the dinghy reached the dock, Dagrun jumped out and jogged over to them.

"Calder's fine," she said. "At least he was when I left him in Messanos. He's searching for Inger and Charis." Dagrun frowned. "I'll tell you all about it later, after the goods are sorted out."

"Sture is ready," Nadez said. She waved to him and Sture waved back.

"Good, thanks," Dagrun replied. "Kaja filled me in on the changes to the Treaty. Gustav reported that it worked out."

"Thanks to your suggestion," Lauma replied. "None of the Clan Freeholders are happy, and a few are feeling murderous, but it's done."

"Speaking of murder," Dagrun said. "We really need to talk about your former husband and Fihaldo Pinho. But first we need to discuss Strongrock pirates, like that one." She indicated a bound woman who was being escorted off the dinghy by Kaja. "And a Freeholder loyal to Tavet Timonis who was trying the help the pirates steal the *Tazeyar*."

Nadez stared past the pirate at a second prisoner being led by two sailors. This prisoner she recognized, and he was indeed one of Timonis' most loyal Freeholders.

"Leif Stendhal would never do anything without Timonis' approval," she said. "Take them both to the jail." She turned to Lauma. Even the Interim Grand Freeholder would have to admit this went beyond a country's mandate to manage their own affairs. "I'd like you present when I question Freeholder Stendhal."

"Of course," Lauma said. "If this is true then it's treason against the Alliance."

"I need to see to the goods we brought," Dagrun said to Nadez. "Where shall I meet you? Lauma's office or yours? Kaja can fill you in on everything that happened while you wait for me."

"My office," Lauma said before Nadez could reply.

"Kaja and I will join you once the prisoners have been settled in jail," Nadez said and was relieved when Lauma simply nodded and headed back to the city.

"Kaja, go find a couple of guards to help with the prisoner," Nadez said. "Dagrun and I will keep an eye on these two." Once Kaja was gone, she made a quick hand signal to Dagrun that she wanted to talk to her before they met with Lauma. Dagrun responded yes and sent her a questioning look.

"Nadez Norup."

She turned from Dagrun to see Captain Eklund approaching her. The second dinghy had made it to shore.

"Just the person I wanted to see," he said. "And thank. I, my crew, and my ship are free because of the brave actions of your Intelligencer, and I wanted to make sure you knew what he did.

And that I will be forever in debt to you and Gustav Gunnarson. Any time you need my help you just have to ask."

"Thank you," Nadez said. She wasn't really surprised that Gustav had done something brave: he'd proven to be smart, courageous, and resourceful. "I'm sure it's a tale I would love to hear from you, when time permits."

"I don't come out a hero," Eklund said. "But young Gustav does." He turned to Dagrun. "Captain Demer signalled that she would send the First Mate ashore. Between the two of us we'll get the *Atlaine* unloaded. I have some Byholter woodcutters that I can put to good use. Shall I send the list of goods to you, Master Intelligencer?"

"Yes," she said. "That would be very helpful. Please send a copy to the Interim Grand Freeholder." She and Lauma had already decided that these goods were destined for Nordmere and Swyford. She didn't want Lauma to change that and decide to ship more food to Byholt simply because the *Tazeyar* was here. Or because Clan Freeholder Timonis seemed to have committed treason. It was the regular Swyfordians who would suffer, not the Freeholders, if food was scarce.

Kaja returned with three guards, and soon Nadez was left on the dock with Dagrun.

"This way," she said, leading the way off the dock and into the city.

She hadn't been here in a while but the little stable was quiet. She pushed aside the plank and crawled in, Dagrun right behind her. The lamp and flint were where she'd left them, and soon light cast a glow over her little hideout.

"You're hiding from Lauma," Dag said. "Why?"

Nadez sighed. "I'm not sure I trust her." She put up her hand. "Sorry, I do trust her in most things, but I think she has a blind spot. I think that since the Treaty was renegotiated, she feels that she has all the power she needs and that whatever the other Clan Freeholders do can't affect her." She paced the small space. "She seems more willing to let each country manage their own affairs without what she calls *interference* from her."

"That's what got us into this mess in the first place," Dagrun said. "Joosep standing by while Tarmo Holt and the other Clan Freeholders worked against each other and the Alliance."

"Yes, exactly." Nadez relaxed. Of course, Dagrun could see the issue. "I'm not even sure Lauma will stand by our original plans for the distribution of the goods that just arrived. They are scheduled to go to northern Nordmere and Swyford, not Byholt."

"That's why you asked for a record of the shipment," Dagrun said. "Do you really think she'll change what has already been agreed to?"

"She mentioned that it was good that the *Tazeyar* was here," she replied. "Because it can take goods north. She could have meant to northern Nordmere."

"But you don't think so," Dagrun said. "And in light of Timonis' apparent deceit, she might find her justification." Dagrun nodded. "All right, but you were feeling this way before we arrived with food. Why?"

"I'm worried that Saulia Holt is truly her father's daughter," she said. "I found out something disturbing, and when I approached Lauma, she said it was not Alliance business."

"You think it is."

"I know it is," Nadez said. "A few days ago, I was visiting Saulia and overheard a man promise to deliver children to her. Seven children: two sets of twins and triplets. From the Sapphire Sea."

"*Skit*. They have Traits," Dagrun stated. "That's the only reason they would be here. Tarmo Holt . . . what, recruited them?" She frowned. "Or bought them or stole them. Where are they now?"

"At Saulia Holt's house in Tarklee, I assume," Nadez replied. "Although by this time she might have moved them somewhere else in the city. I wanted to give Saulia time to report this to me, but she hasn't."

"How can Lauma think this isn't Alliance business?" Dagrun asked. "Children, possibly stolen children, from other countries? How is that not something for the Grand Freeholder to deal with?"

"The only thing I can think of," Nadez said. "Is that she does not want to set a precedent of the Grand Freeholder interfering with how each Alliance member country operates. And the reason for that would be so that the next Grand Freeholder doesn't try to manage Byholt. Come on, we need to check on the prisoners, collect Kaja, and then meet with Lauma."

DAG FOLLOWED NADEZ out of the little stable, through a few

streets, and into the Hall. She couldn't stop thinking about the children. How could Lauma not see them being here, in Tarklee, as a problem? Her own son had a Trait and a father from the Sapphire Sea; it couldn't possibly hit closer to home for her. And yet, from what Nadez said, Lauma thought it acceptable to let Saulia Holt keep and probably train children with Traits. More than likely *stolen* children with Traits.

The prisoners were safely housed in cells and guards posted at the door to the jail. Kaja had already left, so they headed up to Lauma's office.

Kaja was halfway through her report. Nadez sat down and listened while Dag roamed around the room.

She had almost forgotten that Holt had wanted Inger to have children with a man of his choosing. That he had offered to provide for her and any children. She'd assumed that the person he'd had in mind had a Trait, but she had barely given a thought to where that man came from; perhaps he too was from the Sapphire Sea.

Tarmo Holt must have found people with Traits in one or more countries along the Sapphire Sea. One was the man he had wanted Inger to have children with. Others he'd brought here in secret this past summer.

"I'll start from the beginning," Kaja said. "So the Master Intelligencer can hear it all too."

"That's fine," Lauma said. "I'll have a quick word with Dagrun about my son."

"Why is my son looking for your sister?" Lauma said, pulling her into the outer office.

Dag suppressed a frown. Lauma didn't seem angry, but she was sensing an undercurrent of impatience.

"Because I had to navigate the *Atlaine* through the Teeth, and Calder and Esma thought Rahm might listen to his children," she paused. "And not kill my sister's beloved, and possibly my sister, if she gets in the way."

"What?"

Dag was relieved to see Lauma's shock. She didn't want to suspect her intentions, but Nadez's comments had alarmed her.

"It seems that Rahm was redirected from the assassination of Pinho and sent after Charis," Dag said. "By one of the Messanos council members. Do you think he'll listen to them?" She wanted to believe that Rahm wouldn't hurt Inger, but he *was* a Resolute.

"I'm not sure," Lauma said. "This is a part of Rahm that I don't know."

Dag sighed. "All right. I'll continue to put my faith in Calder and Esma."

"What's she like?" Lauma asked. "Calder's other sister."

"She's nice," Dag replied. "And tough, as you'd expect a daughter of Rahm to be. But honest and caring as well."

"She must get that from her mother. Have you met *her*?"

Dag shook her head. "She doesn't live in Messanos. Kaja must be finished," she said, grateful to change the subject. "Nadez is waving at me." She could understand Lauma's curiosity about Rahm's other family, but she didn't feel that it was her place to discuss it.

"What do you think?" Nadez asked when they rejoined her and Kaja in the inner office. "About Stendhal and Timonis?"

"Without proof," Lauma said. "I can't act against Timonis. Unless he no longer has the backing of the other Swyfordian Clan Freeholders."

"Gustav will get proof," Kaja said.

"I hope so," Lauma replied. "Until he returns here with it, I will send a record of this to the other Swyford Clan Freeholders. They will understand what I do: that there is no way Leif Stendhal acted without Timonis' direction and approval."

"Freeholder Skala is in Tarklee," Nadez said. "But Nowack and Kozlow are on their freeholds in the south. Will you send someone by road? It's risky this time of year."

"By ship, I think," Lauma said. "But we'll have to wait for Captain Eklund to return from heading north. Or perhaps one of the log haulers is due in?"

Nadez shook her head. "The log haulers will have anchored for the winter. All right, the *Tazeyar* will only take a few days to deliver food to the Nordmerian coast. They can be back here within a week if the weather holds."

"Add a few days for a trip to Cutterstown," Lauma said. "I wish to send my son a message."

"I'm not sure that's safe," Dag said. "Ice is forming as far south as the Teeth. Sailing that far north could trap the *Tazeyar* in ice, or worse, damage or even sink it."

"They're going to Cutterstown anyway," Lauma said. "Captain

Eklund has Byholt woodcutters on board."

"The woodcutters can take iceboats north," Dag replied. "And deliver your message. We can't afford to lose the *Tazeyar*."

Lauma stared at her, and Dag wondered what she wanted to tell Yakop that was worth such a risk to a ship.

"I'll leave it to Captain Eklund's discretion," Lauma said finally. "If he feels it's unwise to take the ship north, he can send my message by iceboat."

"Agreed," Dag said. Eklund was fond of Lauma Strauskas, but she didn't think he'd risk his ship to gain her favour.

"Kaja," Dag said. "I think that's all you are needed for. Please make a written report. I think we'll need at least two copies." She turned to Lauma and Nadez. "Does anyone think Kaja should stay? I need some rest before I try to find out what secrets the prisoners are hiding."

"That's fine," Lauma said. "Thank you, Kaja. Excellent work, as always. And I would like to have you as my assistant for as long as Nadez can spare you."

"She's yours," Nadez agreed. "I'll let you know if I need her help with anything."

Kaja left and Nadez stood up, but Dag sat watching Lauma, and after a moment, Nadez sat back down.

"Nadez tells me that Saulia Holt is harbouring children from the Sapphire Sea who probably have Traits," she said. "And that despite being given time to disclose this information, she has not."

"I don't feel it's any concern of the Interim Grand Freeholder," Lauma said. She turned and fixed her frown on Nadez. "We discussed this."

"And you made a decision that I did not agree with," Nadez replied. "So, I asked Dagrun for her opinion."

"I see," Lauma turned to look at Dag. "Well?"

"This may not be the business of the Interim Grand Freeholder," Dag said carefully. "But it *is* the business of the Intelligencers. I will be visiting Saulia Holt to meet and assess these children."

"No," Lauma said. "I need Saulia on my side."

"But don't you see?" Dag asked. "If she is hiding and planning on training children with Traits, she is already *not* on your side. I *will* see those children before I leave. Then I need to get back to the Sapphire Sea as soon as possible and meet up with Calder."

Lauma turned her frown on her for a moment. "Then do it," she said. "But please don't treat Saulia as though she's not trusted even if you don't trust her."

"I won't," Dag said. She knew she could fool Saulia because she was fooling Lauma right now. Her Trait hadn't activated, but Nadez was right, something about Lauma's position didn't make sense. She nodded and rose, planning to find her and Inger's old apartment and get some sleep. Nadez led the way out of the office, but they didn't say a word to each other until they reached the hallway that led to her old rooms.

"Thank you," Nadez said. "You see what I mean about Lauma?"

"Yes," Dag replied. "I do. At least I'll have a chance to assess the children. I'll go tomorrow. I'll be able to figure out what Traits they have and find out if they are here against their will." And if they were, she was putting them on the *Atlaine* and returning them home. Dag didn't care if it made Saulia Holt think she wasn't trusted or if that made Calder's mother angry.

She slipped into her old room, shook the dust out of the bedcovers, and fell, exhausted, into her old bed.

CALDER AND ESMA followed Steen along the passageway and up to the deck.

The pirate had told them the truth: they were anchored just off of Messanos.

"We'll give you a dinghy, but none of my crew is rowing you across," Steen said.

"Thank you, Captain." Calder preferred to leave all the pirates on the ship anyway. "I appreciate the swift passage."

"Lucky the wind was with us," Steen said.

"Lucky," Esma repeated and looked over at him. Calder shrugged. If his Luck wanted him here fast, all he could do was hope it would help find him Rahm's token and get it back to Zelesso within the two weeks.

"If you're not back aboard by the time the two weeks is up, we're leaving," Steen said. "I know you probably won't trust my word, but you kept yours by staying below, being respectful, and teaching Cook how to make a better stew. Now get off my ship."

"Aye, Captain." Calder didn't waste any time and headed

straight to the lowered dinghy. Esma climbed down into it and he followed.

"You take the tiller," he said as he settled a pair of oars into the oarlocks. A few minutes later they were skimming away from the *Vassan* towards the harbour. He looked over his shoulder at the city. Rahm's token was there somewhere.

Esma steered them to the northern part of the city and the little hidden dock. It meant a longer row, but it was worth it to dock in a safe place, rather than on the main pier. They followed the narrow channel, and a few moments later they reached the dock where the *Hakon* usually moored.

"The people I need to speak to are nearby," she said.

While on board the *Vassan*, they had agreed that Esma would talk to some people she knew and find out more about Councilwoman Floros and the political situation.

They didn't think Floros would have the token with her, but who better to keep it than the ones who had stolen it from Rahm? Unfortunately, he expected the suicide assassins to be hard to find.

While Esma asked her contacts for information, Calder would simply wander the streets and see if his Luck would help him.

"We'll meet back here in two hours," Calder said. He stowed the oars in the bottom of the dinghy and stepped out onto the dock. Esma waved and sprinted up the steps and he lost sight of her.

He took his time as he left the dock, studying his surroundings and hoping his Trait activated. He wandered down an alley to a busier street, following the scent of cooking meat: he could almost taste the Pilalian spices.

His gaze narrowed, and Calder followed his nose to a street vendor who was grilling mutton on a brazier at the side of a busy road.

"How much?" Calder asked in Pilalian. "For a taste of my homeland?"

"For a fellow Pilalian?" the vendor replied. "A small coin for the spiciest grilled meat in all of Messanos."

Calder fished out a coin and was handed a skewer of meat. He took a bite and chewed slowly, savouring the spicy heat. "The best I've had in a long time," he said. "Better than I make myself." He rattled off half a dozen spices. "But there's something extra that I don't use." He took another bite of meat.

"It's my secret ingredient," the vendor said. "If I tell you then there's no reason for you to come back here."

"But I have the rest of them correct?"

The vendor sighed. "You already know you do." He grinned. "But it's nice to know I can still challenge a fellow spice enthusiast."

"It might take me years," Calder said. "But I will figure it out."

"Not a terrible life goal," the vendor replied.

Calder pulled the last bite of meat off the skewer and tossed the sliver of wood onto the fire. "One of many," he said. "You ever sell to a man named Rahm?"

The vendor's face stilled, and he nodded. "Most Pilalians find me eventually. Do you know him?"

"He's my father," Calder said. "But I can't really say that I know him." He looked around the street, but no one seemed to be paying any attention to them. "He lost something around here, and I've been tasked with trying to find it."

"That's an impossible task," the vendor said.

"Impossible," he repeated. "Why?"

"Because it wasn't lost," the vendor said. "As I think you know."

Calder leaned closer to the man's ear. "Do you happen to know where the suicide assassins train?"

The vendor stilled and sighed. "For Rahm's son, I will say again, every Pilalian eventually finds their way to me."

"Thank you," Calder said more loudly. "Your grilled meat has been a welcome taste of home. I'm here for a few days, so I'm sure you'll see me again." He nodded and headed down the street. He turned a corner, stopped in the shadow of a building, and stared back at the vendor.

He didn't pack up and leave, which was what Calder had been afraid of. Instead, he was busy serving another customer.

Calder watched the vendor until it was time to meet Esma. No young women or girls had visited the grill, but the vendor had as much as told him that a Pilalian was a suicide assassin.

He took a roundabout way back to the dock and found Esma waiting for him.

"Come on," she said. "My room is close by. It's as safe a place as any in the city. We can talk there."

"You found out something," he said.

"Not here," she said, looking around. She headed back up into the city, and Calder followed her down a few narrow streets to a dilapidated gate. The building behind the gate sported a row of faded wooden doors. Esma headed to one, pulled a key from her pocket, and unlocked the door. Upstairs she stopped at the third door along a hallway. Another key opened this door, and he followed his sister into a small room.

A bed hugged one wall and a window opposite the door looked out onto ragged rocks.

"It's one of the smallest rooms in the building," she apologized. "But I can get out that window if I have to." She moved a pile of clothes off a chair before sitting on the bed.

"Do you think you were followed?" he asked, peering out the window. There was a rocky outcrop a few feet from the window, and it looked like there were foot and handholds that would allow someone to climb up to the ridge above. You could escape the room without going through the building or returning to the street.

"No, just letting you know that there is a way out. In case."

"All right." He sat in the chair. "What did you find out?"

"As we suspected, Councilwoman Floros has taken full control of the council," Esma said. "The rumour is that Fihaldo Pinho has returned, but my sources have not spoken to anyone who has seen him in person."

"Keeping out of sight?"

"Probably at sea," she said. "But Floros and Pinho seem to have struck some sort of bargain. Floros does not have extensive property or wealth."

"But Pinho does," Calder said.

"Yes, and rumours say that Pinho has signed over authority of his holdings to her. He still owns everything, but she is making all the decisions."

"And what decisions is she making?" He wished Dag was here; her Trait would uncover Floros' reasons before he would.

"I haven't found out anything threatening so far," Esma said. "My sources seem to think it's more because Pinho expected to be away for a while, perhaps even for the entire winter."

"Was he planning to spend it in Tarklee with Saulia Holt?" Calder asked.

"Maybe," Esma replied. "But it also gave Floros access to Pinho's guards. Apparently, they accompany her everywhere." She paused. "But they are not stationed at her home unless she's there."

"Meaning the token isn't there," Calder said. "Which was what we expected. Originally Pinho hid it far away from both himself and Rahm. Do you know why?"

"Not from Father," she said. "But there are always rumours about Resolutes. One is that the token has some sort of power over whoever wields it and that it compels them to return it to the Resolute."

"Dag didn't mention feeling anything from it," Calder said. "And she carried it for days."

"Maybe it takes more than a few days for it to affect the holder," Esma said. "Or maybe her Trait counteracted the effect."

"Or maybe it didn't need to do anything because as soon as she knew what it was, Dag planned to return it," Calder said. "And she knew who it belonged to." He nodded. "Rahm told me that he *had* to fulfil the contract; that there was some sort of pressure or coercion from the token. That I had no idea what he'd gone through when he'd been separated from it. We have to assume that whatever powers the token has, it can affect someone who holds it and is not trying to return it. Pinho stayed far away from the token, so maybe the compulsion is stronger when you're close to it."

"So, you still think the suicide assassins are holding it for Floros?" Esma asked.

"It makes sense," Calder said. "Even if someone knew how to find the token, who would steal from an assassin?"

"Other than you, you mean," Esma said. "More phantoms to chase."

"Resolutes are real," Calder said. "And so are suicide assassins. I think I know how to find one. I just hope she shows up before we run out of time." And that Luck helped him survive stealing from a school for assassins.

PIA CONCENTRATED ON the house at the end of the track. It belonged to Leif Stendhal; the man Timonis had blamed for working with pirates and attempting to steal the *Tazeyar*.

Gustav had seen the pirates at Timonis' estate, but there was no way they were there now. Even Clan Freeholder Timonis must realize that he had to keep his distance from them.

But they were still in Nurmi, and Gustav had argued that the Strongrock pirates would be here, in Stendhal's vacant house, out of sight but still living in comfort. Neither of them thought the pirates would settle for anything less comfortable, not when they could expose Timonis as a traitor to the Three.

But she had been here for three hours and had still not seen any signs of them. Last night's snow had blanketed everything, and neither the track that led to the house nor the space between the house and the outbuildings showed signs of being disturbed.

She pulled her hat down on her head and shoved her hands into her armpits. She had gone from feeling chilled to being stiff with cold and knew that despite using her Trait to block out the discomfort, she'd have to get warm soon or risk frostbite.

The scent of smoke wafted to her, and she sighed. Finally, a sign that someone was in the house. She shivered, but it wasn't from the cold: her Trait had just reacted to something.

She spotted someone at the side of the house and watched them run across to an outbuilding. A few minutes later a figure walked beyond the outbuilding and out into the woods.

Someone had snuck out of the house. Pia's grin turned into a grimace when she stood up on numb feet. It took her longer than she wanted to make her way to the trees that lined the road. From behind a tree, she saw a man step out of the woods onto the road. Staying in the trees, she followed him into Nurmi where he entered what looked like a small tavern.

Head down, she walked past the tavern and continued east to the old warehouse.

Gustav was stretched out beside the fire.

"Someone left the house," she said. She held her hands out to the low flames and rubbed them together, trying to force warmth back into her tingling fingers. "They snuck out and went to a tavern. I don't think they wanted to be seen by the other pirates and I don't think they were."

"I'll go see what I can find out from him," Gustav said, standing up.

"Be careful," Pia said. "In case this pirate recognizes you." She'd do it if she could, but she doubted a pirate would even talk to her in a tavern, let alone trust her with a secret. Gustav's Trait was needed for this as long as he wasn't recognized.

"They only saw me once," Gustav replied.

"But it wasn't that long ago," Pia said. "How many people do you think they've talked to lately?"

"I'll be careful," he said. "I'll try to buy us something else to eat, too."

"Don't risk it on my account," she replied. "I'm grateful for the fish: it's filling, and we have plenty." It didn't taste great, but she and her sister had gone hungry enough times that she wasn't about to turn away food. Besides, by now everyone on the Pale Sea knew that rations would be in short supply this winter. "And don't use your Trait to take food out of the mouths of some drunkard's children."

"You're right," Gustav replied. "I didn't think about that. Any food we buy will mean less for someone else in town. I might be a while," he said. He jingled a few coins. "I'm going to see if I can get my new pirate friend drunk and then help him get home."

"Be careful," she repeated.

Gustav nodded and then he was gone. She pulled her pack over to the fire and sat down on it before taking off her boots. Eventually her toes stopped tingling and warmth spread over the parts of her that faced the fire. She fed the fire small bits of wood before grabbing a piece of dried fish.

Unlike the fish she and Frida had helped Solvig salt and preserve, this fish had been dried in the sun and didn't need to be cooked. It flaked apart in her hands as she pulled off a piece to eat.

When she finished eating, she put her boots and mitts back on and wandered over to the window they'd been using to get in and out of the building.

The sky was clouding over. More snow would hide her and Gustav's tracks, but she hoped it didn't make his task harder.

CHAPTER 12

Gustav squared his shoulders and pasted a smile on his face before opening the door to the tavern and stepping inside.

The space was small. Just four rough tables with benches pulled up to them. Besides the man tending the bar, there were only three other people inside: all men and all sitting by themselves. His heart pounded when he recognized the pirate; he was one of the ones he'd met along the road. He let his gaze slide over him and come to rest on the barman, worried that the pirate would raise an alarm.

"A mug of whatever you're serving, if you please," he said, stepping up to the bar. He wasn't going to take more than a sip, but buying ale was part of his plan. Did he need to change his plan? He'd told the pirates he was on his way to Lavais. If he was recognized, he could lie and say he couldn't find a boat.

He placed a coin on the scarred wood of the bar and waited while the man poured an ale. It was worth a try. And from the looks of the pirate, he'd already had a bit to drink.

Turning around with his drink in hand, he made a show of looking over the other patrons before heading to the pirate's table.

"I hope you don't mind if I join you," he said, trying to infuse his words with Charisma. He waited for the man to look up and recognize him, but the pirate barely glanced at him.

"Sit, you're most welcome," the pirate said, his words slurring.

"Especially if you like to talk. Been having the same conversations with the same seven people for so long now that I don't barely remember what else can be talked about."

"I do like to talk," Gustav said. Was his companion too drunk to recognize him? Or had been drunk when the pirates had met him on the road? This one had been rolling a barrel of ale.

Gustav took a drink and made a face. "I'm not much for ale, and this tastes sour." He pushed the mug away and hid a smile when the pirate's eyes followed it. "It's yours if you want it," he said. "It's already paid for, and there's no sense having it go to waste just because it's not to my liking. Especially these days when everything is in such short supply."

"You're not gonna drink it?" the pirate asked.

Gustav shook his head and moved the mug a little closer to the pirate. "Feel free," he said. "Although I don't know how you can stomach it."

"I've had worse, believe me." The pirate took a long drink and set the mug down. "And once I've drunk enough, I don't hardly taste it."

"Have you had enough?" Gustav asked.

"Not nearly to make up for this *Jebris* cursed weather." He took another long drink. "Can't stand being stuck inside for so long."

"It's hard during winter," Gustav agreed. "Especially if the ones you're stuck inside with aren't people you're fond of."

"*Fond of*," the pirate muttered into the mug. "I'd settle for people I don't want to murder."

"I'm from Lavais Port," Gustav said, pretending he hadn't heard the other man's last comment. He didn't want to be caught in a lie, so he had to tell him what he'd told the pirates before, which was the truth. "I'm Gustav."

"Benil," the pirate said. "I'm a sailor."

"Your ship leave you behind?" Gustav asked. He knew it happened, and mostly to sailors like Benil who might have stayed too long in a tavern. He'd already declared himself from a shipbuilding community: there was no way he could ignore a sailor without a ship.

"Yeah," Benil said. "Ship left me behind. Now I gotta stay here probably all winter. And I'm gonna hate every minute of it." He lifted the mug and drained it. "Especially once this skit town runs out of ale."

"It's not out of ale yet," Gustav said.

"I'm outta coin." Benil sighed and stared at the tabletop.

"It's on me," Gustav said and waved at the barkeep. "Oh, I think he thought we both wanted one," Gustav said when the barkeep delivered two mugs. He fished out coins to pay for it and pushed both mugs in front of Benil. "I can keep you company if you want both."

"That's generous of you," Benil said. He took a drink and wiped his mouth with the sleeve of his coat. "So, you grew up in this cold?"

"I did," Gustav replied. Benil did not seem to remember meeting him before. Or maybe his Trait was working. Or both. "Winter is not my favourite season, I'll tell you. How about you?"

"I grew up on a ship," Benil said. "And when it got cold in the Pale Sea most times the ship I was on headed to the Sapphire Sea. It's warm there all the time, and when you're out at sea there's often a cool breeze to counter the hot sun." He sighed. "Wish I was there now, not stuck here." He took a long swallow that emptied his mug and pulled the second one closer.

"That sounds really fine right now," Gustav said. "Warm sun and cool breezes. Too bad your ship left you behind."

"I made the wrong choice is what happened," Benil said. "I could be sailing the Sapphire Sea right now. But I made the wrong choice. Now I'm stuck here where I'm as like to die from the cold as from hunger. And for what?" He took another drink of ale. "For what? So some Freeholder can go back on his word to us about giving us a ship? We had a ship. Now it's in the Sapphire Sea, and I'm a sailor stranded on land."

"That doesn't sound fair," Gustav said quietly. He motioned to the barkeep for one more mug of ale. Benil barely seemed to notice when it was delivered and Gustav paid for it. He pulled the mug close and stared down at it.

"It's not fair," Benil said. "We're owed. Even have a promise to pay note. And now we're told there's no ship."

"Hard to believe anyone can get out of a debt like that," Gustav said. "I always thought a promise to pay note was binding." He doubted Benil had that note with him. Could he ask him to bring it here later?

"That's what we all thought," Benil said. "Everyone except the

Freeholder who's breaking his promise."

"Can I see it?" Gustav asked. "The promise to pay note? I've seen a promise to pay note before. I could tell you if this one is legitimate."

"What good will that do?" Benil asked. "We know it is, and the Freeholder still won't pay."

"A legitimate promise to pay note can be enforced by the Fair Seas Treaty Alliance," Gustav said. It was probably true, but he wanted this one as proof of Timonis' treachery.

"It can?" Benil asked. "Really?"

"Really, but I'd need to see it to know if it's real."

"Come on." Benil stood up quickly. He swayed and almost fell before grabbing the edge of the tabletop and righting himself. "I'll get it for you." He picked up his mug and drained it. "Then you can help us get the Alliance to make the Freeholder give us what we're owed."

"Sure," Gustav said as he followed Benil out of the tavern. "As long as it doesn't take too long." As they headed along the road towards Stendhal's freehold, Gustav worried that Benil would come to his senses and realize how unlikely it was that the Alliance would defend pirates in any matter. Especially after those same pirates had destroyed so many ships, an act that had led directly to the impending food shortages.

But Benil hadn't recognized him, and it seemed he was incapable of making the connection. When they stopped on the road near the freehold, the pirate still didn't seem aware that the plan didn't make sense.

"I'll wait here," Gustav said. "You go in and get the note and bring it to me."

"You need to meet the captain," Benil said. "And explain to her about the Alliance helping us get a ship."

"I'd hate to disturb your captain without knowing whether I have good news or bad," Gustav said. "Don't you think it would be better if I made sure the note is real before I talk to her?"

"I guess," Benil said. "It means I'll have to sneak in and out with the note." He grinned. "I'm getting real good at that. I'll do it." He pulled Gustav along the road until the freehold was obscured by some woods. "You wait here. I'll be back as soon as I can."

When Benil headed off through the woods, Gustav walked

back along the road until he could see the house and outbuildings. A few moments later a shadow crossed from behind an outbuilding to the house.

Gustav quietly stamped his feet, trying to stay warm. Even at dusk there was no light coming from inside the house. He hoped it stayed that way. If Benil was caught or decided to speak to his captain, the pirates would come after him.

Half an hour later it started to snow, and he was ready to give up hope. Either Benil had forgotten about him or he hadn't been able to get the promise to pay note.

Wait, someone was running out of the house. Was it Benil?

Snow was coming down hard now, making it difficult to see, but a second person was standing outside the front door.

The first figure was now in the woods, and Gustav lost sight of him. Hoping that it was Benil with the note, he jogged back along the road. He hid behind a tree a few yards from where he and the pirate had parted.

"I got it," Benil called. "I got it. We gotta be quick though. Captain saw me."

"That's great," Gustav said, stepping out from behind the tree. "Can I see it before the light fails?"

Benil grinned and passed a leather wallet to him. Gustav pulled out a piece of paper and read a few lines.

"It's real, right?" Benil asked. "I know it's real. So, the Alliance will help us get our ship?"

"You fool."

As he turned to face the woman who'd spoken, Gustav pulled the note from the wallet and shoved it into his pocket. He recognized Ursa Ozlinch.

"The Alliance is never going to help us," she said. "Benil, get that note and bring me the prisoner."

"You must be the captain Benil's been talking about," Gustav said.

"I am." She raised her hand, and he saw that she was pointing a pistol at him. "And I want the note."

He held up the leather wallet. "Sure." Then he threw the wallet at her and spun to one side. She fired the gun, but he wasn't hit. Without waiting to see if she was readying another shot, he sprinted as fast as he could down the road towards the town.

"Get him, Benil!" Ursa yelled.

Gustav plunged into the woods.

Even sober, a lifelong sailor like Benil would probably not have great tracking skills. Between the snow, dusk, and the trees, he was reasonably certain that he could escape them and make it back to the warehouse and Pia. He had the proof of Timonis' deceit. Now all he needed to do was get it back to Tarklee.

DAG LEFT HER apartment and made her way out into the city. It had taken all day for the goods to be unloaded, and now they were safely divided and stored in warehouses or on the *Tazeyar*.

Normally, she would have left that task to Darya and Rafael. Unfortunately, after Nadez's concerns and her own experience with the Interim Grand Freeholder, she'd been worried Lauma would try to redirect some of the supplies on the *Tazeyar* destined for Nordmere to Byholt.

And she had. Lauma's justification was that by the time any other food was delivered from the Sapphire Sea, the route to Byholt would be closed by ice.

Arguments that the original plan they'd agreed on meant that Byholt already had their share of food had not changed her mind. Finally, Dag told Lauma that another shipment this winter was unlikely. The weather was colder than usual, and instead of risking the ship, she and Calder would spend the season on the Sapphire Sea. And *that* possibility had been taken into account when they'd made their decision on how and where to send the supplies they had.

She frowned as she headed out into the night. Why had Lauma tried to change their well-thought-out plan? Did she even realize that what she was asking would benefit her own people while increasing the risk for Nordmerians? Perhaps there was something about the position, and the decisions a Grand Freeholder had to make, that meant it was next to impossible to not put your own interests first.

Now, far later than she'd wanted, she was on her way to the Holt estate to confront Saulia about the children.

Nadez had offered to join her, but she'd declined. Not only did Nadez need to maintain a good relationship with Saulia on behalf of both the Alliance and the Interim Grand Freeholder, but this felt personal to Dag.

She'd saved Saulia Holt from either death or a life as Pinho's pawn. And just weeks later, she was keeping dangerous, and cruel, secrets from the Three.

Dag would do her best to not insult the new Clan Freeholder, but it would be a struggle. And if she did get angry, Saulia Holt would know that it was *her* anger, not Nadez's or Lauma's.

The gate was closed and locked, but after a moment searching, Dag found a loose hinge and was able to open the gate enough to allow her to slip through it. She strode along the short walkway and up three stairs to the unlit door.

She rapped hard on the door and took a step back. Nothing. She knocked again.

"Who's there?" someone called from the other side of the door.

"Dagrun Lund, Intelligencer, to see Saulia Holt," she said. "I apologize for the late hour, but I am on official Alliance business."

"The Clan Freeholder has retired for the night and is not to be disturbed."

"Let her know I am here," Dag said. "Intelligencer Dagrun Lund."

"Come back in the morning."

"Saulia Holt will not be happy when I find another way in," Dag said. "Tell her I am here and that I insist on speaking with her. You have five minutes before I enter this house."

She stepped back and started scanning the front of the building for a way in. In this bitter cold it was unlikely there were any windows open, but she would find a way in eventually.

The lock on the front door rattled and then the door opened. A sleepy Mykol held up a lamp.

"Dagrun Lund," Mykol said. "It's late. Can't this wait until morning?"

"No." Dag pushed her way past him into a large hall. Closed doors led off it, and a worried woman stared at her. "I need to leave for the Sapphire Sea in the morning," she said, turning to Mykol. "And my issue must be resolved before then."

"Go wake the Clan Freeholder, Maeve," Mykol said to the woman. "Tell her I gave you the order."

The woman left through one of the doors, and Mykol set the lamp on a table.

"We'll wait for Clan Freeholder Holt here," he said.

"All right." She studied him. She'd never trusted Mykol: he'd been Tarmo Holt's assistant for years. She didn't believe he hadn't understood at least some of the consequences of his superior's actions. But he was loyal to Saulia. So much so that it would be dangerous to have him assigned to anyone else. She hoped it didn't also turn out to be dangerous to have him work for Saulia.

She paced the small space, looking for secrets to keep herself occupied, but her Trait remained quiet.

Finally, a door opened, and Saulia Holt stood frowning at her.

"Dagrun, if I'd known you needed to see me, I would have waited up for you," she said. "Come on into the parlour. Maeve is getting a fire going."

Dag followed Saulia into a large room filled with comfortable chairs and settees.

"Don't worry about the fire," she said, staying on her feet when Saulia sat down. "I'm here for the children."

"What children?" Saulia asked, but the housekeeper Maeve had let out a small gasp.

"The children from the Sapphire Sea," Dag replied. "The twins and triplets with Traits. The ones your father searched out and brought here."

"How do you know?" Saulia asked. She didn't seem worried, which made Dag wonder if she'd been expecting this.

"Because of *my Trait*," Dag lied. "The Trait that allowed me to track you down and save you from Fihaldo Pinho."

"You were looking for your sister," Saulia said.

"I was searching for you too," Dag replied. "And saved you both. Where are they?"

"They're being looked after," Saulia said.

"I need to see them," Dag said. She looked around the room and met Maeve's eyes. Tarmo Holt's housekeeper; Dag remembered the name now. Very likely involved in poisoning young Gustav. The housekeeper lowered her eyes but not before she glanced at a small door.

"They're downstairs then?" Dag asked. She took a step and tried to open the door, but it was locked. She sighed and turned to Saulia.

"If you are locking children in, then I must assume that they are not here willingly. Open the door."

"You don't seem afraid of me," Saulia said, getting to her feet.

"You're in my home, all alone."

"Are you really threatening me?" Dag asked. "Do you really think no one knows that I'm here. Or why?" She shook her head. "Or that I'm not prepared? Now, unless you think Mykol and Maeve can defeat me in a fight, I suggest you open the door and let me see the children."

"Fine," Saulia said. "I see no reason to make this physical. And I know that Nadez jailed a woman who has very little responsibility for any of this. Mykol?"

Dag moved aside so Mykol could open the door.

"I spoke to that woman," Dag said. She'd been in the jail to confirm that neither the pirate nor Leif Stendhal had any other secrets. "And if by *little responsibility* you mean she kept the children locked up, then yes, she is practically faultless." She had to try very hard to keep her anger out of her voice.

"And the Master Intelligencer," Dag continued. "Also knows that she has not been informed about children with Traits." She paused. "But this is about *you* and *me*. I saved you—the resources of the Three saved you—and yet you have chosen deceit and lies over the truth. You did know that Traits are the responsibility of the Master Intelligencer, didn't you?"

"Then why are you here instead of her?"

"Because I can identify what Traits these children have," Dag said, and Saulia perked up. "And determine if any of them are dangerous."

"They're not dangerous," Saulia said.

"Then why are they locked up in the cellar?" Dag asked. Her Trait triggered: was Saulia lying? She headed through the door and down a set of stairs. She half expected the door to be shut and for her to be locked in. Instead, when she looked back, Saulia was following her with Mykol trailing behind.

"I am very curious about their Traits," Saulia said. "They haven't learned enough Nordmerian to tell us."

Saulia's careless comment made Dag even angrier, but she pushed that feeling away. "I don't need them to tell me." Stolen children who couldn't even communicate with their captors locked up in a cellar. This was more than cruel.

"Oh, I see," Saulia said. "They're in here."

Dag knocked softly on the door before lifting the wooden bar from the brackets. She handed the bar to Mykol and took his lamp and dimmed the flame before opening the door.

"Hello," she said in Pilalian, followed by Arressan. She'd whiled away some time on board ships speaking with the crew, and she was better at both languages, but not good enough for a boy's rapid-fire questions in Arressan.

"Slow," she replied in Arressan. She didn't have a lot of experience with children, but she thought this boy and his twin brother, who both stared at her with sad eyes, were about ten.

"Who are you?" someone asked her in halting Arressan.

Dag turned to find a girl of about twelve watching her. She was Yedrissian, as were her brothers, their dark skin reflecting the low lamplight.

"Dagrun," Dag replied. Another set of twins, girls, peered up at her from a narrow bed. All of the children looked to be the same age, around ten or twelve. "I've come to help."

"Get us out of here," the Arressan boy who had first spoken said.

"Go home?" Dag asked, wishing she had thought to bring Rafael with her. At least then so much wouldn't depend on her very poor Arressan.

"Yes." All seven children replied in unison.

"Get their coats," she said turning to Saulia. "The children are coming with me."

"Then you owe me money," Saulia replied. "My father paid their families for these children."

"Talk to Nadez," Dag said. "She'll let you know if there's any coin left after the costs of me rescuing you are deducted." She might even ask Nadez to send Saulia a bill for that anyway. "Now get me their coats."

Saulia shrugged, making Dag wonder why she was letting them go so easily. But the Clan Freeholder nodded to Mykol, who left and went back upstairs.

Dag turned her gaze on the children, studying them. "Twin," she said and pointed to herself. "What do you do?"

The Yedrissian girl grinned. "My name is Adjoa," she said. "I Heal. Baako and Chike," she pointed at her brothers. "Not Heal."

"Oh." Dag took a step back from them.

"It's all right," Adjoa said. "I'm here."

"And if not?" Dag asked even though she had a sinking feeling about it.

"Don't," Adjoa said, shaking her head. "Very bad. Not Heal."

"*Skit*," Dag swore and nodded. All right, she would do her best to keep the three of them together.

"What is it?" Saulia asked her. "Did she tell you her Trait?"

"Yes, and you and your people are lucky to be alive," Dag said and shuddered. "Adjoa Heals. Her brothers do the opposite."

"Oh," Saulia said. "I'll just see where Mykol is."

"Warm coats," Dag called after her. "I'm not leaving until they have warm coats and boots." She sighed and turned back to the children. She hadn't thought it through—how taking these children out of this house in the middle of the night would work.

"Are you taking us home?" the Arressan boy asked. "To Arressa?"

"If that's what you want," Dag said. "Then yes. I have a ship, and I can take you home." The Arressan twins grinned at each other, but the Tobeian girls and the triplets just stared at her.

If Saulia had told her the truth and these children had been sold by their parents, then home wasn't a safe place. Or even a choice.

THE KNOCKING TURNED to pounding before Nadez could make it to the door.

"Who is it?" she called, regretting her decision to not have a live-in housekeeper.

"It's Dag, and I have the children with me."

Nadez unlocked the door and stood aside to let half a dozen, no seven, children into her apartment. Dagrun followed and she shut the door.

"How are your language skills?" Dagrun asked as she herded the children into her sitting room. "They all speak at least a little Arressan, but mine's very limited and I know only a few words in Tobeian or Yedrissian."

"I didn't expect you to fetch them tonight," Nadez said. The children huddled in the middle of the room, and she walked around them lighting lamps. "Lauma will be angry if you've upset Saulia." She bent over the fireplace and added some wood chips to the banked fire and stirred the embers. Once the wood caught and the flames flickered, she added a couple of logs.

"Saulia didn't really seem angry," Dagrun replied. "Although, I am. They were locked in a room in the cellar."

"What?" Nadez was shocked. "Why would she do that?"

"To keep them hidden, I assume." Dagrun turned to the children. "You're safe now," she said to them in halting Arressan. "Nadez is a friend." She took off her coat and put it on a chair. After a moment, a couple of the children took off their coats.

"I'm not sure what all of their Traits are yet," Dagrun said to her. "But Adjoa." She indicated the Yedrissian girl. "Heals and her brothers Baako and Chike do the opposite. Not Heal, she called it, and said that we're only safe if she's with them."

"Did Saulia know?"

"I told her," Dagrun replied. "But she knew something already. I think that's one reason why she let me take them."

"Then she knew," Nadez said. "Or at least had some idea. That's why they were in the cellar. To protect her and her household."

"Then why didn't she just tell you she had them?" Dagrun asked. "If she didn't want them?" She shook her head. "My Trait just triggered, so there's something there, some hidden reason for wanting me to come and take the children instead of her surrendering them."

"Maybe the children know?" Nadez asked. The Yedrissian girl had been intently following their conversation. "Are you sure they don't understand Nordmerian?"

"No, but they've only spoken Arressan so far."

"Your name is Adjoa?" Nadez asked in Yedrissian, and the three Yedrissian children looked at her. At one time, her Yedrissian had been good enough for trade talks, but it had been years since she'd spoken it. "Do you know why you were allowed to be taken by Dagrun?" She pointed to Dagrun.

"The other lady was afraid of my brothers," Adjoa said. "I had to Heal the man who brought us to her after he was alone with Chike."

"I see," Nadez said. "Why did she keep you if she was afraid of you?"

"Honour requires that she keep the oath her father swore to mine," Adjoa said. "To feed and house us. Breaking that oath will have dire consequences for her house and her descendants for all eternity."

"And since you were taken from Saulia's house against her will, the oath was not broken?"

"That is correct." She grinned. "She is smart. She no longer has us, and there will be no consequences for her."

"What did she say?" Dagrun asked. "My Trait just eased up."

"Adjoa says that Saulia was bound by a Yedrissian oath that Tarmo Holt made. Since you took the children from her, Saulia has not broken the oath. And yet she is free of children she feared."

"I see," Dagrun replied. "I was taught that the curse on a Yedrissian oath breaker was a myth." But she'd also been taught that Resolutes didn't exist, and she knew that was wrong.

"Perhaps it's not," Nadez replied. "It seems that Saulia believed it." She turned back to Adjoa. "Do you want to return home?"

"Yes, very much, we all do," Adjoa replied. "Although my brothers and I cannot return to our father's village. He sent us away because my brothers are dangerous."

"But you have somewhere to go?"

"Our aunt is not afraid of us," Adjoa said. "Even though her only sister died giving us life."

"Dagrun," Nadez said. "Do you feel comfortable taking these children on the *Atlaine* when you leave?"

"Yes. Can they go back to their families?"

"Some of them can't," Nadez replied. She sighed. "It's late. Why don't we find everyone a place to sleep? You as well, and we can sort it all out in the morning."

"Thank you. I still need to figure out what Traits the two sets of twins have."

Once the children were all settled in two rooms and Dagrun had stretched out on the settee in the sitting room, Nadez headed back to her own bed.

AFTER TWO DAYS of fruitless waiting, Calder was so bored that he almost missed it when his Trait activated.

He stepped out from the shadow of a building and into the street. A small person in a hooded cloak took a skewer from the vendor and hurried away.

The figure ahead turned right, and Calder followed them down a narrow set of stairs. He lost sight of them when he reached an intersecting alley at the bottom.

His focus narrowed on a wooden gate halfway down the alley

on his right. He pushed the gate inward, and he found himself in an even narrower alley.

Something about the way the curtain moved in the window set into the building on his right caught his attention. He pushed the curtain aside and grinned. It wasn't a house or a place of business. Instead, he was viewing a courtyard.

He climbed through the opening and stood at the edge of what looked like a practice ring for fighting.

"You're not welcome here," someone said from above in Arressan.

He looked up to find a girl staring down at him. Her colouring was Pilalian, and she held a skewer of meat in one hand.

"You have something that is not yours," he said in Pilalian. "I'm here to retrieve it for its owner. Or . . ." he paused. "I can just tell him where to find it."

"By the time he arrives, it will no longer be here," the girl replied.

"Will you also be gone?" he asked. "Are you fully trained and able to defend against one who is?"

She stared at him as she ate her skewer of meat. She tossed the skewer down onto the ground when she was finished.

"That is the last time I will be able to enjoy that vendor's Pilalian grilled meat," she said to him. "I might kill you just for that."

"Then my father will come after you for a second reason," he said. "Even when what he owns has been returned to him."

"He won't know what happened to you."

"Are you so sure that a man who was able to follow you and discover where you train has not made certain that someone knows who he was looking for?" He stared up at her wondering if Esma really would tell Rahm what happened. And if Rahm would seek revenge for his son's death.

"Enough."

Calder turned to see a woman emerge from the building and cross the practice yard. She made a hand motion, and the girl dropped to the ground and bowed to her.

"The student shall tell the others that we are moving and that it is her fault," the woman said. "Be ready in an hour."

Head bowed, the girl hurried past the woman and into the house. Calder looked up from watching her leave and met cold, calculating eyes. She was Tobeian, he thought, and she was not happy.

"I've come for—"

"I know what you've come for," she said, cutting him off. "We are holding it for another."

"Floros," he said. "And Pinho. I know."

"Then you know that I cannot simply let you have it."

"But you could let me steal it," he said and grinned. "I'm sure you don't want to be in the middle of a fight between the unlawful Arressan council." He pulled his patch out of his pocket and held it up. "The Fair Seas Treaty Alliance. And my father, Rahm."

The woman frowned at him. "Rahm is your father?"

"He is," Calder replied. "There are a few of us. In fact, I'm not the only child of Rahm's in Messanos right now. Which is why I am certain he would find out if you killed me."

If anything, her frown deepened, and Calder shrugged. If she was intent on killing him, he would have to trust Luck to save him.

"I do not like the kind of trouble you bring," she said. "But agreeing with you brings its own problems."

"The stolen item can redirect certain actions," he said. "You can choose." It meant Fihaldo Pinho would not be his father's target, but he'd never liked the idea of being the one to decide who his father assassinated.

Her face brightened at his words. "My choice?" she replied. "You offer something I have barely dared to dream of. Truly? My choice?"

"I promise," he said, hoping that the person she wanted dead wasn't someone he cared about.

"There is someone," she said. "In the Pale Sea."

Calder's heart constricted. "As long as it's not my family," he said.

"Then it's not really my choice, is it?"

"You forget that Rahm is also my family," Calder said. "I would not expect my father to honour a contract against his own kin."

"Yes, of course," she said with real contrition. "We would not ask that either, and in fact, we would never take such a commission. I agree to that condition. Besides, I don't believe my choice is your family. I will be busy packing the practice gear and will not visit my study for half an hour. I will leave the name of my choice out here in the dust. Make sure you erase it when you leave." She nodded and headed into a small shed.

Calder dashed across the yard and into the building. A girl stared at him when he walked past an open door, but she didn't raise an alarm. When he got to what looked like a study, he entered and stood in the middle of the room.

Something as dangerous as the token would be hidden even inside this building. He took a couple of steps towards a desk and his foot caught on something. When he looked down, his focus narrowed on a specific tile.

He pried it up and pulled out a small piece of linen. He could feel the token, but to be certain, he unwrapped it. This was it. He tucked the rewrapped token into his pocket right beside his patch.

He retraced his path out of the building to the practice yard without encountering anyone. And there, written in the dirt just below the window was a name, thankfully not that of either family or friend, but a name he recognized.

He scuffed the dirt and erased the name and climbed out and into the narrow alley. It seemed to prove who had sent a suicide assassin after his mother. As he made his way back to Esma's place, he wondered what exactly Henrik Ottosen had done to anger the woman who trained assassins.

CHAPTER 13

PIA CROUCHED IN a dark corner, a broken table leg in her hands.

Someone was inside the old warehouse, and they were making a lot of noise.

"Pia!"

She relaxed and stood up just as Gustav rushed into the main room.

"We need to go, now!"

"Did you get it?" Gustav nodded, and she grabbed her coat and pulled it on. "How far behind you are they?" She assumed the urgency was because he was being chased.

"I'm not sure," Gustav said. He picked up his pack and shoved the waterskin under his coat. "It's snowing hard, but they still might be able to follow my tracks."

She looped her pack across her shoulders and stamped at the fire, doing her best to put it out.

"I'm ready," she said and stood by the open doorway.

"Let's go."

Pia led the way to the window. The snow was coming down hard, and Gustav's footprints were already almost filled in. Once outside, she let him lead. She hadn't spent much time outdoors and never in winter. The snow was making it hard for her to figure out which direction to take, but Gustav set off confidently.

Walking was difficult. The snow was much deeper than it had been on their way into Nurmi, and the cold wind blew flakes into her eyes.

Gustav stopped and looked behind them. "At least this snow will make it hard for them to follow us," he said.

"You can still find the boat, right?" Being stuck out here in a storm sounded dangerous. But so did being caught by pirates.

"I'll find the boat," he said. "Come on." He looked up at the swirling snow. "I'd rather not be walking around in the dark."

Pia followed behind him, placing her boots in the footprints he left. Wind whipped in off the sea, blowing the snow sideways. She did her best to keep her eyes clear, but a few times she lost sight of Gustav even though he was just a few feet in front of her.

She Concentrated on the task at hand and was so focused on putting one foot in front of the other that she didn't notice that Gustav had stopped until she bumped into him.

"Watch it." He grabbed her arm and pulled her away from the edge of a drop off. She looked out, but all she could see was swirling snow.

"I don't hear any waves," she said.

"The sea is ice right to the shore," he replied. "As long as the boat's not frozen in too deep, the ice will be easier to manage than open water. I'll go first and make sure it can be sailed." He placed her hand on a rope. "When I tell you to, follow this to the boat."

"All right." The rope bucked under her hand as Gustav used it to guide him as he slid down the slope. She hadn't even known enough to be worried about the boat. What if it couldn't be sailed? Returning to Nurmi didn't seem like a safe option, not with pirates looking for them.

The rope moved under her hand, and a moment later Gustav climbed up beside her.

"I think we'll be able to get the runners unstuck," he said. "But it will take both of us. Come on."

He headed back down the slope, and she followed, hanging onto the rope as she slid down to the beach below.

The wind had swept the snow off the sailboat in places, and as far as she could tell, it looked undamaged. Gustav waved her out to join him at the stern, and she tentatively stepped onto the ice. It was rough underfoot, and she had to tread carefully or risk losing her footing on the chunks of ice.

"Help me push from this side," Gustav said.

She joined him and put both hands on the side of the boat.

"Push!"

She pushed against the wood, her boots slipping as she tried to find solid footing on the rough ice. Her right foot held, and she put all of her weight on it.

"Stop," Gustav said. "That's good. We loosened it a little. Now we do the same thing on the other side."

She hadn't felt the boat move at all, but she followed Gustav around the stern. This time she made sure of her footing before she pushed and was rewarded when she felt the boat shift slightly.

"Now the bow."

It was easier this time, and she felt the boat shift. Now that the runners were loose, Gustav had them lift the boat up out of the grooves and onto smoother ice.

"I'll get the sail ready," Gustav said.

"I'll untie us," she said.

She grabbed the rope and hauled herself up to the top of the slope. After spending a few fruitless minutes trying to undo the frozen knot, she pulled out her knife and cut the rope. With the stiff rope in hand, she slid back down the slope. She looped the half-frozen rope and wedged it into the tip of the bow.

Gustav had unfolded the sail, but the wind had caught it before he had a chance to secure it to the mast. Pia climbed into the boat and grabbed a corner of the canvas. A gust of wind almost blew it from her grasp, and she tightened her grip. The little boat moved before she had a chance to secure the sail, and she wondered if she'd untied them from the tree too soon.

If she hadn't glanced back to the tree, she wouldn't have seen them in time. Three figures stood at the top of the slope, and as she watched, one of them started down.

"Gustav," she shouted. "They're here!"

He looked over his shoulder and swore.

"Hold the sail right here," he said, and she placed her hand where his had been. "And when I tell you to, move it over here." He moved his hand about a foot away, and she nodded. Then he jumped out of the boat and pushed the stern.

"Now," he yelled, and she moved her hand.

Immediately the wind caught the sail, almost ripping it from her hands. The boat lurched and started inching away from shore. Gustav was still pushing from the stern, just steps away from the pirate who was now on the beach.

The boat was gaining speed, and Gustav heaved himself over the gunwale. The pirate grabbed onto the stern and tried to dig his boots into the ice, but the wind was too strong, and instead of stopping the boat, he was being towed behind them.

"I've got this," Gustav said as he took hold of the sail.

Pia stepped aside and stared at the pirate who was trying to pull himself into the boat. She reached down and grabbed an oar, but before she could swing it, the boat hit a chunk of ice and bucked. Thrown off balance, she dropped to her knees. The pirate lost his grip on the gunwale and stumbled and fell. In moments, all sight of him was lost in the swirling snow.

She put the oar down and crawled over to the mast where Gustav was still holding the corner of the sail.

"He's gone," she said. "We got away."

"Just barely," he replied. "We need to stop and get the rudder in place. I can't sail the whole way to Tarklee without being able to steer properly."

"How long will it take?" she asked. "To get to Tarklee?"

"Less than a day if the ice is good." He looked up at the sky, and Pia followed his gaze. Snow was still falling, and it was getting dark. "But it will be cold out there. It might be smarter to land north of Nurmi and take the road to Pavil Barda's house."

"And we always make the smarter choice?"

Gustav laughed. "All right. I'll keep us within sight of shore for tonight, anyway. If we get too cold, we can find a place to land and make a fire."

"Agreed." Pia huddled down and tucked her hands into her armpits. It would be a long cold night, but so far, they'd done what they had set out to do. They had proof that Timonis was working with the pirates, and they'd escaped capture. Unfortunately, delivering that proof would also be dangerous.

"We're ready," Dag said to Lauma and Nadez. They were on the dock, staring out at the *Atlaine*. The *Tazeyar* had already hauled anchor and left Tarklee harbour on its way to northern Nordmere. And Byholt, if possible, but just to deliver the woodcutters and Lauma's note to Yakop. No food was heading that far north.

"You were right about the children," Lauma said, turning to

look first at Nadez and then at her. "I should have listened. I had two sons with Traits, so you'd think I would care about the way children with Traits could be forced from their families." She shook her head. "And how those children could be exploited. I'll speak with Saulia, but it sounds like she had no choice even though she didn't want the children."

"She kept them locked in a cellar," Dag said. "That was a choice."

"She was afraid of them," Nadez replied, seeming to agree with Lauma although she hand signalled to Dag that she wasn't about to trust Saulia.

"I would have been too," Lauma said. "Two children with Traits the opposite of Healing. Who knows what terrible tragedies that could cause? I admit that I am happy to have them out of the city."

"As long as all three are together, everyone is safe," Dag said. "At least that's what Adjoa says, and she should know." The girl had also said that they couldn't return home. Dag briefly wondered if the negative Traits could be modified, the way Inger's seemed to have been. But hers had been changed by Ansdottir's combination of Traits. It was unlikely she could find someone else with Traits that could do the same for the triplets.

"Did you figure out what Traits the others have?" Lauma asked. "The Arressans and the Tobeians?"

"Of course," Dag said. She'd spent some time with the children this morning, and their Traits had become very apparent to her. "Pavlos' Trait is related to Kaja's. He doesn't have her total recall, but he is extremely accurate. Stavlos is the opposite, of course. I'm not sure you'd ever want to trust what he says. He doesn't lie, he just can't seem to remember things the way they really are." She shrugged. The boy hadn't even been able to tell her what he'd eaten for breakfast without getting it mixed up. "Anahita is Fearless and Minoo is Fearful, and I can't tell you which Trait I would consider negative."

"Surely Fearless is the positive one," Lauma said.

"Not in all situations," Nadez replied. "Someone with an unjustified sense of fearlessness could get into trouble very quickly."

"That's what I think," Dag said. "I don't yet know what we're doing with them. The two boys say they were stolen, so them we'll take home, but the others were sold." She caught a signal from Rafael, who had been charged with getting the children settled into the dinghy.

"I'm being told it's time to go," Dag said. She hugged Nadez before turning to Lauma.

"Tell my son I said hello," Lauma said as she embraced her. "And that I'm doing the best I can."

"I will." Dag stepped away and sighed. "And you are doing well despite having been talked into becoming the Interim Grand Freeholder."

"Talked into!" Lauma said. "That sounds like I had a choice." She smiled to soften her words. "Safe journey."

"Keep well, all of you." Dag turned and hurried to the dinghy.

She settled in amongst the children, who were all bundled up against the cold, and watched the shore as they were rowed out to the *Atlaine*. The harbour was starting to ice over, but there was still a clear path out to the sea.

Now it was time to worry about Calder and Inger. And hope that Rahm had been reasonable and had stopped his pursuit of Charis.

CALDER HANDED THE packet of spices to Cook and sat down and started dicing squash for the stew.

"More flavourings?" Cook asked. "The crew is already happy with the one you taught me on the way here."

"Sailors get tired of eating the same thing all the time," Calder replied. He and Esma had stayed in their cabin while Steen got the *Vassan* underway, but he had promised to help with the meals again. He'd bought the spices in order to keep Cook and Steen happy. Now that they were on their way back to Zelesso with the token, he didn't want anything to go wrong.

"Don't I know it," Cook said. "At least in the Sapphire Sea we can fish. I hate serving dried fish almost as much as the crew hates eating it."

"I can tell you how to prepare that too, if you want."

"Won't need it," Cook replied. "Captain says we're to stay on the Sapphire Sea until summer: Strongrock isn't going anywhere."

"All right," Calder replied. "Just the new spices for stew then."

Once the stew was simmering, he grabbed a couple of bowls

of it and headed back to the cabin.

"It's me," he said at the door. "With supper."

He heard the lock turn, and then Esma peered out at him. She stepped aside and opened the door wider. As soon as he was inside, she closed and relocked the door.

"That smells good," she said taking a bowl from him. She grabbed the spoon that rested in the stew and ate a bite before sitting down in one of the hammocks that stretched across the room. "Tastes good too," she said.

"An easy way to keep everyone friendly," Calder said as he sat down on the other hammock. The room they had was small, but it was a luxury on any ship. He didn't know which sailors they had displaced, and he wanted to keep it that way. He had no wish to be confronted by angry pirates who resented being kicked out of their cabin for the man who'd killed Margit Ansdottir. Hopefully good food and staying out of sight, per Steen's orders, would continue to keep any resentment under control.

They ate in silence for a few minutes. When he'd finished his stew, Calder set his bowl on the floor beside the door. He would take the empty dishes back to the mess in the morning, when it was time to start breakfast.

"We should be in Zelesso by noon tomorrow," he said. "Do you think Rahm is still there?"

"You really don't trust him," Esma said. She slipped off her hammock to stack her empty bowl on top of his. "I'd be shocked if he wasn't. He's always kept his word to me."

"He might keep his word, but he also has many secrets," Calder said.

"You think he still has some?"

"You think he doesn't?" he asked. "Where did he grow up? How did he even become what he is? I don't know, do you?"

"I don't," Esma said. "He always claimed he was born in the Pilalian town of Shiori."

"Perhaps he really was," Calder said. "Because that's where he told us he was from too. But I've been there, and I did not meet anyone who claimed to have known Rahm as a boy."

"Maybe his family moved away when he was young," Esma said. "Or maybe they know what he is and refuse to acknowledge him."

"Or maybe it's a lie." Calder sighed. "We might never know."

He shrugged. "Although it would be nice to set foot on the land of our father's people."

"That's not a very Pilalian sentiment," Esma said. "At least, not as far as I know. Like you I'm only half Pilalian and did not grow up there. But Pilalians are seafarers, tied to the water more than the land."

"That's what they—" a loud boom sounded nearby, and Calder swore.

"What was that?" Esma asked.

"Cannon," he replied. "And not from this ship. Someone is firing at us." He strained to listen for sounds from above, but they were too far below deck for him to hear what orders were being given. "We weren't hit." The ship pitched as it made a sharp turn, and the hammocks swung wildly. The bowls skidded across the floor and crashed into the far wall, shattering.

"Should we stay here?" Esma asked. "Are we safe?"

"No," Calder replied to both questions. "We need to get on deck and see what's happening." He stood up, careful not to step on broken pottery, and made his way to the small closet. He tossed Esma her boots and slipped his own on. "Come on."

The hallway was quiet: all sailors would have headed up top as soon as the cannon was heard. He led the way past a couple of open doors—quarters left in a hurry—to the stairs that led up to the deck.

Now he could hear shouts and running feet on deck. Was the *Vassan* retreating, or was it engaging? Knowing which was key to his and Esma's safety.

He pushed the door open and stepped into chaos. A quick look around showed that the *Vassan* was trying to flee. It also showed that they had very little hope of doing it. Three ships flying familiar flags were behind them, almost in position to flank the *Vassan*.

A cannon roared from on deck, and he gestured Esma forward. They needed to get off the ship before it was either captured or sunk.

He led the way to the prow, away from the cannon and most of the pirates. It was almost dark, and he could see land off to port.

"Can you swim?" he asked his sister.

She followed his gaze. "I can, and the sea is still warm at this time of year, but a dinghy would be better."

"A dinghy would be seen," he replied. "Those ships belong to Pinho. We can't be caught, not with the token in my pocket." He patted his pocket to make sure he still had it and sighed when he felt the solid shape beneath his hand.

"We'll need some supplies," Esma said. "Full waterskins, flint, a knife. There's not much along this coast."

"You stay here." He shook his head when she started to protest. "I know the kitchen, and I can count on Luck."

She frowned but nodded, and Calder hurried back the way they'd come. He ran into the kitchen. Cook grunted at him but didn't say a word when he grabbed two knives. He had to search two cabins before he found three waterskins, and once back up on deck, he filled them at a freshwater cask.

"For you," he said when he rejoined Esma. He handed her a waterskin and a knife. "Let's go." He led the way over the gunwale, splashing into the sea feet first. Esma landed beside him.

He looked up, but there were no faces peering down at them from above. If anyone had noticed them jump ship, they either didn't care or were too busy trying to defend the *Vassan* from Pinho.

He nodded to Esma, who was a few feet from him, and then struck out for shore.

Esma was a much better swimmer than he was. He was still a dozen feet behind when she stood up in waist high water.

By the time he felt solid land under his boots, he was shivering despite the warm sea. Esma was ahead, already walking through knee-high surf towards a beach. He realized that he hadn't heard cannon shots since they left the *Vassan* and looked back out at the ships.

The *Vassan* had been captured. One of Pinho's ships was already along her starboard side and a second was easing up to her on port. A third vessel, one he recognized as the *Neas*, Tarmo Holt's old ship, was blocking it in. The *Vassan* was lost.

And he and Esma had just a few days to get back to Zelesso with Rahm's token.

The snow had stopped, but the cloudy sky was still dark and grey. Gustav rubbed a mitten against his face. He was cold, but he didn't think he had any frostbite. And it was finally light enough for him to see the shoreline.

Pia had Concentrated all night, calling out directions to keep them safely on ice and out of the huge snowdrifts that dotted the frozen sea. Now he thought they were just a few hours from Tarklee Harbour.

"Pia!" he called. "Pia!"

When she finally turned to him, her face was blank. Then she shuddered and blinked.

"What is it?" she asked.

"I'm going to stop for a few minutes," he said. "I want to find us a snowdrift and refill my waterskin." He also needed to relieve his bladder and assumed she would too.

"All right." She turned and looked ahead and pointed to starboard. He steered towards the drift she was pointing at. When they were close enough, he pulled up the tiller and climbed over to the sail.

The canvas was stiff with cold: he pulled it down without folding it and draped it over the port gunwale. The boat slid to a stop a few yards from the snowdrift.

The wind buffeted him as he made his way to the bow. He leaned past Pia and grabbed the painter and uncoiled it. He looped the end around his waist and knotted it.

"One of us needs to stay with the boat," he said. "And when you leave it, you need to be tied to it." She nodded, and he stepped out onto the rough ice.

The painter stretched out taut as he rounded the snowdrift far enough for some privacy. Even though he was as quick as he could be, his fingers were almost too cold to get his trousers laced up. Back at the boat, he pulled out his waterskin and did his best to shove snow into it. He shivered when he placed the cold skin inside his coat.

He stepped into the boat and untied the rope from around his waist. "Your turn if you need to, you know." She nodded, and he tied her in.

He checked the sail while she headed around the snowdrift.

She was back a few moments later, and as soon as she climbed into the boat, he raised the sail. The wind caught it immediately, and they were moving before he had a chance to tie the sail to the mast.

Pia came to help, and between them they wrestled the sail into place and secured it.

Gustav lurched to the stern and dropped the tiller. He felt the blade of the tiller bite into ice as he turned them towards the shoreline.

The sun came up an hour later. At first the light was welcome, but when it rose higher in the sky, the reflection off the ice made his eyes water.

It didn't seem to bother Pia: she didn't take her eyes off their path forward as she confidently directed him past snowdrifts and the odd heap of ice as they followed the shore.

At midmorning they were at the mouth to Tarklee harbour. Once they rounded a point, he could see that the harbour wasn't completely frozen. He hugged the south shore where the cold wind out of the north pushed the waves up onto land.

"We're here," he called out to Pia. "But hang on. This might be tricky." He squinted out across the ice, trying to see what their path to the city looked like.

Pia pointed, and he steered to starboard. They passed a drift of snow, and ahead of them a section of windswept ice stretched towards a series of snow drifts.

Gustav crawled to the mast and did his best to shorten the sail.

Pia pointed to port, and he hurried back to the stern and maneuvered them around another drift. The ice was rough but solid along the south shore, and in ten minutes they were close enough to a dock to tie up.

They were at the very edge of the city, but it was safe, and he hadn't had to sail off the ice into open water. A few minutes of walking was a fine trade-off for not having to attempt that.

He sighed when he stepped onto solid ground. "Let's go," he said to Pia as she tied the boat up. "I want to get somewhere warm, and we need to find Nadez and report."

"I DON'T THINK anyone told Pinho's men that we were on board," Calder said, easing away from the edge of the beach.

It was just after dawn, and they'd spent a restless night watching for any signs that they'd been missed. He slapped at an insect as he turned towards Esma. She had her back against a tree and was looking past him.

"I almost wish they would," Esma said. "Maybe they'd send a

dinghy after us." She waved away the cloud of tiny insects that swarmed in front of her face.

"I'll take my chances on land," Calder replied. "I'm sure we have enough time to make it to Zelesso." He stuck his hand in his pocket for what seemed like the hundredth time since they came ashore to make sure that the token was still there.

Esma snorted. "If only we were dealing with land," she said. "And not what's between us and Zelesso. Swamp and wetlands, and way upstream is a river that is as wide as the city of Messanos." She slapped her arm. "And more biting and stinging insects than you've ever seen."

"Now that it's light, we can leave as soon as the ships are gone," he said. He knew from maps what the shoreline was made up of, but he had never been there. The way Esma described it, it sounded like they would need Luck to make it to Zelesso. "Is there anything dangerous we need to watch out for? I mean besides Pinho?"

"Snakes," she replied. "The ones that swim are poisonous, but some of the others grow as big around as your thigh and can crush you if they catch you." She swiped at more bugs. "Other than that, insects, sun, and dehydration. You have to go a long way upstream to find drinkable water."

"Do people come here by choice?"

"Fishermen mostly," Esma said. "Some of the tastiest shellfish are found only here, and a good catch can be worth a quarter of what a dock worker can earn in a year. Three or four experienced fishing crews regularly fish out here, but there's always someone foolish enough or desperate enough to try their hand."

"And then there's us." He crawled up to look out at the sea. Only two ships remained, and neither one was the *Vassan*. The *Neas* was gone as well, and he wondered if any of Holt's crew were still on board. A series of flags was run up the mast of one of the ships, and soon the sails were raised.

"They're leaving," he said over his shoulder. "We should too. The beach goes south a ways; I think we should be safe enough on it."

By the time they had walked a dozen steps down the beach, he could barely see the sails of the two ships.

At midday, the beach gave way to marshland. Calder stared out across the mounds of grasses that dotted the wetlands. He couldn't see the other side from here.

"Do we swim?" he asked Esma. The marsh extended far out into the Sapphire Sea, but it had to end somewhere.

"We wade," she replied. "Try to go from mound to mound but be careful. Some of them won't be very solid."

"How do you know?" he asked. "You said you've never been here before."

"One of the fishing crews that comes out here docks near the *Hakon*," she said. "And I ask a lot of questions." She waded through brackish water and stood up on a small lump of ground. "I am really glad you made me wear my boots." She left the high ground and headed for a second mound of grass.

Calder stepped into the marsh, and water soaked his trousers up to his knees. He couldn't imagine walking through this in bare feet no matter how toughened they might be.

They took turns leading as they slowly made their way through the marsh. A few times they had to head further inland in order to find a path of mounds and hillocks to cross over.

Calder stepped from a tiny lump of solid ground into water that rose up to his waist. Something slithered past him, and he stopped, not wanting to startle anything into taking a bite out of him. A moment later it was gone, but the water was noticeably flowing towards the sea. They must be in the river now. He glanced upstream, and then his focus narrowed.

"Stay here," he said, turning to Esma. "I think there's something there." The current was slow, but it still took some effort to walk against it.

He stared at a large mound of land covered in a thatch of grass. There was something there that Luck wanted him to see. He had to climb up onto the mound and pull the grass aside before he saw the thin white lengths glinting in the sun.

Bones. Human bones with a few scraps of fabric still clinging to them.

"Someone died here," he called out over his shoulder. His gaze skimmed past the bones, and his eyes fixed on something wooden buried deeper in the thatch of grass.

He reached into the thicket and grabbed what looked like a trap of some kind. He got it halfway out of the thicket before it got stuck and he couldn't budge it no matter how hard he tugged.

He stepped past the former owner of the trap and pushed

more grass out of the way.

And stood up and grinned. A boat. The trap was tied to one end of a long narrow boat that had either been purposely beached here or had washed up on this clump of earth.

He backed up past the bones and waved Esma over.

"What did you find?" she asked as she joined him. She eyed the exposed bones. "Besides the remains of this poor soul."

"How the poor soul got here," he replied. "There's a boat in there, and I have some hope that it's still seaworthy."

"He's been here a while," she said. "As has his boat."

"I think he only came here this summer," Calder said. "Spring at the earliest. Heat, water, insects, and whatever else calls this marsh home would make short work of him. And his trap hasn't yet been damaged by the water. Here." He handed her the trap and headed deeper into the thicket until he could grab the boat.

It felt solid beneath his hands and there was relatively clean water in the bottom of it. Hopefully, it was rainwater that hadn't drained out rather than swamp water that had leaked in.

"Start pulling," he said. Esma hauled on the rope and it went taut. He rocked the boat a few times and then tugged it hard. It jerked forward a foot, and he stepped back and pulled again.

Esma joined him beside the floating boat.

"Help me empty it." They lifted one side of the boat and tipped the water out before setting it back down. Now that he could see the bottom, he realized that the boat had been carved out of a single tree. He put one foot in it and pressed down for a moment, but the little boat didn't sink, and swamp water didn't leak into it.

"Does this always happen?" Esma asked. "You just find the thing you need the most?"

"Not always," he replied. "But often. And remember, the only reason we're here to find this is because the *Vassan* was attacked by Pinho and we had to jump ship. None of that seems Lucky."

"No, but this sure does," she said. "Just not for the boat's former owner." She looked back at the thicket of grass. "Did you see any paddles in there? We still need a way to power this thing."

Chapter 14

DAG STOOD IN the stern and looked back at the Teeth. The weather had turned cold just as they entered them, and thin ice had stretched between some of the spires that were close together.

About halfway through, the ice had disappeared, but the worry was that a return trip could see them get part of the way through and then be frozen in.

She wasn't going to risk the *Atlaine*. She'd talk it over with Calder, but she very much thought they'd be wintering on the Sapphire Sea.

Much as she might wish otherwise, she couldn't change the weather. Lauma and Nadez and everyone else in the Three would just have to manage without her.

"The children are asking for you," Rafael said as he joined her at the stern. "I've taken them to the mess for some tea." He shook his head. "They were very impressed by seeing the Teeth up close and then sailing through them."

"At least they get to have some adventures," she replied. The children had told her they'd been kept below on their separate trips to Tarklee, probably an order from Tarmo Holt. Then they'd been kept inside the whole time they were in the city. "Can you spare a few minutes to translate?"

"I have some time," Rafael said and led the way to the door that led below deck.

It turned out that Rafael spoke fluent Tobeian and passable

Yedrissian, courtesy of his time working on his uncle's spice ship. A few sailors were Yedrissian, and others could speak it better, but Dag wanted as few people as possible to know what Traits the children had. The triplets' own family had been afraid of them; she wasn't willing to trust that sailors on board wouldn't fear them too. And the two boys *were* dangerous, if separated from their sister.

She had told the crew most of the truth though. That the children had been taken from their homes by Holt and she was returning them to their families. At least she would return the ones she could to their families.

The triplets, Adjoa, Chike, and Baako, had been handed over to Holt because their father feared the boys. Adjoa claimed an aunt would care for them, but was it true?

The Arressan boys, Pavlos and Stavlos, said that they had been stolen; taken from the streets of Zelesso and that their mother would never have allowed them to leave home.

But the Tobeian girl Anahita, whose Trait was Fearlessness, got very quiet and sad when asked how Tarmo Holt acquired her and her sister. They'd been sold by their parents, and Dag still wasn't clear why. Neither of their Traits were dangerous, not like Chike and Baako's. She supposed that the why didn't matter: she wouldn't send children back to a situation like that. They could be sold a second time and not because they had Traits but because they were girls.

Dag followed Rafael into the mess and then stopped, a smile on her lips.

Cook stood beside a table of sailors, Anahita at his side with a tray of bowls. Cook took a bowl from her, dipped a ladle into the pot that sat on the table, and filled the bowl.

They went around the table until each sailor had a bowl of stew or soup before carrying the pot to a second table.

The rest of the children were sitting at a table in the corner.

"Anahita is working to pay for her passage," Adjoa said in Arressan when Dag and Rafael joined them. "Chike and I wanted to help too but Baako didn't, and I can't leave him by himself."

"Even if you're in the same room?" Dag asked.

Adjoa shook her head. "Sometimes the Not Healing is deadly. I cannot risk it." She brightened. "But Anahita said she'd work enough for all of us."

"That's very kind of her," Dag replied. She pulled up a chair and sat down. "The captain needs to decide where we're heading first," she said. "Adjoa, where does your aunt live?" She looked at Rafael who was still standing.

He nodded and spoke to the girl in Yedrissian. She answered, and Rafael turned to her.

"Her aunt lives in a small fishing village along the coast; at this time of year, it will be just past the main city of Wekesa. She says it is not the village of their mother, nor of their father, and that their aunt would have them live at the edge of the village, away from other people."

"Is that what you want?" Dag asked Adjoa in Arressan.

The girl nodded. "My brothers cannot be around anyone without me. It is not an ideal life, but it will let me leave them at times to use my gift, my Trait, to help Heal people in the village."

"All right." Adjoa was correct that her brothers couldn't be around other people; no one would be safe. And at least they would all be together.

"Pavlos? You and your brother will rejoin your family in Zelesso," she said.

"Yes!" Pavlos said. "We can't wait to get home. Our mother will be so happy."

"Our older sister might not be!" Stavlos said, and the boys broke into giggles.

"That leaves you Minoo," Dag said to the quiet girl. Her eyes widened, and she searched for Anahita who was still helping Cook. "Don't worry, I'm not leaving you anywhere unless you're safe. Would you be all right in Arressa, or would you prefer to return to Tobei?"

Rafael spoke in Tobeian, translating Dag's words, and the girl relaxed a little, although she still darted worried looks at her sister. She said a few quiet words to Rafael, who nodded and turned to Dag.

"She says that she would feel safer in Arressa and is worried that her sister will insist on Tobei."

"We'll see if we can find a home for them when we reach Zelesso," Dag said, and Minoo nodded.

"Captain Demer mentioned someone she can contact," Rafael said.

"Thank you," Dag said. Speaking Arressan, she turned to the

children. "You can stay here or in your cabins. And if you want to go on deck, ask Cook or another sailor to come and fetch me. You're my responsibility while on board."

Rafael spoke in Tobeian and Yedrissian and then Dag stood up. She waved goodbye as she and Rafael went on deck to speak to Darya.

Darya decided to head to Zelesso first. They could get the boys settled, and she confirmed that she had a friend who could help find a home for Anahita and Minoo. After Zelesso they would head to Yedris and then, finally, to Messanos.

Dag hated that her search for Calder and Inger would be delayed, but she was the one who had decided to be responsible for returning the children to the Sapphire Sea. She couldn't complain when Darya agreed to do just that.

NADEZ HEARD RUNNING feet outside her office and looked up to find a panting Kaja in her doorway.

"What's happened?" she asked, her heart pounding. Had there been another attempt on Lauma's life?

"It's Gustav," Kaja said and smiled. "He sent word that he's here. He needs to see you right away. He's in Joosep's safe apartment."

"What ship did he arrive on?" She'd need to see about keeping the harbour clear of ice. They couldn't afford to lose a single ship to ice over the winter.

"He didn't arrive by ship." Kaja said.

"Oh." She was surprised. Taking the road this time of year was dangerous. "I'll go right away." She grabbed her coat from the peg near the door. Why hadn't Gustav come directly to her office? Was he hurt? Or followed? She turned to Kaja.

"Are you coming? I'd like a record of everything Gustav says." She led the way out through the narrow passageway, into the alley, and then to the street where Joosep's safe apartment was.

The sun shone on the nearly empty street, doing little to chase the cold away. She knocked on the door, and a moment later Gustav opened it.

She stepped into an overly warm room and shrugged out of her jacket.

"Why didn't you come to me?" she asked after she'd looked him over. His cheeks were red, probably because of the heat, but other than that he seemed healthy.

"We needed to be warm," he said. "And unlike the Hall, here I can keep the fire as hot as I want it." He headed further into the apartment.

"What news?" she asked. She supposed it was true about the Hall. The entire building was heated, but not all rooms had fireplaces. Although this heat seemed excessive. "Pia," she said when she spotted the girl sitting by the fire. "I did not expect to see you. Is your sister all right?"

"She was last time I saw her," Pia said. "I left her with Solvig Madsen."

"The warehouse owner," Nadez said. "Where the pirate Tilde was captured." Interesting that Pia had chosen to leave her sister behind. Keeping Frida safe was the whole reason for sending the two of them south. She turned to Gustav. "Did you get it?"

"Yes," he said. "We got it." He picked a piece of paper up off the table and handed it to her.

"*I, Tavet Timonis,*" she read. "*Clan Freeholder of Swyford, and Freeholder of the Lavais shipyards, pledge and promise a ship to Captain Margit Ansdottir and her crew for assistance given now and in the future.*" She stared down at the signature on the paper. It looked real to her. She passed the paper to Kaja who studied it for a moment before handing it back.

"Is it his signature?" she asked Kaja.

"It's identical to what I've seen before," Kaja said. "So, it's either his or a very good forgery."

"All right," Nadez said. "I'll take this to Lauma." She smiled at Gustav. "Well done. I hope your trip along the road wasn't too difficult."

"We didn't come by road," Gustav said. "We sailed an iceboat from Nurmi." He glanced over at Pia. "And I wouldn't have been able to do any of this without Pia's help."

"I would have expected you to return to your sister after delivering the pirate to Lavais," she said to Pia.

"That's what I expected too," Pia replied with a shrug. "It turns out all that schooling and training has made me an Intelligencer after all."

"Has it?" She met Gustav's solemn gaze, and he nodded. "I can always use good Intelligencers." There was also the matter of Pia and Frida Engen being the rightful heirs to Henrik Ottosen's freeholdings. At some point she'd have to talk to Pia about that, but there always seemed to be other priorities.

"Good," Gustav said. "That's the real reason why we came here. The fire was just a bonus. I wasn't sure how you'd feel about Pia since . . ." he trailed off.

"Since I tried to assassinate Lauma Strauskas," Pia finished. "I know exactly what I did and why. And I would understand if no one can trust me." She looked down at her hands. "I probably wouldn't."

"You can be my assistant," Nadez said. "I need one, and since we're being honest, it will give me a chance to get to know you."

"And a chance for me to earn your trust," Pia said. "I accept. Not everyone will be happy that I'm here. What will you do about Clan Freeholder Ottosen?"

"Ignore him, I think." She got to her feet. "And if he presses the issue, I will make him regret it. Gustav can bring you to my office later. I need to get this to Lauma immediately." She waved the promise to pay note. "You both can report everything to Kaja. I'll either speak to you later about your mission or read Kaja's account."

"Thank you, Master Intelligencer," Pia said. "I won't let you down."

"You haven't yet," Nadez said. She nodded and headed back outside. Initially the cold air was welcome, but soon enough she was huddled into her coat against the wind.

Traveling the road at this time of year would be hard enough, she couldn't imagine being out on the ice in a small boat. She really did need to see about ice breaking in the harbour. Better yet, she'd ask Lauma. It was more a duty for the Grand Freeholder than for her anyway.

Lauma looked up from her desk when she knocked on her half open door.

"Nadez, come in. I'm not sure where Kaja is, if you're looking for her."

"I've just come from meeting with her," Nadez said. She sat down across from Lauma. "And Gustav. He's back in Tarklee, and he brought this." She handed the promise to pay note to Lauma and watched her face while she read it. Surprise and interest flitted across her face, and then she smiled in satisfaction.

"This is very good," Lauma said. "I will be able to make

Timonis behave with this."

"It's enough to imprison him, I thought," Nadez said. Did Lauma mean that she wasn't going to charge Timonis with treason?

"It's proof that he is working against the Alliance," Lauma replied. "Of course, it's enough to imprison him. And I will use it to do that if he doesn't comply with my orders."

Nadez didn't reply, but her expression must have given away her disagreement because Lauma sighed and shook her head at her.

"We are heading into a potential famine," Lauma said. "And I can't be certain that Tavet Timonis has not hidden a supply of food somewhere that we don't know about. If I imprison him, that food will not be found, and people will face a bigger threat of hunger than they already face."

"You think a threat will make him give up that food?"

"No," Lauma said. "But the right incentive might persuade him to at least feed his people."

"You're willing to let him get away with treason?" Nadez could see Lauma's reasoning, up to a point, but treason was too serious a transgression to be forgiven.

"There will be conditions," Lauma said. "I will strip him of some of his Freeholdings, including the shipyards, but yes, I am willing to ignore this attempt at treason in order to secure the wellbeing of thousands of people. Can I count on your support?"

Nadez met Lauma's eyes. There was nothing except determination there. But was it determination that a fellow Freeholder should not be held accountable? Was it related to her unwillingness to do anything about the murderous way Henrik Ottosen had inherited? Or was it determination to do whatever she could to ensure that Swyfordians had the best chance at surviving the winter.

She nodded. "You have my support." In the end, Lauma's true intentions didn't matter. What did matter was that this way would give more people a better chance of living until spring. Because she was certain that Lauma was right: Tavet Timonis almost certainly had extra stores of food that no one else knew about. And she was just as certain that once imprisoned, he would feel no obligation to tell anyone where it was. And because of that, people might starve.

"Good. I'll need some time to draft a letter to Timonis. Do you have someone who can deliver it? Gustav, perhaps?"

"He needs a day or so to rest," Nadez said, hating that she had to send him back out in the cold. And so much for finally having an assistant: there was no way she was letting Gustav travel alone in this weather. Pia would have to go with him.

CALDER WOULDN'T SAY he'd gotten used to the insects; it was more that trying to chase them away was such a fruitless endeavour that he'd given up. Now, unless they were in his eyes or nose, he did his best to ignore them.

He and Esma had spent a restless night in the dugout. Not wanting to drift into danger during the night, they'd tied up to a clump of bushes and had taken turns on watch.

He used his stick and pushed against what he'd thought was solid land, but the stick sunk in a foot and he had to fight to pull it back out, which dipped the boat dangerously low in the water.

"*Skit*," he said. "Why couldn't Luck let us find paddles?" They'd searched the area where they'd found the boat, but no paddles had been found. Instead, they'd had to cut the thickest and longest branches they could find and had been using them to push themselves along from hillock to hillock. But eventually they were going to be free of the swamp, and then the lack of paddles would make travelling in the dugout even more difficult.

"How long until we reach solid land?" he asked Esma, who was leaning out of the bow trying to push them away from a tangle of grass.

"At this pace?" Esma replied. "Not until afternoon. And even then, I'm not sure we can actually walk all the way to Zelesso."

"*Skit!*" she swore as the branch she was holding almost slipped out of her hand. She grabbed it and the boat swung towards the mound of grass.

Calder pushed at a clump of bushes, and the dugout headed into a stretch of unbroken water. The slow current of the river sent them towards the sea, and he dug his branch into the soft dirt under the boat and tried to steer them to the closest mound of bushes.

Esma leaned out again, trying to reach a clump of earth under some bushes with her branch. This time it stuck in the muck, and instead of letting go, she hung on to it and slid out of the boat.

"I got you," Calder said. He reached out a hand and grabbed hers. The current was still dragging the boat out to sea and it pulled at them. The side of the boat dipped dangerously close to the water, and then he had both hands on Esma's arm.

"*Skit!*" This time her curse was almost a scream. He pulled her closer and helped her into the boat.

"Something bit me!" she said, holding out her arm. Blood trickled from two small puncture wounds in the flesh of her forearm. "Get a knife!"

He pulled out his knife while she huddled in the bottom of the boat.

"Tie something around my arm," she told him. "Skit, skit, *skit!* My arm is tingling. I think whatever bit me is poisonous."

They'd taken the trap apart and had used the rope from it to tie the boat to a bush at night. He tied that around her forearm as tight as he dared.

"Now cut out the bite marks," Esma said. "Hurry!"

Calder braced himself against her side and swiftly cut a wedge of flesh from her arm. Esma screamed once and then quieted.

He'd heard of this way to deal with a poisonous bite, but he'd never seen it done, let alone done it himself. "Now what do I do?"

"Stay back," Esma said. "If you do it wrong, we'll both be poisoned." She leaned over her arm for a moment and then sat up and spat blood over the side of the boat. After sucking at her wound half a dozen times, she wiped the blood off her lips with the back of her good hand.

"I think that's all I can do," she said. "You'll need to do your best to get me to Zelesso and a healer." She wrapped the hem of her shirt around her forearm and slumped in the bottom of the boat.

And for the first time since they'd left the *Vassan*, Calder was terrified. His sister was pale and shaking, and he was afraid that she was dying.

He looked around to see that the current had pushed them almost out of the marsh. He could see the clear water of the Sapphire Sea ahead. He took his branch and tried to steer towards the open water.

There was no way he would be able to carry Esma through the marsh and swamp or even along a beach for very long. The only way he would get her to Zelesso and help, would be in this little boat.

As soon as the water looked clear enough to be safe, he tied the rope around his waist and slipped over the side of the boat into the water. With the boat containing his sister trailing behind, he started swimming.

DAG ROLLED HER shoulders to try to relieve the itch between her shoulder blades. A while ago, her Trait had activated. She stared out at the sea: something must be out there, but she couldn't see anything. Neither could anyone else on board: not with a spyglass nor from the highest point up in the rigging.

"Sorry I can't be any more definite," she said to Darya, who was standing beside her at the starboard gunwale.

Darya lowered the spyglass and turned to her. "I've been around you and Calder long enough to know that what Traits do and how they work doesn't matter as much as the fact that they *do* work. I just want to make sure that whatever is out there doesn't see us before we see them."

"It's probably the pirates," Dag said even though her Trait didn't react when she said that. "We know they're in the Sapphire Sea, and it makes sense to stay away from them." She paused. "It could also be that my Trait is warning us away from Zelesso."

"Say the word and we can head north to Messanos," Darya said and turned to her.

"No, we need to take the two boys home." She sighed. "And I don't think Zelesso is the problem. It's not triggering my Trait."

"We'll be at the marsh at the mouth of the Valtanum River soon," Darya said. "We'll head south along the coast from there." She looked up at the late day sky. "And reach Zelesso before the sun goes down."

"Thank you," Dag said. Darya nodded and headed back to the bridge where Rafael was at the wheel.

An hour later, the ship slowly turned towards shore. A huge marsh stretched along the shoreline. Sailors scrambled in the rigging above her head, shortening sails as the ship finished its change of course to go south.

A few seagulls screeched above, and she watched for a while before making her way to the bow.

She'd been looking seaward, away from shore, when the itch between her shoulders twitched back to life. Was something out there? She stared, trying to make out any sails on the horizon, but she didn't see a thing. She glanced behind her, wondering if she should say something to Darya. The itch intensified when she faced starboard. She hurried over to the gunwale and looked out.

Was that? Yes, there was something in the water.

"Darya," she called as she ran back to the bridge. "Captain. I saw something."

"A sail?" Darya asked. She put the spyglass to her eye and looked out to port.

"No, something in the water between us and the shore."

"*Jebris*," Darya said. "Someone is swimming, and they're trailing a boat of some kind behind them." She turned to her. "We'll get a dinghy in the water right away." She called out orders as she hurried away, and Dag stood at the gunwale, staring as they got closer to the boat and the swimmer.

A moment later, the swimmer stopped and lifted their head, and after a confused moment, they waved.

Dag's heart clenched. It was Calder. She didn't know why or how, but Calder was swimming, far from any ship or village or city, towing a boat. And now that they were closer, she could see someone lying in the bottom of the boat. It was a woman, and she didn't wave or sit up or even move. Before the dark hair registered, Dag's heart clenched again, thinking that it was Inger and that her sister was dead.

But it wasn't *her* sister, it was *Calder's*. As the ship closed in on Calder and the little boat he towed, she saw how still Esma was. A dinghy had been launched, and soon a weary Calder was helped into it.

She hurried to the stern and was staring down when the dinghy arrived.

"Dag," Calder called up to her. "Thank *Jebris*. Esma's been bitten by something poisonous. Is there anything on board that might help?" he sent a worried look towards his sister who was being lifted out of the boat and handed towards the rope ladder. "I'm not sure she'll make it to Zelesso."

"Yes!" she called. "There is. Wait on deck and I'll set it up." She ran across the ship and went below and knocked on the door to the cabin the triplets were staying in.

"Adjoa!" she called "Adjoa, I need your help. I need your Trait on deck right now."

The girl opened the door. "My brothers and I will come," she said.

"No," Dag put her hand on the door when the girl would have opened it wider. "Just you. They limit your Trait, and right now we need it full strength."

"But the danger," the girl whispered.

Dag nodded and pounded on every door in the hallway. "Everyone out," she said. "Go to the mess and stay there until I say it's safe to return."

The two sets of twins exited their room and headed along the corridor, and a few sailors grumbled and followed them.

"What is this?"

The sailor staring at her rubbed sleep from his eyes.

"You need to get to the mess," Dag said. "It won't be safe here for a while."

"I'm off duty," he said. "And I need my sleep." He turned to go back into his cabin.

"Adjoa," Dag called, watching the sailor. "Will you be able to Heal this sailor if your brother's Traits make him ill?"

"Probably," Adjoa called from the open door to her cabin. "As long as he doesn't die first."

The sailor had turned back to her with a startled look on his face.

"Your choice," she said to him. "Either get out now or stay inside and away from the door."

The sailor looked past her shoulder. "Knew there was something odd about those children." He stepped out of the cabin, closed the door, and headed along the passageway.

"Come on," Dag called out to Adjoa. "Tell your brothers to stay inside until you return."

By the time Dag arrived on deck with Adjoa in tow, Esma had been laid out and Calder was kneeling at her side, shaking her.

"ESMA, WAKE UP." Calder stared down at her. She was cold under his hand, but he thought she was still breathing. But for how long?

"Oh."

He looked up to see a girl of about twelve staring at Esma with a serious look on her face. Dag hovered behind her.

"Adjoa is a triplet with a Healing Trait," Dag said, and he

almost wept in relief.

"Snake bite," Adjoa said in Arressan. She knelt down beside Esma and peeled away the fabric that covered Esma's wound. "I have seen many of these in Wekesa."

Calder sucked in a breath at the angry looking wound. The skin around the cuts he'd made was turning black, and dark purple was spreading to the surrounding tissue.

The girl placed a hand on the wound, and Esma flinched and cried out, although she didn't wake up.

"Can she be saved?" Dag asked, sliding to the deck beside him. She gripped his arm as they both stared at the girl.

"She'll have a scar," the girl said. "But I am a very powerful Healer, and you did all of the right things to help her. See?" She lifted her hand, and Calder thought the wound looked less dark and angry.

A crowd had gathered around them, and Calder looked up and met Darya's concerned gaze. He nodded at her, and when she nodded back, more of his worry and fear subsided.

He'd done his best for Esma. And it looked as though, against all the odds, it would be enough.

It seemed like more than just Luck had brought them here, on board the *Atlaine*, surrounded by people he trusted. With Dag and a girl child with the exact Trait Esma needed.

Dag's hand found its way into his, and he squeezed it, not able to look her in the eye just yet. But even if Esma didn't survive, he would know that it wasn't because Luck had let him down.

"She can be moved now," the girl said.

She pulled her hands away, and the wound Calder looked at was just a wound. There was no black tissue, no purple skin.

"I need to get back to my brothers," the girl said. "Dagrun?"

"Yes, thank you Adjoa." Dag rose when the girl did. "I'll come with you and make sure no one has taken ill." She turned to him. "Have them take Esma to the captain's cabin. I'll join you when I can."

He watched her walk away before returning his attention to his sister.

"We'll get her settled, Sir," Darya said. "I'll have Cook get her some broth and tea."

"Thank you." Now that the crisis was over, his exhaustion settled over him, and he slumped down on the deck.

"I'll have Cook send a meal for you too," Darya said. She leaned over him and helped him to his feet. "Dagrun will join you as soon as she can. Adjoa is a powerful Healer, but she's a triplet, and both her brothers have the opposite Trait. Before she brought them on board, Dagrun warned that separating the girl from her brothers was extremely dangerous."

"Oh." He wasn't too tired to understand the threat two children with the opposite Trait to Healing could be. "I can make it to the cabin," he said. "We're not putting you out?"

"Dagrun's been using the captain's cabin with my permission," Darya said. "We knew we were coming back for you."

"Thank you."

"We are heading for Zelesso," Darya said. "Unless you request a different destination?"

"No, Zelesso is exactly where I need to be." He patted his pocket and was relieved to feel the outline of the token still there. "Thank you again, Darya, for everything."

She nodded, and he made his way across the deck and down the stairs. The door to his cabin was open, and he entered to find Esma laid out on the bed in the sleeping quarters.

Her face was relaxed, and her breathing seemed steady. He sat down on the side of the bed and blew out a breath.

"You scared me, sister," he said out loud. "I didn't think we had a chance."

She turned her head and opened her eyes. "Can't lie," she whispered. "I'm surprised to be alive. Where are we?"

"We're on the *Atlaine*," he said. "With Dag. And a child with a Trait who Healed you." He smiled. "I still have the token and," he paused. "We're on our way to Zelesso."

Her laugh ended in a coughing fit, but she grinned at him. "You and your gods-given Luck. Perhaps I should almost die more often."

"No." He couldn't laugh at that because she almost *had* died. "Don't ever do that again. Besides, I need your help with Father. Now that we have his token, he'll have to stop chasing Charis." And Dag would be able to find her sister. After almost losing his, he would do everything in his power to reunite Dag with hers.

Chapter 15

Pia stamped her feet, flattening the snow beneath them as she shaded her eyes against the sun's reflection off the snow.

"Almost ready," Gustav said. He grabbed his pack from the back of the wagon, waved to the lad who had brought them here, and joined her at the edge of the city. The road south was under the snow somewhere, they just couldn't see it.

"Are you sure you're all right taking the road?" Between the road and the iceboat, her choice had been the road. And it wasn't because she didn't know how to sail and had felt almost useless on the trip to Tarklee, although she had.

No. She'd asked Kaja to recite every single thing she knew about travel during winter and then she'd Concentrated. The road was the safest route to take.

"Don't you trust your Trait?" he asked.

"I do, but I'm asking you to trust it." She shifted her pack so that it was centred on her back. Not only did they both have warm clothing and boots, they each had a supply of food and a simple shelter. If they were lost or separated during bad weather, each of them could settle in and stay safe for a few days.

"Come on," Gustav said. "It's clear now, and we should take advantage of that." He set off south, and she hurried to catch up to him.

"You have all the letters?" Pia asked. Nadez hadn't exactly kept her instructions a secret, but she'd directed all of her comments to Gustav. "I need to know the plan too."

"Sure." He patted a pack that was tied around his waist. "There's a message to Tavet Timonis telling him that Lauma won't charge him with treason if he complies with her demands."

"That one I know. He has to give management of the shipyards over to Berna," Pia said. "Until the spring, probably, when the Swyfordian Clan Freeholders can meet and hold a vote. There's a note for Berna telling her that, but I saw more letters than those two. What about the others?"

"Notices to the other Swyfordian Clan Freeholders," he said. "Clan Freeholder Skala is in Tarklee, but we need to deliver notes to Kozlow and Nowack."

She'd spent some time studying the map she had in her pack. "We'll need another ice boat to get to Setberg," she said.

"Yes." Gustav didn't look very happy, and she laughed.

"Is your da going to hold you responsible for the loss of the one we left in Tarklee?" she asked.

"Probably."

"Can't you use your Trait on him?"

"I wouldn't do that to my da," Gustav replied. "Would you like me to use it on you to get you to go along with what I wanted?"

"No, but it wouldn't work anyway," she said. "I'd be able to Concentrate and see past your Charisma. Oh, you've already tried it on your da and it didn't work."

Gustav frowned at her. "It did work," he said. "But when Ma found out she was furious. And my Trait *didn't* work on her."

"You tried using Charisma on her while she was angry that you'd used it on your da?" Pia shook her head. "That wasn't very smart."

"I know." He grinned. "But I never did that again. So no, I can't use my Trait to get my da to give me another ice boat."

"We'll have Berna find us one," Pia said. "We're on official Treaty Alliance business." She had a brand new patch to prove it. It was tucked away in her trouser pocket. She'd had a patch before, every student was given one, but this was different. Not only was it *not* a student patch, but accepting it had been her choice.

And that, it being her choice, had made a much bigger difference to her than even she'd thought it would, and she'd spent years hoping and planning and waiting for the day when she could choose.

It was still a surprise to her that she'd chosen to be an Intelligencer.

They walked in silence until they passed the last farm along the road leading south. Forest lay ahead, and the sun was starting to sink below the trees.

"We won't make it to Pavil Barda's for hours," she said to Gustav. "Do you want to keep going or find a place to stop for the night?"

"I'm not sure I can put up the shelter in the dark," Gustav replied. "Will you be able to?"

She Concentrated on remembering the instructions and the demonstration they'd been given. It seemed simple enough, but that had been inside where it was warm and there was no wind to contend with. Finally, she nodded.

"With both of us working on it, yes," she said.

"Then let's keep going while the sky is clear," Gustav said.

It was clear and cold, but her new coat and boots kept her warm enough. The sun set, and a half moon rose, giving them more than enough light to see by. The road was very clearly defined by the trees on either side.

A gust of wind blew in from the sea, and she grabbed Gustav's arm to make him stop. She pulled her scarf from her face and stared out across the frozen water and Concentrated.

"How much farther?" she asked Gustav. "I think a storm is building."

"A few hours," he replied. He stared out at the Pale Sea. "Will it be a bad one?"

"I don't know enough about storms to be able to predict how bad it will be." Another thing she should learn about. Her Trait meant that she noticed details and could piece them together to see patterns, but she had to know what to look for, what might be significant, before the pattern was apparent. She Concentrated on the sky again. Clouds were starting to roll in, but the wind was still relatively gentle. "I think we have a few hours."

They turned back to the road, this time moving faster. An hour later, the wind picked up and gusted through the trees, dropping clumps of snow on them. An hour after that the snow started, gently at first, but soon it was so thick that Pia grabbed Gustav's belt just to make sure they didn't get separated.

Gustav slipped, and she pulled at him, keeping him upright. He lost his balance and scrambled backwards and then stumbled and fell on top of her, sending them both sprawling to the ground.

"Sorry," he said, rolling off her and sitting up. "You saved me from going over a cliff. I didn't see it."

Carefully, she stood up and peered past him. Somehow, he'd stepped off the road. His last footprint had left a long skid mark in the snow that led to a drop. Beyond that was the icy sea.

"I'll lead," she said. She fumbled with the strap on her pack and finally handed one end to Gustav. Then she Concentrated on the path ahead.

Like always when she used her Trait, a shiver that had nothing to do with the cold travelled down her spine. And then everything else was blocked out. The snow, the wind, the cold, even the feel of Gustav tugging on her pack, it all went away until there was nothing other than the road through the trees.

She had no idea how long it took, but she was shaken out of her Concentration to find herself standing in front of the door to Pavil's house.

"You did it," Gustav said. "Come on, let's wake up Pavil." He trudged up to the door and started pounding on it.

Pia followed more slowly, her joints stiff with cold. By the time she joined him the glow of a lamp came through the window. The door opened, and Pavil Barda stared out at them.

"Come in," he said. "And get out of this storm. Been expecting it to hit all day and here it is."

She huddled inside with Gustav while Pavil got the door closed, shutting out the howling sound of the wind.

"Gustav, that you?" he shook his head before heading down the hall. "I'll get the fire built up. Get out of your coats and come get warm."

Pia shrugged out of her coat and hung it on a peg and slipped off her boots. With her pack in hand, she followed Gustav to the kitchen.

"We appreciate your hospitality," Gustav said.

"You're welcome, you know that," Pavil said. "And you have Pia with you. It's no time to be outside day or night. Intelligencer business, I assume." He put a pot on the stove and turned back to them. "Tea will be ready soon."

"Thank you," Pia said. She crept closer to the stove and

reached her hands out to the warmth. "We'll just warm up and get a few hours sleep and then be on our way."

"I can't make you stay," Pavil said. "But this storm will not be gone in a few hours. Days more like." He grinned. "And it might be bad for you, but I can't say I won't enjoy some company. Winter's set in early this year, and there's hardly been any travellers on the road."

"We won't leave until it's safe," Gustav said. "So, we really appreciate this."

"Tell me that when you've had nothing but salt fish for a few meals," Pavil said. "Although it's passable thanks to another Intelligencer. Did I tell you about the time Calder and Dagrun stayed with me? Has some good ideas about cooking, that Calder does. Oh, water's boiled for tea."

While Pavil set about getting the tea ready, Pia sent a questioning look at Gustav. She didn't know much about Intelligencers besides the ones she'd met: Gustav, Kaja, and the Breck twins. It would be good to hear about others. And if they were stuck here for days, she'd ask Pavil how he knew the storm was coming. And if he was right about how long it lasted, how he knew that. As someone who never gave much thought to the weather, she was realising that knowing what was coming could be the difference between life and death.

"Here's the tea." Pavil set the pot on the table and grabbed three mugs from a cupboard. "Sit down, come on."

Gustav sat and Pia pulled up a chair.

"I'd like to hear about Calder and Dagrun," Gustav said. It was in response to Pavil's earlier comment, but he was looking right at her when he said it. He nodded. "And it's good to be in the company of such a true friend of Intelligencers."

"Well, I didn't know they were Intelligencers when I picked them up," Pavil said. "In Nurmi, it was, right after the warehouses and docks were burned."

Pia took a sip of tea as she listened. It wasn't just the tea and the fire that warmed her. Gustav was allowing Pavil to talk about Intelligencers. These were people that she knew had been working against the threats to the Alliance for months. There had always been so much secrecy around Intelligencers: they didn't even know each other. But Gustav trusted her. All she could do in return was do her best to be worthy of that trust.

Chapter 16

DAG STOOD IN the doorway. Calder had climbed into the bed and was now fast asleep beside his sister.

"I hear I have you to thank for being alive," Esma said. She carefully slipped off the bed.

Dag stepped out of the room, and Esma joined her, sitting down heavily at the table.

"I think it was Luck," Dag replied. "Along with determination. Both yours and his."

"Calder's determination, yes," Esma agreed. "I assume he told you about our business in Zelesso and that's why we're heading there."

"We're less than an hour out," Dag replied. "But Zelesso was already our destination. Darya told me that Calder said that he was fine going there." She sighed. "I haven't had a chance to talk to him. I didn't want to wake him up, and I was dealing with a few minor issues." Baako and Chike had stayed in their cabin, but a sailor crossing the deck above them had collapsed. Once she'd reunited Adjoa with her brothers, Dag had the sailor taken to their cabin to be Healed.

According to Adjoa, he would recover. She'd placed her hands on his chest before prescribing a tincture of herbs. The sailor had been awake and alert when Dag had left him in his hammock in the hold.

"Zelesso is where our father is," Esma said. "When we return his token to him, he will stop searching for Charis and your sister."

"Thank you." Dag heaved a sigh of relief. Inger was safe. "You have no idea how grateful I am to you."

"I do."

She looked up to see Calder standing in the doorway to the sleeping quarters.

"After almost losing Esma, I believe I know how relieved you are." He stepped into the room, and she walked into his arms.

She stood for a moment, wrapped in his warmth, just breathing in his scent. She leaned back, and he kissed her lightly before stepping away.

He sat down, and she returned to her chair.

"I was just telling Dagrun about our agreement with Father," Esma said.

Calder frowned. "We shouldn't have had to make that deal, he should have just done as we asked, because he is our father. I want Saba to know that he almost cost you your life."

"That would mean telling her what he is," Esma said. "Saba is my mother," she said to Dag. "We cannot break the agreement, not when we can fulfil our part of it."

"You're right," Calder said. "And I have a promise to fulfil." He looked at Dag with a serious expression. "The token was being held by the suicide assassins. They let me take it when I promised to let them name a replacement target."

"A replacement target?" Dag repeated. "For assassination? Who?" Her Trait triggered, and she rolled her shoulders.

"Henrik Ottosen," Calder replied, and Dag nodded.

"Because he was the one who sent the suicide assassin to kill your mother," she said. "And I suppose that how he contracted the assassin was not appreciated." The itch subsided but didn't completely disappear. "At least that's part of it. Do you need to tell Rahm? Of course you do. You can't break a promise to a suicide assassin." Though there was some justice in the Resolute avenging an attempt on his first wife's life, she didn't like that it was Calder who was giving Rahm a new target.

"I wouldn't anyway," Calder said. "I think Ottosen truly wronged them. But we don't need to help Rahm, either." He tilted his head as though he heard something. "I think we just sighted Zelesso."

"I'll meet you on deck," Dag said. "I'll be taking a set of twins with Traits to their home here in Zelesso. Darya will take the other pair to a friend of hers who can help find them a new home."

"There are more children on board than Adjoa and her brothers?" Calder asked. "Never mind. Esma and I need to find Rahm. You can tell me all about that later."

"I will." Dag nodded and left.

She knocked on the door of the cabin the triplets were in.

"It's time to say goodbye to the others," she said in Arressan when Adjoa opened the door. "They are all leaving this ship now."

"We are happy they are going home," Adjoa said. "But I will miss them."

"I'm sure they'll miss you too." No doubt the seven of them helped each other get through the frightening months of being locked up together. Dag knocked on a door farther down the hall. "It's time to leave, boys and girls."

"Finally," Pavlos said. "Stavlos said we were here. I just want to go home."

Anahita and Minoo stood in the open door to their cabin, and he waved at them. He spoke a few words in Yedrissian, and Anahita waved while Minoo buried her head against her sister's shoulder.

"Pavlos," Adjoa called. "Stavlos!" The two boys entered the other room for a moment before returning to the hallway.

"Let's go," Stavlos said. "I can tell you exactly how to get to our house."

Dag led the way up to the deck. Calder and Esma were already there.

"Pavlos and Stavlos, Anahita and Minoo," Dag said. "Meet Calder and Esma."

"Are you twins?" Pavlos asked.

"They're not twins," Anahita said before the adults could answer. "But they are brother and sister."

"We are," Calder replied. He looked from the boys to the girls. "I hear that you are all going to stay in Zelesso."

"Yes, and I'm grateful to Dagrun Lund and Captain Demer," Stavlos said. "For returning us to our parents after we were stolen."

"Our mother is going to be very happy to see us," Pavlos said.

"Father too," Stavlos added. "Although he might try to hide it."

"No, he won't," Pavlos replied.

"And my friend will be very excited to meet Minoo and Anahita," Darya said as she joined them. She placed a hand on each girl's shoulder. Minoo leaned into her, and Anahita looked up and grinned.

"Come on," Dag said. "The dinghy's ready." She met Calder's raised brow as the boys argued over who was going to get into the dinghy first. The girls patiently waited their turn before climbing down after them.

"Have they been like this the whole trip?" Calder asked.

"No. They were all pretty subdued at first. Until we were through the Teeth, I don't think the boys really believed they were going home." She grinned. "Since then, those two have reminded me of me and Inger."

"You'll be able to argue with her soon," Calder said.

"I hope so," she replied. "Thanks to you and Esma." Once in the dinghy and sitting between the two boys, she looked out at the town of Zelesso. As soon as both she and Calder completed their respective tasks, the *Atlaine* would be on its way. But not to find Inger, not yet. Now that she knew her sister and Charis were safe from Rahm, she needed to deliver the triplets into the hands of their aunt. She really hoped she *did* want them.

CALDER WAS ABOUT to knock when Esma brushed past him and opened the door.

"Mother," she called as she entered. "Father, we're back."

"Did you get it?" Kasim asked, coming from the kitchen.

"Get what?" Calder asked. Unless Rahm had told him, his half-brother didn't know their father was a Resolute. Or that they'd gone to retrieve his token.

"Whatever it is that father needs in order to not be so anxious," Kasim said. "Honestly, I thought he was going to leave even though he promised to stay another four days."

"Esma, are you well?" Saba asked. She put her hands on Esma's shoulders and frowned. "You look very pale. Come, I'll make tea." She shepherded her daughter towards the kitchen, and Calder followed.

"Is Rahm here?" he asked.

"I am."

He turned to see his father come through the front door. He came close and leaned in. "I don't even have to ask if you have it." He sighed and smiled. "I could feel it as soon as the ship entered the harbour. Not the *Vassan*, though. Did the pirates strand you?"

"They were captured by Pinho," Calder said. "Esma and I were forced to jump ship." He glanced over at Saba, who was fussing over Esma. He drew Rahm away from the kitchen and into the sitting room.

"Esma almost died because you couldn't agree to a simple request from your own children," he said. "I've half a mind to destroy your token and see what happens to you then."

"You can't destroy it," Rahm said bitterly. "Do you think I haven't tried? It can only be destroyed when I'm dead." He closed his eyes. "The last thing I want is for any harm to come to my children. Now that you have the token, you can change my target. Now that Pinho is free, it would give me pleasure to fulfil that original contract. Or perhaps Councilwoman Floros? She is the one who sent me after Charis Diakos."

Calder stared at his father for a moment. "You're certain the token can't be destroyed? What have you tried?"

"I've tried putting it in a fire, pouring acid on it, hammering it," Rahm said. "Better to ask what I haven't tried."

"All right, I will," Calder replied. "Have you tried someone with an Unmaking Trait?"

Rahm stepped back. "There is such a person? I would offer a fortune to them if they could Unmake it."

"Bring your token to the Pale Sea," Calder said. "And we'll see if a Trait can do what nothing else can. But do not blame the Unmaker if it can't be Unmade." He didn't want Jarri Breck to have to deal with a disappointed Rahm if it couldn't be done.

"If it can't be Unmade, then it can't be destroyed," Rahm said. "Which is what I already fear; although, I am eager to try this next time I visit the Three," Rahm said. "But I need to complete your task first."

"My task will take you there," Calder replied. "Although Dag and I both agree that we don't have to transport you. You didn't ask where I found your token." He paused. "Or how I retrieved it from them."

"Does it matter? You have it and will give it to me."

"It does matter. As you said, the suicide assassins were the ones who stole it from you," he said. "And they were keeping it safe for Floros."

"You robbed them? They will never let you or Esma live." Rahm was more than worried, he looked frightened. "That is my task, is it? It must be, you need to send me after them, all of them, if you and Esma are ever to be safe again."

"I didn't steal it," Calder said. "Not exactly. And Esma and I are not in danger from them, although it's reassuring to know that you care. After all, you would have killed me to get to Charis."

"I told you, the token compels me," Rahm ran a hand through his hair. "I would have had no choice. So, they just *gave* it to you?"

"Of course not," Calder said. "When I told the woman in charge that I was your son, she recognized that killing me might make you angry enough to avenge me. Instead, I made a bargain. If she let me take the token, the new target would be her choice. She seemed to like that trade."

Rahm laughed and clapped a hand on his shoulder. "You offered her the one thing everyone who is trained as a weapon wants. The chance to pick your own target. Tell me, who did she pick?"

Calder dug the token from his pocket and held it out to his father, whose eyes fixed on the coin. "Nordmere Clan Freeholder Henrik Ottosen."

Rahm nodded and plucked the token from his hand. "I'm not surprised," he said. "I heard recently, from someone who would know, that Ottosen insisted on collecting on an outstanding obligation despite being told many times that there were no weapons ready. So, a weapon was lost without the task being completed. I know that Lauma is alive because of that, and I am grateful, but to an assassin, that is the most unforgivable outcome." He pocketed the token. "Once I have completed this task," he said, "we will see if the curse of my existence can be Unmade."

CHAPTER 17

RAFAEL LED THE way down a narrow lane. The homes here were stacked on top of each other with stairs leading up to walkways that stretched along the upper floors. Laundry had been strung across the lane every few feet. They turned a corner, and Stavlos bolted from her side with Pavlos right behind him.

"Mama, Mama," Stavlos shouted up at a woman who was on the second floor hanging wash. She cried out and dropped her basket and rushed down the stairs to envelope the two boys.

They spoke too fast for Dag to catch more than a few words, but from what she could see, the twins had been missed and this was a happy reunion. Pavlos pointed at her and Rafael, and the woman stood up and headed towards them.

"Thank you," she said. "For returning my boys." Tears streaked her cheeks as she hugged them to her. "Our neighbour said they were taken by a man with pale skin, like you, but we never saw that man or the boys after that." She wiped away tears. "Thank you. Can I offer you something to eat or drink? We don't have much, but whatever we have is yours."

"I'm glad that Pavlos and Stavlos are safe and at home," Dag said. "Thank you for your offer, but we have other children to reunite with their family. I'm sure you understand that we can't delay that more than necessary."

"Of course. But if you ever need anything from me or my family, just ask."

"Where's Papa?" Pavlos asked. "I want to see Papa!"

Stavlos left his mother's side and hugged Dag. "Thank you."

"You're welcome," she said.

Their mother smiled again as she turned to head back up the stairs, the two boys clinging to her.

"That went well," Dag said to Rafael. "Let's hope Darya has luck placing the two girls and that the triplets also have a happy reunion."

"You don't think they will?" Rafael asked. "Adjoa seems certain."

"Adjoa is not the one everyone is afraid of," Dag replied. She sighed. "Let's find something to eat before we return to the dinghy. Darya didn't think she would be long, but I suspect Calder and Esma will be a while."

NADEZ STARED OUT across the harbour. She'd tasked Sture to do his best to keep the ice from forming, but it looked like a losing battle. There was a narrow path close to shore that he assured her was deep enough for the *Atlaine* or the *Tazeyar*, if either were to arrive, but then the challenge would be to keep the ice from crushing the ships before spring.

Even so, she was hoping the *Tazeyar* returned. Surely it would fare worse if it was forced to stay in the north? The loss of a single ship, even with new ones being built, could put the entire region in jeopardy again next winter. She'd send ships further south if she didn't have to worry about Timonis and the pirates.

"I can get a few more fishing boats out," Sture said when he joined her. "But they aren't double hulled like the two we have there now."

"Do it," she said. "Maybe they can fish while they're out there. Or they can tell us if the ice is thick enough to ice fish."

"I'll organize the fishing either off the boats or once the ice is safe," Sture said. "Ice fishing isn't something we do much around here, so I'll need to hunt down experienced people and equipment."

"Lauma knows how to ice fish, so check with her. And can we have crews work those two reinforced boats day and night?" She'd learned more than she wanted to know about boats with hulls thick enough to survive ice. The most important lesson was that they didn't have enough of them in Tarklee Harbour.

"Aye, already being done," Sture said.

"Thank you, Sture," Nadez said. "I know this is not something you would usually do, but your efforts are appreciated. And important."

"Same for you," Sture said. "I'll let you and the Interim Grand Freeholder know if we have more trouble."

"Good." Nadez nodded and turned and left. Sture was correct in that this wasn't really her task, but she and Lauma were both doing whatever was needed to get through the crisis.

Lauma had her hands full making sure the food distribution was being managed fairly and efficiently. And that no one—including any Clan Freeholders—was hoarding food.

She shook her head. Even though keeping the harbour clear of ice seemed impossible, she thought Lauma's task was the more difficult one.

She didn't even make it to her office before Kaja tracked her down with a request from Lauma for her help.

She followed the Intelligencer student through the halls to Lauma's office and sighed in relief. If she'd been taken to a warehouse, she would have worried that something had gone wrong with the food distribution. Problems could mean chaos or worse when they still had weeks to go until midwinter.

"Is something wrong?" she asked as she entered the office.

Lauma looked up from her desk and gestured for Nadez to take a chair. Kaja sat down as well.

"Not more than usual," Lauma said. She put down the papers she was reading. "I've been looking through the records to see if the past can help me predict the future. Namely, is this really going to be a bad winter in Tarklee?" She sighed. "This weather is normal for Cutterstown. By this time of year, only iceboats can access Cutterstown, and the seasonal business of logging has long been shut down. But here?" She waved a hand at the window that overlooked the harbour. "The harbour does freeze over some years, but I've searched the records for the last thirty years, and it's never frozen over this early."

"That's what I'm hearing from the fishermen," Nadez replied. "I fear we may lose the *Tazeyar*; that we may have already lost it, and that will mean food shortages well into spring and even beyond."

"And worse if the *Atlaine* returns," Lauma said. "I hope Dag meant it when she warned us that she thought they would need to stay in the Sapphire Sea."

"I do too," Nadez said. "Have you made a decision, or do you want my advice on something?"

"Both," Lauma said. "If we assume the worst and that the *Tazeyar* is lost over the winter, then we need to cut rations in the food halls."

"Making people nervous and worried," Nadez said. "We need to stop them from panicking."

"Yes." Lauma frowned. "But how to tell a mother that her children must go to bed hungry and that the best-case scenario is that they will live with hunger for many more months?"

"Sture is looking for people who know how to ice fish," she said. "We are doing everything we can."

"But will it be enough?"

A bell rang out from the harbour, and expecting the worst, a fire, Nadez hurried over to the window.

A ship was just entering the harbour. It was too far away for Nadez to see if it was the *Tazeyar* back from up north or the *Atlaine* home from the Sapphire Sea.

"Let's go greet them," Lauma said.

"Yes." Nadez followed her out of the office. She wasn't sure which ship she hoped was here, or which would help them the most.

Chapter 18

GUSTAV BRUSHED SNOW off his hat as he stared at the house. Clan Freeholder Timonis' house.

Someone had been out near the road recently; a single set of footprints led along the fence, but he hadn't seen anyone.

He edged back under the trees and joined Pia. She was leaning against a tree trunk and staring at the house, Concentrating.

She was getting really good at using her Trait, and he had to admit to being a little bit jealous. When they'd needed to know when it was safe to leave Pavil Barda's house, she'd used her Trait to figure it out. When Pavil had harnessed his horse to a sleigh, she'd Concentrated to make sure they stayed on the road.

Now she was using her Trait to see what or who Gustav might be dealing with at Timonis' freeholding.

The last thing he wanted to do was run across the pirates; not after he'd stolen the promise to pay note from them. They knew what he looked like, but sending Pia to bargain and maybe even threaten Timonis wasn't much of an option. Timonis knew he represented both Lauma Strauskas and Nadez Norup and still treated him with contempt. He had no reason to believe the Clan Freeholder would treat Pia and her message any better.

"No pirates," Pia said. "And just the one guard doing rounds. There are only three fires lit in the house, so I think it's just the family. He has a wife and children, right?"

"Yes." He squared his shoulders. "There will be a housekeeper, but what other staff?"

"Ottosen always had someone to look after the children along with his personal assistant," Pia replied. "When he was in town, he had a couple of guards, but when he was in his freeholding, he counted on the groundskeepers to help keep unwanted visitors away."

"I haven't seen a groundskeeper today," Gustav said. "All right, if I'm not back in an hour, head to Lavais and let Berna know what happened."

"No. I'll come get you," Pia replied.

"You'll leave me here and go and tell Berna." They'd been arguing about this for hours, and she still wouldn't promise to follow his directions. "The Alliance can't afford to lose both of us and not have this task completed," he said for what he hoped was the last time. "Timonis won't hurt me." He hoped he wouldn't, but if Timonis did hurt him, well, that was the risk he took as an Intelligencer.

Pia didn't reply, but her chin went up, and he shook his head. He'd just have to make sure that he was successful.

"One hour," he said and headed out from under the trees and onto the road.

It was a long way from the gate to the house. The window coverings to the left of the door twitched when he reached the halfway point. Three steps led up to the porch. He stopped on the top step, pulled off his mitten, and held up his patch.

"Intelligencer Gustav Gunnarson here to see Clan Freeholder Tavet Timonis," he called out, trying to infuse his words with Charisma. "I have official correspondence from Interim Grand Freeholder Lauma Strauskas."

The door opened, and Tavet Timonis glared at him.

"I know who you are," he said. "What does she want this time?"

Gustav held out the sealed letter and waited while Timonis grabbed it, ripped the seal off it, and scanned the contents. The Clan Freeholder's frown deepened.

"She's threatening me again," he said and took a step towards Gustav. "With something you stole. And don't tell me it wasn't you. I have eyewitness accounts."

"Do you?" Gustav asked. "And these are citizens of the Alliance countries who can testify against me?" They both knew his eyewitness accounts were proof that he was working with the pirates and that Lauma's accusations were true.

Timonis took another step out, and Gustav backed down the stairs.

"What would happen if you weren't able to send Lauma Strauskas my answer?" Timonis asked. "After all, the weather makes travelling treacherous this time of year."

"Berna Strauskas is already being advised of her mother's decision," Gustav lied. "And when to expect me. If I don't arrive on time, she will visit you herself."

"I'll deal with the child when she arrives," he said. "If she arrives." He looked over Gustav's head and smiled. "There you are. Take this arrogant boy into custody."

Gustav turned to see a man in a heavy coat walking towards him, and without a second thought, he started running towards the side of the house.

He turned the corner and saw Pia crouching in the snow beside a woodpile. She waved him forward and he ran past and slid to the ground behind her. The man chasing him rounded the corner, and Pia swung a log. It hit him just below his knees, and he went down with a grunt.

Pia rose to a crouch and pulled a single log from the woodpile. The rest of the logs started tumbling off, half of them landing on top of the fallen man.

"Run," Gustav said. He followed what he assumed were Pia's footprints back through the woods to the road. They didn't stop running until they were on the outskirts of the small town.

Down near the shore, they found an old dinghy leaning against a weathered warehouse wall and they huddled under it.

"Thanks," Gustav said. "Even though it wasn't the plan."

"It was *my* plan," Pia said. "I figured it out using my Trait, so I knew it was a good one. Although the firewood stack being there and one single log holding it all up was lucky."

"Next you'll have me wondering if you have Calder's Trait," Gustav said. He leaned out to scan the docks. "We need to find an iceboat before Timonis gets his men here."

"I'll look," Pia said and was gone before he could argue with her. She was back a couple of minutes later.

"I didn't see one, but I think our best chance to find one is on the other side of town. The ice near the shore is more solid due to the way the winds blow in off the sea."

"Do you know that because of your Trait?" He stepped out from under the boat. Timonis and his people might already be here.

"I think so," Pia said. "I'm getting good at putting things together. I'll lead. I can find a path."

Gustav nodded. When she stepped past him, he followed as she took a roundabout route through the town.

Pia kept them away from the harbour as they travelled through narrow alleys and laneways. In some cases, theirs were the only tracks in the snow, but there were enough places with other footprints that he knew it would slow down anyone in pursuit.

He almost stopped when Pia headed across an open square, but he followed her. He had to trust her Trait: trust that she'd already determined that no one would see them. They made it safely to the other side of the square without anyone raising an alarm.

Another circuitous route brought them to the very end of the dock. Pia stopped at the side of a rough shack and motioned him forward.

He grinned and nodded at her. Just ahead was a small sailboat that had been fitted with runners. It was on the dock up on blocks. He frowned. The two of them might not be able to get the boat onto the ice.

Not to mention it was probably up on blocks for a reason.

His gaze swept over the boat. From this angle, he didn't see what the issue might be, and worse, he didn't see a sail or a place where it might be stored.

He sucked in a breath. But he did see Timonis' man across the harbour.

"You two gonna stay here all day or are ya gonna let me get on with my work."

Gustav plastered a smile on his face as he turned around. A weathered man in a waterproof coat stood staring at them.

"My friend and I would be willing to help you do your work in exchange for a bit of bread," he said, hoping his Charisma was working.

"No one around here has any bread to spare," the man said. "Grain was all destroyed by *skit karl* pirates." He spat to one side.

"Them same pirates the Clan Freeholder thinks he's hiding from everyone, but I coulda told him pirates don't do what they're told: don't stay away from the tavern, don't stay hidden in someone else's house, and they sure don't pretend they're anything other than pirates."

"I've seen them," Gustav said. "In the tavern and at the house of Leif Stendhal."

"Aye, that's where they are." The man studied him for a moment. "This way," he said. "Unless you want Timonis' lackeys to find you." He turned into a narrow alley.

Gustav met Pia's eyes and she shrugged, so they followed the man through a small door and into a fisherman's workshop.

"I'll not tell you my name," the man said. "But if you can prove you're not with Timonis, I'll see what I can do to help you."

Gustav dug out his patch. "We're here on behalf of the Alliance," he said. "The Interim Grand Freeholder is aware of Clan Freeholder Timonis' transgressions and was hoping he would listen to reason."

"And the fact that he's chasing you means he didn't," the man said. "Why not just send guards to fetch him?"

"I can't tell you that," Gustav said.

"We think he has food hidden and that if he's in jail, he'll never tell anyone where it is," Pia said.

"Pia!" Gustav said. "You can't tell him that. *We're* not even supposed to know."

Pia glared at him but turned back to the man. "Lauma Strauskas thinks that the hidden food is more important than locking Timonis up. And so do I."

"Me too." The man seemed to relax. "All right, so you're trying to get away from the Clan Freeholder. How?"

"We were hoping to steal your ice boat," Pia said. "But now I hope you'll give it to us."

"Do you? Why should I?"

"Because we want what you want," Pia said. "For everyone to make it to spring and for shipping to resume and for everyone to prosper."

"And what do you want?" the man turned to Gustav.

"For the Alliance to work the way it's supposed to," he said. "For it to help better the lives of all people, not just a few Freeholders."

"You ever sailed an iceboat before?"

"Just last week we sailed all the way to Tarklee," Gustav said. "Not the best idea I've ever had." The man snorted. "But we were being chased by pirates."

"That's how you knew they were in Leif's house," he said.

"Yes," Gustav replied.

"Are you planning on taking my boat to Tarklee too?"

"Lavais Port," Gustav said. "And the representative of the Interim Grand Freeholder."

"I hear they're making good work repairing the shipyards. You know anything about that?"

"My da's on the crew there," Gustav said. "And two fellow Intelligencers are using their skills to make the work go faster. They'll be starting to build a ship any day now."

"Your da? You're Lavaisian?" he asked. "No, don't tell me. I can't tell what I don't know."

He paced the small shed for a few minutes before he grabbed a bundle off a shelf and tossed it to Gustav.

"Stay here until I say so," he said. "The boat will be ready then." He abruptly left the workshop, and Gustav and Pia stared at each other.

"Looks like we talked ourselves into a boat," he said, shaking out the bundle to show her the sails.

CHAPTER 19

CALDER JOINED DAG at the bow and stared out at the shoreline.

They were a day out of Zelesso and approaching the coast of Yedris. He'd declined Darya's offer to take control of the ship and instead had been content to spend his time on board with Dag.

"Rafael says we should see Wekesa soon," he said. He looped an arm around her shoulder, and she leaned into him.

"Have you been here before?" she asked. "Is that it?"

He followed her finger and stared out at a smudge on the horizon.

"That's it," he said. "And I've been to Wekesa once before, although it wasn't exactly here at the time." Wekesa was the main Yedrissian floating city, although in truth it was made up of smaller villages that collected and disbanded according to the season.

"Adjoa said her aunt would be on the edge," Dag said. "I hope she really does want the triplets."

"I don't think Adjoa would lie about that," he said. "Or that she would be mistaken about her aunt."

"You're right." She sighed. "I'm just worried that we'll end up trying to find another place for them."

"Which would not be easy." He'd been thinking a lot about the sacrifice Adjoa was making for her brothers. Her Trait meant that she would be welcome anywhere, that she could live whatever type of life she wanted in exchange for Healing.

Instead, she was willing to stay with her brothers in order to keep them safe. Sadly, he could easily see the boys being abandoned or even killed if their negative Traits were not kept in check.

And he wasn't sure he would be able to blame anyone for doing that. Would he risk Dag's health, or his sister Berna's, for the sake of two children who were never going to be able to live a normal life?

He hated that the answer was no. Hated that it made him grateful that he didn't have to make the choice Adjoa was making.

Because if Hakon had lived, he might have been in the exact same position. Able to keep his brother alive but at the cost of having a life he could call his own. He would have been forced to live an isolated life with Hakon, and he would never have seen the world or met Dag or any number of things that had shaped him into the person he was today.

He would have had his twin, but *he* would have been a very different person. He knew he would have come to resent his brother. And Calder knew himself well enough to know that he would have eventually left, and Hakon's Bad Luck would have maimed or killed him, and it would have been Calder's fault for leaving.

The sails were dropped before the *Atlaine* got so close to the village that its wake would disturb the platforms.

"We're getting a dinghy ready," Rafael said joining them. "Do either of you want to come?"

"I'll be no help," Dag said. "I don't know the language, and I'm a terrible rower."

"I'll come," Calder said. "My Yedrissian isn't the best, but I can row."

He squeezed Dag's shoulder and followed Rafael to starboard where a dinghy was being lowered. A few minutes later, he was helping row the dinghy towards the nearest platform.

He understood a few words Rafael said to a group of women. One nodded excitedly and left the group, leaping onto the next platform.

"She said she knows the woman Furaha," Rafael said. "And has gone to fetch her."

"Good." Calder tried to track the woman but lost sight of her after she'd jumped onto a fourth platform.

The Yedrissians on the platform nearest him went back to stringing up seaweed. They draped the long strands over lines that ran from poles lashed to each corner of the platform to the hut in the middle.

A woman reached up to pull a dried strand off a line. It was stiff in her hands, and she broke it into sections and took the bundle inside the hut.

His eyes moved to another Yedrissian, a man who was gutting a fish near the side of the platform. He threw the entrails into the water before rinsing the fish off and tossing it into a basket.

His gaze passed over the fisherman and—What? Calder sat up in the boat and stared. Had he really seen that flash of golden hair?

"Inger!" he called out. "Charis! It's Calder, and it's safe. You're safe."

A blonde head peaked from behind a stack of baskets.

"Calder? Is it really you?" Inger looked behind her for a moment before she stood up and headed towards him.

"Dag's here," Calder said, gesturing to the *Atlaine*. "We're looking for you. You know Rafael."

"Yes, hello," Inger stopped a few feet away. "How do you know it's safe?"

"Because my father is no longer looking for Charis," he said, and Inger slumped in relief.

"Are you sure?" she asked. "Of course, you're sure, you know what he is. Did you ask him to stop, is that how you know?"

"I returned his token to him," Calder said. "And changed his target."

"Oh, thank you." Inger looked over her shoulder and waved. A moment later, Charis emerged and headed towards them.

"Calder settled it," Inger said to Charis. She reached out a hand and he took it. "We're safe."

"Safe from my father," Calder said. "Not from Pinho and Floros."

"Your father was the immediate threat," Charis said. "And the reason we fled all the way out here."

A Yedrissian woman rushed up to them speaking quickly.

"This is Aunt Furaha," Rafael said. "She wants to see her niece and nephews."

"Then let's go," Calder said. He moved aside to let Furaha,

Inger, and Charis into the dinghy. He grinned. Dag would be happy about the children's aunt, but she would be overjoyed to see Inger and Charis.

CHAPTER 20

Nadez walked beside Sture as they approached the *Tazeyar*. The ship had been brought in as close to shore as possible, and now the double hulled boats were constantly circling the ship, keeping a ring of water around it clear of ice.

"Will we be able to save the ship?" she asked. Now that the *Tazeyar* was here, she was glad it was this ship and not the *Atlaine*. Extra food would have been welcome, but Captain Eklund had said the Pale Sea was almost completely frozen and that even one extra day delay would have stranded him in ice and threatened the survival of both the crew and the ship.

The crew was safe, and at least they had a chance to save the ship.

"We'll do our best," Sture said. "Everyone knows what's at stake."

"That's all we can do," Nadez replied. "Our best." She wouldn't have minded a bit of Calder's Luck to help them through the winter, but now she hoped the *Atlaine* stayed away.

"I'll let you know if things change," Sture said.

"Thank you. Good or bad, I want to know." She nodded and headed back to the Hall. She turned around before stepping off the docks.

Out past the *Tazeyar*, fishermen dotted the ice. Lauma was out there somewhere showing more people how to fish through the frozen harbour. She had plans to take them out of the harbour once they had a few more sailboats fitted with runners.

Maybe they would make it to spring without a major fight or disease or starvation. Maybe.

DAG FROWNED AS she looked at the dinghy. Then her eyes widened. Inger! It was Inger and Charis. She rushed to the side of the ship and danced from foot to foot as her sister came closer and closer. Inger waved at her, and she waved back.

As soon as her twin was on board, she pulled her into a hug.

"I'm so happy to see you!" she said into Inger's ear. "So, so happy." She leaned back and grinned.

"Not as happy as I am," Inger said. "When we heard that a ship had arrived at Wekesa and a Pilalian was disembarking, we feared the worst. And then I saw Calder, and he said Rahm is no longer targeting Charis." She kissed Dag on the cheek. "You don't know how scared we've been."

"You're safe," Dag said. "We're all safe. Oh, hang on, there's something I need to take care of." A Yedrissian woman stepped onto the deck, and Dag approached her.

"Furaha?" she asked. "This way," she said in Arressan. "Adjoa, Chike, and Baako are this way." She led the woman through the ship, stopping at the door to the children's cabin.

"Adjoa," she called out.

Furaha spoke quickly in Yedrissian, and then the door was flung open and Adjoa and her brothers were in their aunt's arms.

"Come up on deck when you're ready," Dag said in Arressan, and Adjoa nodded.

She headed back to her sister who was with Calder and Charis.

"Calder says you can help us with Floros and Pinho," Inger said. "Will you?"

She met Calder's eyes and nodded. "Winter was early on the Pale Sea, so it's safer if we stay here until spring. We'll need something to do. But we can't go back to Messanos."

"Calder already said we can go to Zelesso," Inger said. "Where he has family."

"So he does."

PIA HELPED GUSTAV tie the iceboat to the dock. By the time they were done and had stepped onto land with the sail, Berna was there.

"I expected you both to stay in Tarklee until spring," Berna said. "Come inside. At least we can be warm while you give me the bad news."

Pia trailed Gustav and Berna into the shipbuilding office. The fire crackled, and she stood close to it, enjoying the warmth. She'd been far too cold for far too many days already this season, and it wasn't even midwinter yet.

And there were more cold days ahead because after Timonis tried to capture him, there was no way she was letting Gustav deliver the letters to the two Clan Freeholders alone. She knew better than most that Clan Freeholders couldn't be trusted. Besides, she was going to make Gustav teach her how to sail that boat on ice. And when the weather was warmer, on the sea as well.

Because she'd learned so much about her Trait. Things that even Joosep Sepp hadn't thought of. The more she knew, the better she could predict events.

So, she was going to spend the whole winter learning everything she could from anyone who could teach her.

Acknowledgements

Thanks to everyone at Tyche Books—especially my editor Karley Hauser and publisher Margaret Curelas.

Author Biography

Jane Glatt loves that along with creating original worlds, writing fantasy allows her to indulge her curiosity about an eclectic group of subjects. So far she's researched synaesthesia, medieval guilds, tidal rivers, cities atop bridges, pirates and privateers, plants used for healing, and the history of spying. For that last one she blames a visit to the International Spy Museum (yes, it's a real place), in Washington D.C.

For news on Jane's future releases visit her website http://janeglatt.com/index.html and sign up for her newsletter

www.ingramcontent.com/pod-product-compliance
Lightning Source LLC
Chambersburg PA
CBHW060545190726
48283CB00003B/871